LO

P

ALSO BY CLAUDIA CAIN

Silver and Bone

Smoke and Mirrors

Shadow and Crow

LOVELY, DARK AND DEEP

CONTENT WARNINGS

This novel includes violence, animal death, mild gore and depictions of injury. It also includes mentions of suicide.

Cover art by Stefanie Saw (Seventhstar Art)

ISBN (paperback): 978-0-473-59426-8

ISBN (epub): 978-0-473-59427-5

For Karli,

who makes the world a brighter place.

1

IT'S A GLORIOUS AUTUMN AFTERNOON, AND THE WOODS are about to swallow a girl whole.

The forest is lovely at this time of year. Sunlight falls splintered through the tangle of branches, the foliage a riot of colour. The green canopy is spotted with blooms of brilliant orange and fiery red and deep, rich browns, intertwining until looking up is like peering into a kaleidoscope. Birdsong rings through the treetops in an endless high scream.

All of this is lost on the girl. She kicks at the ground as she walks, scowling at her feet. Her new jacket scratches at her neck, and her legs are tired. One of her socks is damp. Hiking is boring, and she wants to go home.

She will not be going home.

Her parents walk ahead of her, chattering between themselves. About the scenery, about the birds, about things she doesn't care about. Every so often one of them calls back, "Look, Hannah!"

There is never anything interesting to look at. It's just trees and leaves and leaves and trees, going on forever. They said this would be fun, and that they could get ice cream afterward, but so far there has been an awful lot of walking and no ice cream.

Their steps are long. Her steps are short. They aren't paying attention, and she is falling behind.

A cold wind blows. The sunlight dims.

And the girl stops.

Nothing moves between the trees other than the slow descent of falling leaves. There is nothing to see. Perhaps the shadows fall slightly too long, sliding too swiftly across the earth. Perhaps the birdsong has gone quiet.

But there is nothing to see.

There is no reason for the girl to turn, frowning, and stare into the woods, unmoving for several long moments. No reason for her to step off the well-worn path, marching unhesitatingly into the trees.

One minute she is there.

The next she is not.

Soon the shouting starts. The shouts turn to screams. Leaves drift gently downward, like slivers of gold dappling the ground, but otherwise there is stillness in the woods.

It's a glorious autumn afternoon, and a little girl is gone.

~ 2 ~

EVERYTHING HAS A PRICE.

That's how the world works. Nothing comes for free, and anyone who tells you otherwise is lying. If you want something, you have to pay the price.

In most cases the price is money. Sometimes this is true with magic too, but often the price is something else. There's no avoiding it. Witches don't work for free, and it doesn't matter how well you negotiate; in the end, there is always a cost.

I've never seen negotiations opened with a severed finger before, though.

Will plops it down in front of me. Ring finger. Severed just below the knuckle. It's nestled in a napkin which was originally white and has now achieved a state of soggy redness.

I stare at it.

"Guess I mistook it for a carrot." Will's shirt is bloodstained, and his hand is wrapped in a dishtowel, but he's in a good mood for someone who recently dismembered himself. He's not at all perturbed to be sitting on the back porch of a house inhabited by witches.

His fiancée, on the other hand…

"This is unnatural," Stephanie hisses.

My vision is starting to swim, so I shift my gaze to her. She's pretty: tall, willowy, blonde. She also looks appalled to be in my presence, cringing as if she expects dark forces to rise from beneath the weathered porch and drag her down to Hell.

"I've asked you not to use that word," Will replies.

Stephanie bristles, glaring at me.

She'll go to church this Sunday and tell her friends how Will made her drive him to *that house*, to the lair of the Devil's mistresses. She'll complain how she can feel the sin seeping into her. And they'll cluck, and comfort her, and pretend none of them have ever come knocking on our door, looking for help God didn't see fit to give them.

I look calmly back at her, pondering curses.

"We should go to a hospital," Stephanie continues. "They have surgeons, Will—"

"Surgeons can't grow back fingers."

"They can reattach them!"

"I don't want to go to a hospital."

Stephanie closes her eyes. "We're getting married in less than a month," she whispers. I imagine this never featured in her wedding plans. "How can you wear a wedding ring without a ring finger?"

"He could wear it on a different finger," I offer. "Or his thumb."

Will's mouth jerks like he's fighting a smile, and Stephanie makes a sound like a choking budgie.

The backyard is quiet. Vines climb the painted porch railings, the leaves perfectly green despite the changing season. Bees hum lazily through the lavender, weaving among the reaching strands of rosemary bushes. Will's blood is staining the wooden steps.

"Well?" he asks. "Can you fix it? I could go to a hospital, but I thought you might be able to do it… better."

Stephanie refuses to look at us, staring angrily at an oblivious bee. I swallow hard, preparing myself, and pull the napkin closer.

I've never seen an unattached finger before. If I pretend it's fake I feel less nauseous, but I hold my breath as I examine it. It's a clean cut. I can imagine how it happened: too much enthusiasm, not enough attention.

Chop.

"Cleaver?" I ask weakly.

"A big knife."

"How long ago?"

"About twenty minutes."

"Does this mean we should avoid the food at the diner this week?"

Will scowls at me. "You're hilarious."

"I know." I straighten, my head spinning. "I can do it."

A flash of relief crosses his face, and then his expression darkens. "What's the price?"

The air seems to still.

This is always the question: the one that keeps people away from our door, that makes seeking help from a witch more dangerous than juggling knives. All magic—every spell, every rite, every ward—has a price, proportional to the spell's power. If I perform magic for someone else, they're required to pay me for the trouble. I can ask for anything I want. They can refuse to pay, but the consequences will be unpleasant. Maybe Will develops a sudden and severe case of gangrene. Maybe he heals perfectly, but Stephanie's finger falls off. Likewise, if I get greedy and ask for too much, *my* finger might fall off. Magic likes balance.

Stephanie still won't look at me. I consider asking for their firstborn child, if only to see her reaction, but that's not how it works. Besides, I already know the price I'll name. With Will, it's always the same.

"No price," I tell him.

Will's tension evaporates. He doesn't question it. He never does.

From there things progress smoothly. Will unwinds the bloody towel, and he and I get his finger aligned as it should be, with only a slight whitening of his cheeks.

"You're doing well for someone who lopped off his own finger," I mutter, battling the urge to retch.

"Thanks," he says tightly. "Is it sanitary to be doing this outside?"

"Probably not, but Louisa doesn't allow bloodwork in the house."

He snorts, and while he's distracted I dab my finger in his blood and draw a symbol on the back of his hand.

It means nothing to him, or to anyone else. Stephanie looks disgusted, but she doesn't understand what the symbol means. She only knows it's magic, and therefore, it shouldn't exist.

But if the finger gets reattached, people don't usually complain about the methods.

And then it's done.

I sit back, relieved. "Congratulations. You have ten fingers again."

Will tentatively stretches his hand. "It works."

"That's the point."

He keeps admiring it. I did a good job, to be fair. His finger is nice and straight. "I can see the mark," he says. "Where you joined it."

"It will fade. Just don't put your hand under any stress for a while. In fact, don't do anything to mess it up until *after* you get married. I don't want to do this again on the big day because you did something stupid and your finger fell off."

"*It could fall off?*"

I grin at him. "Not if you look after it."

"There's really no price?" Stephanie's hazel eyes are squinted with suspicion, her hands pulled close to her chest as if witchcraft is contagious. "This isn't a trick?"

I'm all too familiar with the distrust on her face. It's how most people look at me, but today it rankles, and my smile dies. "Do you *want* a price?" I ask coldly. "I could send a horde of crows to knock at your windows for the next month. It would make your wedding interesting."

The terror on her face is immensely satisfying.

Will gives me an exasperated look. "No price?"

I sigh. "No."

As I say it I curl my hands into fists, hoping he won't notice the scar appearing below my knuckle, unfurling in a straight white line. He certainly won't notice the new, dull ache gnawing into my finger, but he'd feel guilty if he knew about it.

Someone had to pay the price for the healing, though.

He gets to his feet, pulling me up with him, and I take a deep breath. The air smells like herbs and blood, the shadows lengthening as the afternoon deepens.

At the bottom of the backyard, the garden gate is locked. Beyond it the woods loom.

Stephanie storms inside without saying goodbye, the screen door slamming shut behind her. Will lets her go, glowering at me. “Really? Crows? Now she’ll have a meltdown if she sees a single bird on the wedding day. I’m surprised she didn’t uninvite you.”

I scoff. “She doesn’t want me there anyway.”

“*I* want you there.” His expression softens. “She’ll get used to you, Cass. She’s really a lovely person, you two just don’t know each other yet. I’m sure you’ll be friends one day.”

The idea is almost funny. Stephanie crosses herself if she sees me in the street, and if they still burned witches she’d have hurled me onto a pyre the day Will introduced us. He’s the only reason she tolerates me. Without him she’d pretend I didn’t exist, and we’d likely both be happier that way.

But the obstinate set to Will’s jaw tells me any argument is futile. I know how stubborn he can be, and how naïve.

So I roll my eyes, as if in begrudging acceptance, and he smiles.

He really is handsome. His eyes are a beautiful deep blue, his hair a dusty brown. He hasn’t changed much over the years. He’s taller, and broader across the shoulders, but he’s still the kid I grew up with, with a smile like a slice of sunshine.

A small scar curls in the hollow of his throat, a vicious little twist. My eyes catch on it. They always do.

“I’d better go after her,” Will says, waving the bloodstained towel at me. “Thanks, Cass. I owe you one.”

“Nah.”

He pauses at the door. “You should come down to the diner sometime. Get out more.”

"Maybe," I lie, and he nods, a bitter quirk to his lips, before heading inside.

I wait a moment longer, until I hear their car start out front. Then I run into the house to wash Will's blood off my hands.

•••

That afternoon, a girl goes missing in the Fallow Creek woods.

The woods are hungry this year. Dogs run in and never run out. A few too many hikers stray off the path and come to grief. And every so often families venture in for a walk, towing their children behind them.

Sometimes they emerge with one less child.

Hannah is six. It's the third day of October, and she's the fourth child to go missing in two months.

Evening falls quickly, swallowing the search party as they comb the woods behind the house. They appear like ghosts past the treeline, their flashlights casting beams of white through the deepening shadows, their calls echoing and fading.

I stand on the back porch, watching the night slide out of the woods. Later it will bring mist, creeping between the trees like grasping fingers.

The lights flicker, growing distant. Hannah's name is a whisper in the air.

"How sad," Louisa sighs.

My aunt looks tired tonight. Her golden hair falls loose from her ponytail, framing her fine-boned face.

"We should be out there," I reply. "We should be helping."

Will is out searching, along with Stephanie. Half the town is, in fact. The candlelit vigils stopped after the second child went missing, but there's a routine to each disappearance: the leaflets left in mailboxes, the *MISSING CHILD* posters plastered on every wall, the search teams amassing to drag themselves through the undergrowth. At some point people started to whisper about anyone who *wasn't* out there looking. Four children vanishing in two months is suspicious, after all. Who would be content to do nothing? Why *wouldn't* you want to help?

Unless you had something to hide.

But Louisa is immune to whispers, and in this house, she's the one in charge. And she always says the same thing.

"No."

Theo watches us like he's waiting for a bomb to go off, leaning back against the porch railing as if he hopes to escape the blast. He doesn't comment as I turn to Louisa, my irritation rising.

"Come on. *Four* kids."

She doesn't look at me. "The woods aren't safe."

"Did you tell them that?" I gesture to the distant lights. "After the first kid disappeared, or the second?"

"They wouldn't have believed us," she says softly. "They never do."

Maybe there's some truth to her words. The fact we're witches is no secret, but most people in Fallow Creek think we're either frauds or in league with the Devil. We're not exactly considered trustworthy, so any warnings would probably have gone unheeded. But when we heard another child was missing, Louisa didn't seem surprised.

So I continue. "Did you know this would happen? Did you know another kid would go missing?"

"It was inevitable."

"Nothing is inevitable if you know it's going to happen," I snap. "That just means you're *letting* it happen. I want to go out there. There must be something we can do to help."

Louisa finally looks at me, her eyes narrowing to slits of blue. "It *was* inevitable," she says. "Don't insinuate that I had anything to do with this. Until this town has a Witch, bad things will continue to happen. I didn't know another child would go missing, but I knew something would happen, because there's nobody to stop it."

Theo grimaces, turning back to the woods. This conversation is familiar territory, gone over so many times that we already know how this will end. Even so, I can't stop my hands from clenching into fists, my knuckle throbbing along the scar from Will's knife.

"Fallow Creek *has* witches," I point out. "You don't let us do anything."

"You know that's not what I meant," Louisa says tautly. "One of you will have to make this commitment—"

"Why don't *you* become the Witch, then! You're the one obsessed with it."

"Oh God," Theo mumbles.

But the words are already said. Louisa draws herself up, her lips pressing thin. "If I were suitable for the role, I'd have become the Witch years ago," she says, her voice as cold as the evening. "I am not *obsessed* with it, Cassandra. I'm just the only one who seems to recognise what is needed. Don't act like this is a shock to you. You knew this day was coming. This town needs a Witch, so one of you has to step up, and soon." She gives me a hard look. "You may be an adult, but I am in charge here. Nobody asked for our help, so we will stay out of the woods."

Then she turns and strides inside, closing the screen door with more force than necessary.

My fingernails are biting into my palms, the sting reaching me from a distance. I count back from ten, letting my grip ease.

Theo watches the woods, a grim set to his mouth. "This is bad."

"Obviously," I mutter, leaning against the railing beside him.

Everyone knows the Fallow Creek woods run a little too deep. By day they're pretty enough. Light filters through the leaves until the ground seems dappled, and the air is thick with the scent of damp earth and greenery. Deer step through on spindling legs, and the canopy rings with birdsong.

It's different at night. The silence is heavy. The trees are too tall and dark to be lovely, their boughs hanging low and twisting. Things move in the shadows.

There's a reason our garden gate stays locked.

I glance at it. The gate sits at the bottom of the garden, a pale shape in the growing gloom. Small symbols are scratched into each white post. Every year Louisa redraws the wards, enlisting one of us to help her layer the house in magic. I know each mark by heart: protection, deterrence, alarm.

When the news reached us I went out and unlocked it, just in case. Nobody approached it. People are afraid to know what help from a witch will cost them.

Theo sighs, plucking at the sleeve of his sweater. "Do you think she's right? I mean, you and me, we're old enough."

"You want to risk the rite?"

He doesn't respond.

I pick angrily at my thumbnail, Louisa's words echoing in my ears. "This shouldn't fall on us! This shouldn't be our responsibility—we don't want this!"

"That girl probably didn't want to be missing," he points out.

It shouldn't be our job to make sure kids don't go missing, I think. But there's no point in saying it; Theo is only older by a year, yet when it comes to being responsible he has decades on me. He might be my brother, but he never sides with me against Louisa.

The flashlights move deeper into the woods. The voices keep calling.

Hannah. Six. I picture her in my head, some imagined child conjured by a name. She probably likes ballet, or horses, or dinosaurs. The news of her disappearance came from a neighbour, announced with a shake of the head and a resigned sigh. As if the case were already closed.

Four kids in two months. They didn't find any trace of the others.

"Don't you hate this?" I ask. "Having to just... sit here?"

"We can't do anything else," Theo says dully. "They don't want our help."

"*They* don't want our help," I shoot back, pointing at the fading flashlights. "A lost six-year-old will take any help they can get! Doesn't it bother you to know what people say about us? Did you know some of them think *we've* got something to do with these disappearances?"

"Cass..."

The words come easily now, as if the frustration seething inside me is forcing them out. "Doesn't it bother you how she makes us sit by while terrible things happen, watching when you know we could help? How is it fair that we're forbidden to do anything unless we make a massive, life-altering decision?"

Theo's expression is bitter. "Louisa always says '*you can do whatever you want if you become the Witch—*'"

"We both know that's a lie," I say sharply. "I think our mother might have wanted to live a bit longer, but she didn't get to do *that*."

There's a pause.

Theo closes his eyes, taking a deep breath. "It's not—she wasn't—Louisa is only looking out for us."

I don't reply, fuming. *Until this town has a Witch, bad things will continue to happen*. Louisa has always kept us separate from the townspeople, urging us not to make waves. We never help unless we're asked, and now, nobody asks.

But there must be something we can do. Something *I* can do.

A spark of defiance flickers to life in my chest. "Maybe I'm tired of being looked out for."

I step off the porch.

"Oh Jesus," Theo hisses. "Cass, *no*!"

I ignore him, crossing the backyard. My feet sink into the dampening grass, my shadow shivering across the light cast from the house as I push open the garden gate. The symbols are stark against the white paint: small, careful black marks. *Protection. Warning. Defence from evil.*

I close it behind me and walk into the woods.

•••

Darkness falls, deep and immediate, the trees looming like the shadows of giants. The house suddenly seems very far away, and I can't tell if the sensation of eyes upon me is imagined or not.

I don't look back, striding further into the unfolding night. The search party has disappeared, their calls now a faint suggestion of sound. I don't bother trying to join them. They'd likely abandon me, and as Louisa said, they didn't ask for help.

But four children have vanished in two months, and no trace of them has been found—no dropped belongings, no bodies, no bones. The parents claim their children would never wander, *didn't* wander. They were simply there, then gone.

No search party has found anything. But none of those search parties included a witch.

Of course, I don't have a flashlight, or even my phone. My first major act of rebellion in twenty-four years is impulsive, stupid, and starts with me tripping over a root and biting my tongue.

I curse, blinking away tears of pain, and glance back in the direction of the house. Theo is probably inside, listening to Louisa rant about me. I could go home. It would mitigate some of the damage.

Still, what's the point of rebelling if you don't see it through?

I extend my hand, striking my thumb across my fingers, and a spot of brilliance splits the gloom.

Magic works around anchor-points. You can't summon it from nothing; all magic must link to something physical, and when you reach for a spell the options for anchor-points light up in your mind like flames in the dark. Reattaching a finger is easy, a matter of linking flesh to flesh. Some spells are anchored to your own energy. To create light, all you need is a point of brightness: the flash off a mirror, the flare of a match. Or, in this case, the glow of moonlight through the trees.

And now a pale sphere hangs in the cradle of my palm, like I've pulled down a star.

The price for the magic is irritating: my peripheral vision goes black. Partial blindness in exchange for partial sight, I suppose, but a witch doesn't get to choose the price for the magic she uses. At least from this distance the sphere will pass for a flashlight, and now I can see the ground and avoid biting off my own tongue.

And everything can see me coming.

I huff out a breath through my teeth. *Stupid.* Now that I'm here, all I want to do is leave, and yet...

Hannah. Six.

The woods are very dark.

I sigh, dropping into a crouch. Without an object linking me to Hannah there's no easy way to locate her, but she must be somewhere in the woods. I brush aside decaying leaves and loose rocks, pressing my free hand to the damp dirt below, and plunge my mind into the earth.

The world around me vanishes, but a hundred sparks of knowledge appear in my consciousness. Off to the west, dozens of pulses mark the location of a search party. There's a similar cluster to the east, moving through the other side of the woods. And to the north—

To the north is *something*. Not a search party. Not even an individual pulse. Instead it's a small, silent spot, a hole in the map.

And it's undeniably magical.

I end the spell, frowning. There shouldn't be anything magical around here. My family are the only witches I know of, and Fallow Creek isn't the kind of place that would welcome anything supernatural. But there it is: a presence in the woods.

Four kids vanishing into thin air. Surely that's not natural.

My heart beating a little faster, I carve a symbol into the soil with a finger, crushing a fallen leaf in my hand. "Show me," I murmur.

A shiver runs through the air.

Then, trembling as they rise, a cluster of leaves lifts off the forest floor. They hover for a moment, like strange butterflies, before spinning away into the trees.

I watch them go.

Louisa told us lots of things as we were growing up. *Don't perform magic you can't pay for. Don't stray too far from home.*

This town needs a Witch.

Jacob. Morgan. Emma. Hannah.

Four kids. Two months. And not a single one of them found.

I don't have to be the Witch to do something useful.

I push to my feet and follow the leaves.

They tumble through the trees like a wheel, picking up speed as they go. I have to move fast to keep up, weaving between gnarled black roots and strips of white moonlight. The faint shouts of a search party echo in the distance, their flashlights briefly breaking the dark, but the spell leads me deeper into the woods and they vanish once more.

As the minutes tick by the terrain becomes more dangerous, and I feel the first hint of doubt. This can't be the way Hannah came. There are no walking paths here, and this isn't a place any sane parent would take a small child. The trees grow twisting and close together, and the ground is steep and uneven, waiting to trip unwary feet. Even if Hannah came this way on her own, she must have turned back.

On my left the moonlight suddenly brightens. I look over and find a clearing.

In the centre, limned silver by the night, is a large round rock.

My blood chills.

Once, magic was everywhere, as natural as air. But as humans pushed forward, the magic drew back, and now it's a shadow of what it was, a puddle where there once was a sea. Even so, there are still places where an old wilderness clings on—where there are still wells of power.

And in those places, there are Witches.

A well of power needs a Witch like a body needs a heart. The Witch is the guardian, the gatekeeper, the hunter. The Witch keeps out the evil that walks in the world, taking responsibility for all things supernatural within their territory. There might be many witches, but there's only one *Witch*.

Louisa has always claimed she's not suitable for the role, insisting the job must fall to me, or to one of my siblings. But to become the Witch of Fallow Creek, to claim the title and the immense power that comes with it, one must first perform the rite. Someone has to come out here, hoping they're strong enough, and—

Pain lances through my skull, and I gasp, swaying. The spell is still going, the leaves spinning onward, and it's draining my energy as I fall behind. I could give up and go home. It seems unlikely Hannah came this way. The magic I sensed is probably unrelated, a bizarre anomaly.

But if there's a chance…

The leaves are a fading flicker of movement.

I run.

The night blurs, the woods jolting in the light cast from my palm. Things rustle and dart in the boughs overhead, the leaves hiding the moon until the darkness is as thick as velvet. Fallen leaves form a slimy track underfoot.

Then, ahead—

Light.

My pace slows.

The leaves tumble into a clearing and disperse, floating to the ground as if carried there by no more than a stray wind. The sudden stillness is startling, as is the silence. The sounds of the night are gone, and all that remains is the whisper of a cold breeze, muffled by the rising mist.

Moonlight pours down into a clearing, transforming it into a pool of silver, and in front of me is a single small shoe.

I stare, trying to make sense of it.

A shoe. Purple. Pink laces.

I wonder if Hannah liked purple.

I edge forward, too afraid to breathe as I lift the light in my hand higher. At any moment I'll find an equally small bare foot, attached to a body.

I step into the clearing.

There is no body.

There is only the gate.

A black, wrought-iron gate stands alone in the centre of the clearing, as if the woods themselves have drawn away from it. The metal bars glint dully, the curlicues bare of rust. It stands slightly ajar, no taller than my hip. There's no sign of how it came to be there. I can't even see how it's remaining upright.

It's only a gate.

But fear turns my veins to ice.

The shoe might not be Hannah's. Even if it is, she's not here now. This gate may be the source of the strange magic I sensed, but I don't see anything promising enough to make me want to linger here for another second.

In the forest behind me there is a low, rattling hiss.

I freeze.

The light in my palm now seems as bright as a beacon. I let the spell die, my heart in my throat as I listen. Leaves whisper. Branches murmur and creak. Otherwise, it's far too quiet.

As if something is watching.

I swallow, forcing myself to turn.

Nothing moves. Darkness hangs in the woods, deep and heavy and still.

Then the iron gate lets out a long, deliberate *squeeeak.*

And the shadows surge.

I bolt, shoes skidding on wet leaves, and race away from the clearing. The undergrowth shudders and snaps as something follows, but I don't look back, leaping over a spray of raised roots and scrambling onward. Trees loom out of the night, invisible until they're only inches away, and I throw myself past them.

Don't stop. If you stop, you die. My breaths come in gasps, my legs burning with effort as the sounds behind me draw closer—

A figure steps out of the darkness ahead.

There's no time to think. I dart sideways, blood roaring in my ears. I don't see the tree until it's directly in front of me, and then my foot slips.

My head cracks against wood, and everything goes black.

3

"THAT WAS WHAT WE WOULD CALL AN *ABSOLUTELY terrible idea.*"

I open my eyes.

Leaves sway overhead, a tangle of branches forming a lattice against a pale sky. I'm sprawled on my back, something sharp digging into my spine. When I flex my hands dirt slides beneath my fingernails.

I'm in the woods. It's morning.

And I'm not dead.

I gingerly sit up, my head pounding in time to my pulse. Wet leaves cling to my skin like scales, raw red scrapes covering my palms, but I don't appear to be badly injured.

The speaker sits a few feet away, lounging among the roots of a tree. A man from the search party, I suppose. His sleeves are rolled up to his elbows, revealing sun-kissed golden skin, and his hair falls to his jaw in untidy waves.

He spins a leaf back and forth between his fingers, an irritated twist to his mouth, and even with my swaying vision I can see he is incredibly, *unfairly* good-looking.

"Racing around in the dark like a lunatic," he continues, in a voice as attractive as he is. "A shockingly stupid idea. Suicidal, one might even say. You could have broken your neck."

There's nobody else around, so I assume he's talking to me. I force my mind into some sort of order. "I didn't mean to cause trouble," I start, searching for an explanation that won't make me sound insane.

He scoffs, not looking up from the leaf. "I'm sure you didn't."

I climb unsteadily to my feet, trying not to vomit as the world rocks. Running face-first into a tree probably wasn't good for my health, but it's not the cause of my unease. Other than the fact I'm still in the woods, possibly concussed, and in the presence of a man who looks like a minor God, there's something off about this situation. "Were you with the search party?" I ask.

"No."

Odd. If he's not with a search party, then what is he doing in the woods? And how did he find me in the first place? It can't have been by coincidence, not if he saw me running.

An image surfaces in my memory. A shadowed figure, emerging from the night moments before I knocked myself out. No flashlight. All alone.

My skin prickles, but before I can speak, the man looks up.

His eyes are black.

And that's *all* they are.

He has no pupils. No whites. His eyes are black from rim to rim, as dark as holes in his head, and fear closes my throat.

I twist my wrist, clawing my fingers. *Freeze*.

The creature stiffens, magic locking his limbs in place, yet a wicked smile spreads across his face. It turns him into something more beautiful, and more terrifying.

"Ah," he says, the word almost a purr. "*Witch.*"

There is no Witch, I think. But if things like this lurk in the woods, I can see why Louisa is so desperate for someone to police them. Is this why she warned us not to wander far from home? Is this why our garden gate stays locked? Though I can't imagine it would have stopped someone like this.

The spell keeping him immobile roots my feet to the spot as well, but I can't risk letting him go. I've trapped myself with him. Panic threatens to overwhelm me, and I clench my fist, the bite of my fingernails keeping me grounded. "Who are you?" I demand.

"Do you mean *who*?" he asks smoothly. "Or *what*?"

"Whichever!"

Whatever he is, he's definitely not human. Now that I'm concentrating I can see the small details in his appearance that made me uneasy even when I was too stunned to identify them. He's still absurdly handsome, but there's an unsettling quality to his features, as if they can't possibly be real. His eyes aren't simply dark, but true black, and the colour of his hair is a rich, luxurious bronze I've only ever seen in statues. It's beautiful, and I feel the sudden, ridiculous urge to touch it.

The creature's smile widens, as if he knows what I'm thinking. "My name is Merich."

Use some sense, I tell myself. I search my memory, sifting through everything Louisa told us about the supernatural entities roaming the world. With his terrifying good looks, and his eyes…

I swallow. "You're… a fairy."

His expression darkens. "A *fairy.* Yes, I live in a toadstool. Fiddly-fucking-dee."

"That's leprechauns."

"What?"

I *must* be concussed. "Leprechauns," I repeat, feeling stupider by the second. "Fiddle dee dee."

Those awful black eyes narrow. "I am *not* a leprechaun," he says. "I am one of the Fae. I am a Warden of the Woods. Both things you would know if you were a halfway decent witch."

Fae. Well, the term *fairy* does seem woefully lacking, though I do have a whole new understanding of why people called them the Fair Folk. "I know what the Fae are!" I protest.

He smiles again, sharp as a knife, and a chill rolls down my spine. "Then you should know to be afraid."

Oh, I am. My legs ache with the urge to run, but the spell keeps me frozen. "If I move three fingers at once, I can give you the plague," I tell him. At least, I hope I can. If this comes to a fight, I won't win. "Where are we?"

"The woods. After you caught the attention of a creature better left alone, I saved your life. You're welcome."

Well, that much seems true. We're in a tiny hollow, surrounded by a thicket of withered brown vines. The trees gather around us so densely I can't pick which direction the town is in. Maybe five feet of space sit between me and the—and Merich.

And around us, in a perfect circle, a ring of symbols is carved into the dirt.

Horror renders me silent. They're wards, markings full of power, but I can't read them. They're as different to the ones I know as

English is from hieroglyphics. They could mean anything, *do* anything.

Louisa never told us much about the Fae. She said she'd never met any, so she only knew they were immortal and unnaturally beautiful. We found plenty of stories to fill the gaps in her knowledge, though. Like the ones where someone steps into a fairy ring and a hundred years slip by…

Merich sighs. "Try not to wet yourself."

"What is this?" I choke out.

"A protective circle," he says irritably. "Your adventures last night angered some very unpleasant things, and they can kill me as easily as they can kill you. Considering you led them straight to me, my options were to save your ungrateful life or to sit here all on my lonesome, watching you get torn limb from limb."

I study the ground. Outside the ring the earth is torn up, scattered with vines and shredded leaves. The thicket itself is ragged, as if something fought to get inside. I remember running, an unseen beast crashing through the dark behind me.

He's telling the truth.

My heart begins to slow. "How long have we been here?"

"All night."

"And… outside the circle?"

Merich sneers. "That's a myth. We don't lurk in separate realms, jumping through mushroom circles to dance around naked and ravish maidens. We've always been here. We don't need to mess with time."

I nod. Slowly. The less I move, the less my head aches. "Why did you save my life?"

"Are you worried about the ravishing? I wouldn't be. You're not the type to be ravished."

It stings. It shouldn't. This entire situation is ridiculous, and I'm not convinced it isn't a hallucination brought on by head trauma. Still, when the words come from someone who looks like him…

"I could make sure you never ravish anyone again," I say coldly.

"Ooh. Harsh." But he grins as he says it.

I let out a breath, watching him. My wrist aches, my fingers cramping, but a niggling worry stops me from releasing the spell. "You wouldn't happen to be stealing children, would you?" I ask.

He raises an eyebrow. "To eat?"

"That's not funny."

"Good lord, you *are* a humourless one. No, I am not stealing children."

"And I don't owe you anything for this, do I?" I continue. "I heard your people only do things in exchange for favours."

The following silence goes on for a long time. Merich's face is unreadable. "Is it so hard to believe we might do things simply because we aren't total assholes?" he asks finally.

I blink. "I—no."

"No," he echoes. "I saved your life because I didn't think you'd *want* to die horribly in the woods, and it seemed like the polite thing to do. If I was wrong, I sincerely apologise, and I promise next time I will leave you to your grisly fate. Either way, witch, would you please let me move? My nose itches."

I bite my lip, considering it. He probably wouldn't save me just to kill me himself. And he seems unarmed.

Unless he can kill me with his cheekbones.

I release the spell.

He groans, shaking himself, then scratches his perfectly formed nose. I jerk my gaze away, stretching my hand.

"I'm not the Witch, by the way," I feel compelled to admit. "Fallow Creek doesn't have a Witch."

"I'm aware. But you're from the family, yes?"

"Yes." Oh God. Theo. Louisa. "Crap, they'll think I'm dead!"

"Probably," he says serenely.

"Do you know the way out of the woods?"

"Yes."

I wait. Nothing follows. "Well, could you tell me?"

Merich shrugs, reclining among the roots once more. "That seems like a *you* problem, to be honest."

I glare at him. He looks impassively back.

"Prolonged unconsciousness is really bad for you," I try. "If I was unconscious all night—"

"Oh no, you weren't out for long at all," he interrupts. "But I didn't want you to start screeching and lure everything in the vicinity straight to us, so I put you to sleep."

"That's even worse!"

"You were perfectly safe." He gives me a hard smile. "No ravishing, remember?"

I'm definitely concussed. This can't be real. Or maybe I'm dead, and this is a special kind of Hell. "I take it you don't have a high opinion of witches."

"Perhaps I just don't like *you*," he says coolly. "Perhaps I don't have a high opinion of abrasive, unpleasant people who saunter into deadly situations with no regard for themselves or others. You could have gotten someone killed."

The words make me flinch. For a moment I'm eleven again.

Broken bones throb under my skin, my hands slick with blood, and the woods are so very, very quiet.

Merich's smile twists. "Touch a nerve, did I?"

"No," I lie, and then, to stop him smirking, "What was that gate I saw?"

He looks wary. "What gate?"

"The one over…"

I look around, but though it felt like I only ran for a few seconds, there's no gate in sight. I'm not even sure which direction it was in.

"Ah," says Merich. "That gate. Invisible, is it?"

I have the irritating urge to stomp like an angry toddler. "I saw it! And there was something wrong with it. It felt evil."

"An evil gate." He gets to his feet, brushing himself free of dirt. He's even more attractive upright, tall and muscular, moving with an eerie grace. "How riveting."

"*Merich*!"

His head snaps up. "You're addressing me as if you know me," he says. "Odd, as you haven't once shown any appreciation for me saving your life, yet you've both threatened me and accused me of stealing children. I don't even know who you are."

I falter. He's right. I haven't thanked him, and I'd be dead if he hadn't intervened. Would Louisa be appalled at my lack of manners, or just appalled I'm talking to him in the first place? I've become so socially inept even someone without a speck of human blood thinks I'm rude.

I extend my hand. "I'm Cassandra Reilly. Thanks for saving my life. I appreciate it."

Merich blinks, unmoving. He stays like that long enough for me to start feeling like an idiot, and then he takes my hand.

"Merich," he replies. "And you are most welcome."

Then he performs a small but undeniable bow.

I take my hand back, hoping I don't look as flustered as I feel. "I know you've done more than enough to help me, but I do have a question."

"You may ask it."

"What's going on in the woods?"

His face stills, and the temperature seems to drop, as if a shadow has fallen over us. "It's not safe to talk about it here," he murmurs. "I'll walk you out."

I glance uneasily at the wards surrounding us. "But outside the circle…"

"It's safe enough by daylight. Just don't use any magic. They notice that."

Merich steps out of the circle, and for the first time I notice what he's wearing: a pair of weathered jeans tucked into battered brown hiking boots, and a white shirt worn to softness. Over that he wears a second shirt of dark flannel, the sleeves rolled up.

I don't know what I expected one of the Fae to dress like, but this wasn't it.

He catches me staring. "People see me from a distance and think *hiker*," he says mildly. "Not *immortal supernatural being*. As a result, I'm not usually threatened with impotency."

I wince, but my embarrassment vanishes as he picks up the object leaning against the tree beside him.

My jaw drops. "That's a sword."

"Yes."

He's holding an actual, honest-to-God sword, with a slender blade formed from a strange silver-blue steel, as bright as sunlight on water.

In contrast the hilt is wrapped in leather, grubby and dark with age.

I remember the other thing Merich called himself. "What exactly did you mean when you said you were a Warden of the Woods?"

He glances at me. "I guard the woods."

"From what?"

His black eyes glint, and the lack of iris, of sclera, of *anything* but that blackness, makes me shiver. "From monsters, of course."

Don't use any magic. They notice that.

I feel far colder than I did a minute ago.

Merich turns away. "Come."

He pushes through the thicket and starts off through the trees, and I follow, struggling to tear my eyes away from the sword. He holds it with ease, and the blade almost glows. I doubt it was made by humans.

"There are monsters in these woods, then?" I ask nervously.

"Yes. Their numbers have grown over the years, as the borders have weakened."

I don't respond, hoping my discomfort doesn't show on my face. A magical boundary surrounds Fallow Creek, one that should have kept those monsters out. But the boundaries are maintained by the Witch. The idea is simple: the stronger the Witch, the stronger the border. Any evil entities are unable to enter, and any within the boundaries are unable to escape into the wider world. But if the Witch is weak, or if there's *no* Witch, those borders fade, until they eventually stop existing at all.

And Fallow Creek hasn't had a Witch for a long time.

This is one of the duties the role involves. If Louisa had her way, it would be me or Theo hunting monsters in the dark, not these

Wardens. If Fallow Creek had a Witch, maybe there wouldn't be monsters at all. Maybe I should feel guilty.

But those borders don't just keep monsters out. They keep the Witch *in*.

And I am *not* getting trapped in this town.

"It wasn't always like this, though," Merich continues.

I emerge from my thoughts. "Like what?"

He ducks some low-hanging branches. "Something happened a few months ago. I don't know what. It was like the world... shook."

I frown. "Like an earthquake?"

"No. This was powerful." His head cocks. "Like a magical disturbance, but... enormous."

"I didn't notice anything."

"Unsurprising," he says, though he doesn't sound snide. "You're human."

"I'm a witch!"

"Still human. The Fae are more inclined to notice these things. Even so, I disregarded it until recently."

Shafts of sunlight pierce through the trees, the undergrowth spreading around us like a rippling green sea, hazed by morning mist. Leaves rustle and sigh. Birds are singing.

It still feels like something is lurking.

I take a few steps closer to Merich. "What happened?"

"The world shook," he repeats. "And I think something cracked."

"*Cracked*?"

His hand tightens on his sword. "You claim you saw a gate. It wouldn't surprise me. Strange things have been happening. More monsters have been appearing, but not the kind we're used to. These are worse. Unnatural. I think a gap has opened between our world and another. I think it formed a pathway for things that shouldn't exist. Now they're here. In the woods."

"What are they?"

Merich halts, looking down at me. The sun strikes his face, and my breath catches as specks of gold burst to life in his eyes.

"Hungry," he says.

Around us the woods whisper.

Without waiting for a response he resumes walking, pushing through the ivy tangling around our feet. I hurry after him. I'm not short, but his legs are long, and I'm forced to move in a trot to keep up.

"You said the world *cracked*," I pant. "How is that possible?"

His broad shoulders shrug. "Hard to say. My guess? Someone, somewhere, meddled with phenomenally powerful magic and accidentally ripped a hole in the world. Now creatures are taking the opportunity to come through."

"Why hasn't anyone seen them?"

"Some monsters can't be seen by mortal eyes. Some can't be seen by immortal eyes, either. Or maybe they're just really good at hiding."

My head is spinning. Monsters. Holes in the world. It shouldn't be possible, but…

Something happened a few months ago.

And a few months ago, seven-year-old Jacob Harris went walking in the woods with his family and never came out.

I struggle to keep my voice even. "Merich, there are four children missing."

"I know."

"You *know*?"

He doesn't stop, forging ahead through the trees. "The woods aren't safe for you. Not for anyone, but especially not you and your family. Magic and power draw dark creatures. You're lucky I was there last night, or you'd know first-hand what I mean."

The thought fills me with terror. "Those kids—"

"Are probably dead."

I seize Merich's arm, tugging him to a halt. He gives me a bemused look, and I'm suddenly wildly aware I'm touching someone who isn't human.

"They're *little kids*," I hiss. "We can't do *nothing*!"

He smiles slightly. Sadly. "You're not the Witch. Nothing you do will be enough."

"We have to try! Just because I'm not some turbo-charged super-witch doesn't mean I'm useless!"

"And if there's nobody there to save you next time? Are you ready to die for this?"

I pause, my bravado vanishing.

Am I?

Does it make me a terrible person if I'm not?

Merich notices my hesitation. "Tell your family. Spread the word that the woods aren't safe. Tell people whatever you like. Tell them animals are snatching children if you think it will work. But keep them out of the woods."

Then he gently shakes me off and keeps walking. I have no choice but to follow.

Soon the trees thin, and before long I can make out the blue walls of the house. The branches part around us, and we step out of the woods and into the clear autumn morning.

"Safe and sound," says Merich. "Mostly."

"Thank you." I raise my face to the sun, trying to erase the chill his words brought on. "I'm sorry if I offended you before."

"I've heard worse."

"Where will you—"

There's a shrill scream, and then a fireball hurtles toward us.

Shield. I step in front of Merich, throwing my arm wide, and the fireball strikes empty air, erupting in a burst of flame and heat. Another follows seconds later, forcing me back a step.

"*Pen*!" I roar. "*Enough*!"

There's a pause.

Then another fireball.

"*Pen*!"

"*Oh my God*, fine!"

As the smoke dissipates, Pen slowly comes into view. She stands on the back porch, dressed in a bathrobe with her black hair wild. One hand points at us.

"You're not dead!" she calls.

"No," I snap. "So stop trying to kill me!"

"Something is following you."

I let my arm fall, the air shimmering as the shield fades. "He's fine."

"This must be your younger sister," Merich says pleasantly. "I can see the family resemblance. Do you all look so irritated?"

Pen watches us approach the fence. "He's not human," she says.

"He's one of the Fae."

"He's hot."

"Pen, *no*."

"But he is!"

"I appreciate the compliment, but now I'll take my leave." Merich turns to me, a small smile playing on his mouth, and my stomach lurches. "A pleasure meeting you, even though you were rude."

"Likewise," I say sourly.

He grins, then performs another low bow, looking up through ridiculously long eyelashes. "Until next time, witchling."

Then he strolls away, disappearing into the trees so quickly it's like he was never there.

"Dibs," says Pen.

I scowl, stalking through the garden gate. It shuts behind me, locking with a brassy *snap*. "You can't call *dibs*."

"Why, did you?"

"No!"

"Then dibs." She eyes me as I climb the porch steps. "Where were you?"

"Unconscious."

"Aunt Louisa is *pissed*."

"I'm sure." I glance at the back door. "Is she in there?"

"Yes." Pen wears the smug expression of someone who knows they're not the one in trouble for once. "He was extremely hot."

"I get it."

"And you have blood all over your face."

I pause. "What?"

"You didn't know?" She looks delighted, ticking things off on her fingers. "Leaves and sticks in your hair, a giant bruise on your forehead, a cut through your eyebrow, blood all over your face, and dirt, like, *everywhere*."

Oh my God. For a moment I'm unsure why this is so horrifying. Then I remember how my stomach lurched when Merich looked at me.

I shove the feeling down.

"Louisa is going to lose it," Pen gloats, and then she skips inside, leaving me standing wearily on the porch.

The back of my neck prickles, and I turn.

The woods wait, looming. Sunlight spills through the canopy, yet what few shadows there are seem unnaturally dark.

I swallow, and before I lose my nerve, I go inside.

4

IT'S BEEN TWO FULL DAYS SINCE I EMERGED FROM THE woods, and I can't help but wonder if it would have been better if I'd died in there.

At the very least it would have been less dramatic.

Louisa spent the first twenty-four hours after my return ranting about my recklessness. I might have escaped with less, but Pen told her I'd been escorted home by a supernatural wood-dweller, a point I had intended to gloss over, and she went predictably ballistic. Telling her I found a shoe and a creepy gate didn't help the situation, and once she finally grew tired of yelling she moved on to icy silence and pointed thumping, which has continued ever since.

There is a muffled *thud* from downstairs, and the mirror rattles on top of my dresser. I wince.

My bedroom is a pleasant place to hide from Louisa. The walls are painted herb green, the woven rug on the floor a cheerful pop of red. Light streams in from the window overlooking the garden, and the air smells like dust and flowers.

The wall over the bed is dotted with pictures: bright snapshots of different places. Italy. New Zealand. Ireland. South America. Will and I had plans to go to those places, once. We thought we'd finish school and go hiking through forests, trekking up mountains. But now he's getting married, and I'm staring out my bedroom window, willing a missing child to walk out of the woods.

There's another *thump*, and the pictures flutter against the wall. For a moment I want it so badly it hurts: to do something, *anything*, as long as it's not being *here*.

One day, I promise myself. *One day I'll go.*

But for now I pick up my phone.

There's an unspoken understanding that nobody is to mention any missing children around Louisa, and since I've spent as much time as possible avoiding her, I haven't had the chance to hear any news. Luckily, I have an external source of information.

Fallow Creek is a small town. There are no secrets, only things too distasteful to discuss in public. The rumour mill turns endlessly, fuelled by the awesome and terrible power of meddling church ladies.

My family regularly features as a topic of scandal. We provide multiple avenues for outrage—like how my siblings and I live with our aunt, not our mother. Or how my mother had four children to different men, but the fathers are neither seen nor mentioned. Or how, even though Theo and I are in our twenties, we still burden Louisa with our presence. Pen's expulsion from the local school fuelled the gossip for two months. The fact Louisa never forced us to attend church fuelled it for two decades.

The word *witch* is rarely used, as though the gossipmongers think it will cause us to rise up in anger. We're treated politely, but mostly we're politely ignored. Other people don't usually acknowledge us unless they need us, and Louisa keeps us so separate from them that we might as well live in our own little bubble. We're always the last to hear anything.

I get my news from Will. His family runs the best diner in town, and right now it's the base of operations for the search teams. Hannah Hendricks remains missing, and Will gives me all the latest updates.

I read over our last messages.

8:13am - ?

8:31am - Search teams started again at 5am

8:34am - So still nothing?

8:45am - Nope. The parents are here waiting

8:48am - Looks really grim 😞

8:50am - Guess you don't have any finding people spells, huh?

8:57am - Funny. When are the search teams due back?

I frown. It's been an hour, but Will hasn't replied. With half the town out looking for Hannah it's unlikely the diner is having a breakfast rush. Maybe the search teams have returned and he's busy being regaled with tales of the freaky gate they found in the woods.

Down in the kitchen there's an ear-splitting *crash,* followed by a shriek of rage. The smell of burning drifts up the stairs, accompanied by Louisa's voice.

"Don't be upset! This level of control is hard to grasp—"

"Which is why we have a *stove*!"

I relax. The noises I've heard don't spring from Louisa's passive-aggressive disapproval, but from the latest episode of kitchen misadventures. Theo and I still live with Louisa, but Pen is the only one under eighteen. While Theo works in IT, spending most of his time in his room, and I take odd jobs where I can find them, Pen has been home-schooled since she was expelled. Occasionally Louisa tries to teach her by combining magic with household tasks, like making breakfast.

This often results in small fires.

I check my phone once more, then go back to trying to fix my face.

My night in the woods resulted in a variety of interesting bruises, but the most prominent one was caused by running face-first into a tree. It sits high on my forehead and is apparently resistant to magic.

Healing is hard. Reattaching fingers is one thing: part of my magical education was learning about anatomy, and reattaching limbs is just putting pieces of a puzzle back together once you get past the blood and screaming. Fading bruises requires more finesse, and finesse is not one of my strong suits.

So far I've managed to move the bruise to my eyebrow.

I examine myself in the mirror, considering my options. Louisa is the best at healing, but she won't help. Theo might, but he's better with written magic and dead languages, and he won't cross Louisa. That only leaves Pen, and she's more likely to accidentally burn my eyebrows off due to her alarming affinity for fire.

I don't have an affinity for anything, really. I know the basic magic Louisa taught us. I can set a fire and put one out. I can summon light, and I have a decent understanding of curses. But I've never excelled in any single discipline. I'm not even really drawn to magic, like Pen is. My talents are more aligned with things like athletic ability and making questionable decisions. As far as witches go, I'm decidedly average.

Nothing you do will be enough.

Merich's voice springs into my head, as it has frequently over the last two days, and I scowl, suddenly conscious of my reflection. Dishevelled black hair, an ancient plaid shirt, a face that alternates between bruised and too pale. I look cold. Grim. Unsmiling.

You're not the type to be ravished.

"Bastard," I tell the mirror. Everything Merich said was intended to annoy me. None of it *mattered*.

And he's wrong. There is something I can do. If I spend any longer in my bedroom I'll go insane, but I can go to the diner. I can join a search party. Sure, they might ignore me, but it's better than sitting around being useless.

I pull on my shoes, seizing my frustratingly silent phone, and dart across the landing. I tip-toe past Theo's closed door and slip downstairs, hoping to go unnoticed.

If there was a fire, it's already been extinguished. Pen stands in the kitchen amid a haze of smoke, looking seconds from violence, but I don't see Louisa. I sneak toward the front door.

"*Cassandra.*"

Shit.

I turn back. Louisa has materialised in the doorway, and Pen is now watching me, holding a spatula in a distinctly threatening way.

"Where are you going?" Louisa asks suspiciously.

"Out," I try.

Her eyes narrow, and I try to calculate whether I can make it out the door before she catches me. It's possible, but Pen is still holding the spatula, and she's got good aim.

"Are you sneaking off to the woods?"

Alternatively, maybe I can run back upstairs instead. "No!"

"I say we let her." Pen examines a small, blackened strip which may originally have been a slice of bacon. "Especially if she brings home more of the Fae. *Especially* if they look like the last one."

"Nobody is bringing home any of the Fae," Louisa snaps. "They're not stray cats." She glares at me. "Don't you think you've caused enough trouble?"

"I'm not causing trouble!" I smother my irritation, choosing my words carefully. "The other day, I did what I thought was right." *Yes. Good start.* "I didn't mean to worry anyone. I was thinking about Hannah. I was trying to help."

"Yes, now we know about the evil gate," Pen mutters. "Very helpful."

But Louisa's expression softens. "The whole situation is very sad, but there's nothing we can do," she says gently. "The police are searching for Hannah, and it's best we don't interfere."

Fallow Creek's police department consists of less than a dozen people, and I wouldn't trust them to find a lost dog, let alone a child. But I don't resist as Louisa guides me away from the door. "What if those kids aren't lost?" I persist. "The police can't help if there's magic involved!"

"We don't know if magic *is* involved," she points out.

"I don't think Merich was lying—"

"*Merich* is one of the Fae. I'm sure he had his reasons for saying what he did, but we can't know he's trustworthy, Warden of the

Woods or not. We can't act on his word, and nobody has asked for our help."

The statement falls with the finality of a judge's gavel. That's Louisa's golden rule: if nobody asks, we don't act. She thinks it's safer that way, so we avoid involving ourselves in situations where we aren't wanted. But nobody approaches us for help, so we never act at all.

She deposits me into one of the chairs around the kitchen table. "So we do nothing," I say bitterly.

Again.

"I'll make you some toast," she says, moving into the kitchen.

I watch her go, a dull burning in my gut. It's always like this. Things always go Louisa's way. It doesn't matter how good an argument might be, it never stands up to hers. Every plan she doesn't like falls through, like when Theo wanted to move out, or when Will and I wanted to go travelling. Everything is brushed aside unless it meets her approval, so our whole lives revolve around this tiny, smothering, *safe* house, where she can always keep an eye on us.

There *is* magic involved in Hannah's disappearance. I know it.

And I know Louisa won't act.

"Why don't you do something to distract yourself?" she asks, not unkindly. "You could invite Will and Stephanie over for dinner."

The pure horror of this idea is distraction enough. "*No.*"

"Have you ever actually had a conversation with Stephanie? She might be nice."

Pen scoffs, perching on the kitchen counter. She's wearing a red dress and some hideous black and white stockings, and the blur of her swinging legs is nauseating. "She thinks we're crimes against God. How can she be *nice*?"

"Even if I did invite them, she wouldn't come," I add. "She's terrified of us. Especially Pen."

Louisa throws some bread into the toaster, rolling her eyes. "Nobody is scared of Penelope."

"*Everybody* is."

"She's seventeen!"

"She burned down a science classroom," I reply. "She threw fireballs at me two days ago, and she's dressed like Beetlejuice. People are *right* to be afraid of her."

"That fire was accidental," Pen protests, though she seems slightly too pleased with herself. "And I like how I dress. Besides, I don't know why they're scared of *me*. I'm barely allowed to leave the house, while Helen—"

"We are *not* discussing your sister," Louisa bites out.

They glare at each other for several long moments, and I hold my breath, pretending to find my shoelaces interesting.

Once upon a time there were four little witches being raised by their aunt. Then, one day, there was an enormous, world-ending fight, and one of them left and never came back. And they never talked about her again.

Luckily, there's no time for an argument to break out.

Outside, someone starts shrieking.

The three of us jump, Louisa releasing a squeak of shock, and footsteps thud down the stairs. Theo appears, looking half-asleep and deeply irritated.

"I don't know if you've noticed," he rasps, "but there's a couple of people freaking out in front of the house."

Dread hits me. "Maybe they want a séance."

Louisa sighs.

"I don't think that's it," says Theo.

"Maybe it's about Helen," Pen mutters sulkily.

"*Stop talking about your sister.*" Louisa pinches the bridge of her nose. "Cass, go and see what's happening."

I gratefully flee the room, making my way to the front door. The screaming has gone quiet, but through the panes of frosted glass I can see figures on the doorstep. Two voices hiss at each other, too low to make out, until a woman screeches, "I don't care! We're doing it!"

Someone knocks.

I close my eyes, directing my thoughts to whatever God might be listening. *Please,* I beg, *don't let it be a séance.*

Witches can't actually speak to the dead, but every so often someone comes looking for a direct line to the afterlife. Those requests usually end in crying and pleading, or cursing and resentment, and occasionally someone throwing eggs at the house.

I open the door.

A man and a woman stand on the doorstep. He's tall and dark-haired, she's petite and blonde. They're both grey with exhaustion, and she looks like she's been weeping for days.

My stomach sinks to my feet. Definitely a séance.

Then I notice the figure behind them. Will looks guiltier than I've ever seen him, cringing down into his jacket.

"Sorry," he says, which means this is worse than I thought.

The woman takes a deep breath, tears shining on her cheeks. "You're a witch, then?"

My brain stalls. "Pardon?"

"A witch," says the man. "He said there were witches here."

Guess you don't have any finding people spells, huh?

I narrow my eyes at Will. He looks like he wants to crawl under the porch and die.

Then—

"Our daughter is Hannah," says the woman. "She's missing. *Help us.*"

•••

For a place housing four witches, our home is very normal. The books on the shelves might be filled with runes and wards and languages incomprehensible to anyone without magical blood, but they fight for space with Theo's sci-fi books and Louisa's romance novels. The herbs in the kitchen are the kind you would expect to find, like rosemary and basil. There is no black cat, or any cat at all, because Pen has allergies.

The main room is a combined kitchen and living area. The kitchen faces the woods at the back of the house, while the seating area is beneath the large window overlooking the front yard. There's a vase of flowers on the coffee table, next to a plate of cookies nobody is touching.

It forms a barricade between the two couches. On one, a woman is sobbing her heart out, her husband holding her hand. On the other sits Louisa, with a hastily dressed Theo beside her.

Will hovers miserably in the doorway, and Pen has been banished for the crime of being underage. I don't mention I can see her eavesdropping from the staircase. I'm fairly certain Louisa is looking for a reason to banish *me*, so I lurk in the kitchen, watching from a safe distance

"Mrs. Hendricks," Louisa says weakly. "I'm not quite sure what you're looking for."

Jane Hendricks likely hasn't stopped crying since Hannah disappeared. Her eyes are swollen, yet tears keep coming, as if she's overflowing from within. It's uncomfortable to watch.

When she gasps for breath she sounds like a woman drowning. "I don't know." She dabs her eyes, sniffing. "You must be able to do something, right? *He* said you were witches. He said you reattached his finger the other day."

Typical Will. He can't resist trying to make us more popular. I shoot him a glare, and he mouths *sorry* for the fifth or sixth time.

"Can't you sense her or something?" Jane asks desperately. "Can't you see where she is?"

Louisa looks wildly out of her depth, but she's looked like that since she offered them coffee and they declined. "You're thinking of psychics," she replies. "We *do* practice magic, but it's not an infallible thing. I don't want you to get the wrong impression. Besides, there are better ways to perform a search. The police—"

"They're just searching the woods." Simon Hendricks has the face of a man staring into his worst nightmare and failing to wake up. There are no tears from him. Maybe they've crystallised into despair. "They have no leads. And the longer a child is missing, the less likely…"

He doesn't continue.

Louisa shuffles, her expression becoming increasingly panicked. *Almost,* the tiny, mean part of my brain thinks, *like she's running out of reasons to avoid helping them.* "Any outside interference could obscure a potential trail," she says.

"Tromping through the woods for days could do that too," I mutter.

Her spine stiffens.

"She's our only child," Jane whispers. "We tried for years. We'd almost given up, and then…"

"I understand," says Louisa. "But I'm sure if you give it more time, the police will find her."

"She's six," Simon replies, his voice hollow. "If she's lost, she's running out of time. If she's been taken…"

A shudder runs across his shoulders, like a tremor through the earth.

"I'm sure they'll find her," Louisa says softly.

Even she doesn't sound convinced.

I stare at her, my throat tight. The police can't help here, not if there's magic involved. The best authority then would be a Witch, and there isn't one. But there *is* magic that could help: tracking spells to trace Hannah's path through the woods, scrying spells to locate her. If she's there to be found, it might work.

Louisa knows this. I see it in her face. Theo knows too. He watches her with dark eyes, jaw set like he wants to speak up but can't quite bring himself to do so. He's the golden boy. He won't argue against her.

We could do something.

But she stays quiet.

I chew the inside of my cheek. *Don't be hasty,* I warn myself. There might be a perfectly reasonable explanation for all of this. Coyotes can be dangerous. Someone might have taken Hannah; people snatch kids all the time. There must be something in the woods that will set the police on the right trail—

Like a lost shoe—

I think of the iron gate. That long, echoing creak.

"Was Hannah wearing purple shoes?"

The question comes out before I even know I'm going to speak. Louisa and Theo look at me like I've sprouted a second head, and Will's eyes widen.

Hannah's parents look up, and with growing horror, I see hope on their faces.

"What?" Jane whispers.

"Purple shoes." I wish I'd never opened my mouth. Judging by Louisa's glare, by the end of the day I may no longer have a tongue. "With—"

"Pink laces," she breathes.

"Do you know something?" Simon gets to his feet, a renewed intensity in his voice. "Did you see her?"

Jane clutches his arm, her gaze fixed on me. "Please."

I shouldn't have spoken. This was a stupid idea. And yet...

Nothing you do will be enough.

Isn't it worse to do nothing at all?

My mouth is dry as I say, "I can't promise anything."

They nod frantically. Jane Hendricks has eyes in a perfect shade of light green, like light through leaves. I wonder if Hannah's are the same colour.

"*Anything*," I stress. "Magic is—it's unpredictable. But I'll try."

Mrs. Hendricks throws herself at me, and then I'm nervously patting her back as she sobs. Louisa's face is stony, and Will beams at me from the doorway, as if he knew it would turn out like this all along.

In the shadows of the staircase, I see Pen extend her hands in the universal symbol of *what-the-fuck*.

•••

It took considerable effort to make Hannah's parents leave. In the end we had to claim their presence would distract me from the task at hand, and only then did they reluctantly depart, still sobbing with thanks.

As soon as the door was closed the air turned icy, and Louisa stalked into the kitchen in ominous silence, with an unspoken order to follow.

And now we're sitting around the kitchen table, enjoying the most hostile late breakfast in history.

"Why would you do something like this?"

Beneath the table my fists clench, my fingernails biting grooves into my palms. "It was the right thing to do," I say stiffly.

Louisa scoffs, slamming a mug of coffee down in front of Will, who looks as though he's regretting his decision to stick around. Her aggressive hospitality makes it clear that although she's not angry enough to ignore him, she definitely blames him for starting this. She also doesn't offer him a cookie, which is a bad sign.

She doesn't give me coffee at all, which is worse.

"I don't understand what you're so angry about." Pen sits on the kitchen counter, chewing thoughtfully on a piece of toast. "Cass never said *we* were going to help. She said *she* would."

"I said I'd *try* to help," I correct.

"You're not helping anyone, Penelope." Louisa's hair is moving ever-so-slightly of its own accord, and I resist the urge to shuffle my chair backward. "You're underage, you stay out of this."

"I don't think they're expecting a miracle, Ms. Reilly," Will says. Perhaps sensing danger, he stays huddled down, his chin tucked into his collar. It makes him look about ten, like the little boy he used to be, as in awe of Louisa now as he was then. "They just want some help. The cops… well, they're stumped."

"That's not our problem," she replies.

"Why are you acting like this is the end of the world?" I demand. "At least we have a lead! Nobody else found anything!"

She gives me a dirty look. "You found a shoe."

"*Hannah's* shoe."

"Where did you find it, anyway?" Will asks. "How did the search teams miss it?"

Louisa puts the coffee pot down in the centre of the table, and I gingerly reach for it. "I don't know. It was pretty deep in the woods. Maybe they haven't looked there yet."

I doubt the words even as I say them. There was something magical about that gate. So many search parties have combed through the woods; someone should have found it. So why haven't they?

"Anyway," I continue, trying to ignore my unease. "It doesn't matter. I already agreed to help."

Louisa grips the back of a chair. "You shouldn't have."

Her bitter tone sends a ripple of anger through me. "You're the one who wanted us to step up," I snap. "They came to us, they asked for our help. That's what we were waiting for, right? What more did you want?" I turn back to Will. "You brought them here. Do you know anything useful?"

Will sighs. "Hannah has been missing for over forty-eight hours. Search parties have swept the woods, but nobody has found anything yet."

"Did anyone see her enter the woods?" Theo asks, finally breaking his silence. He hasn't spoken since Hannah's parents left, and I can't tell what he's thinking. "When was she last seen?"

"She went in with her parents and was with them for most of the walk. She vanished on the way back. They claimed they looked for her for about an hour, then went for help when it started to get dark."

"They *claimed*?"

Will grimaces. "Well..."

"It's a missing child," Louisa says. She takes a seat, looking marginally calmer, but she still won't look at me. "And the parents were the last to see her."

Theo's eyebrows shoot up. "*They're* suspects? *Them*?"

"The parents are always suspects," says Louisa. "And people can be excellent liars."

The thought makes me uncomfortable. It's impossible to imagine Jane Hendricks having anything to do with her daughter's disappearance, but I suppose Louisa is right. "What do the police think happened?" I ask.

Will's diner has the well-deserved reputation of serving the best coffee in town. Cops frequently stop by, so I'm not surprised when he answers immediately. "In normal cases they'd assume it was a lost child. They'd look at the parents, question whether they had any involvement."

"In normal cases," I echo.

"If they were dealing with *one* lost child."

"But Hannah is the fourth."

He nods. "I don't think anyone believes her parents were involved, but they don't believe she simply wandered off, either. Not after the others. They're talking about bringing in special teams. Government, maybe." He glances at me. "Do you think this has something to do with magic?"

I try to keep my expression neutral. As comfortable as Will might be around witches, he's still a normal guy. He knows magic exists, but all he's seen of it is harmless, helpful, *good*. He has no idea about the wider supernatural world. He's never seen the Fae. For him, things like vampires and werewolves are only stories, monsters stay under the bed, and children don't go missing under magical circumstances.

I remember my night in the woods. That rattling hiss in the dark.

If he knew what was really out there, I'm not sure Will would sleep at night.

"I don't know," I say. "I don't think the place I found Hannah's shoe was somewhere she could have found on her own. Maybe she was taken. But I don't think the circumstances were… normal."

"Magic, then?"

"Maybe."

"But there's no proof." Louisa sighs. "There are a few ways of using magic to find a person. One of those would be the best place to start, if Cass decides to do this."

Unbelievable. "If?"

She gives me a pleading look. "Cass, we try so hard to keep a low profile—"

"Pen sets a fire every second week!"

"Accidentally," Pen adds loudly.

"We get by perfectly fine without inserting ourselves into matters that don't involve us," Louisa continues. "We're keeping ourselves *safe*—"

My disbelief turns to anger, lodging in my throat like a swallowed bone. "Safe from *what*?" I demand. "Nobody likes us! Nobody trusts us! Will is the only person who doesn't think we're communing with Satan—"

"Not my business if you are," he interjects.

"Do you really think this is a happy way to live? We are totally alone—"

Louisa reaches across the table, seizing my hands. "Cass, have you thought about what happens if you find this girl and she's dead?"

My words wither in my mouth.

Louisa's gaze is piercing. Desperate. "Nobody likes us," she says, and I realise with a start that she sounds close to tears. "I know, sweetheart, it's hard. But you—all of you—are special, and different, and powerful, and that *terrifies* normal people. They don't trust us because we'll never be like them. They tolerate us if we're helpful when they need us, and if they don't see us any more than necessary. But now they're scared because their children are missing, and scared people are dangerous. Have you thought about how it will look if you find Hannah in any way but alive and well?"

My lips feel numb. Pen and Theo are staring at her, and Will has gone pale. "But it wouldn't be my fault."

"They won't care," she whispers. "They already view us with suspicion. Witches have been killed for less."

I blink at her. "What do you want me to do? Just… leave it?"

Louisa straightens, and a stab of betrayal runs through me as I realise what she's going to say. "Attempt the rite. Become the Witch, and—"

I tear my hands free from hers. "*No*."

The room seems to freeze.

Then Theo leans forward. "This isn't the seventeenth century," he says calmly. "Nobody is killing anyone."

Louisa blinks at him. "You can't think this is a good idea."

I'm equally surprised. Theo's always so *good*. He's never sided with me. But I remember his face earlier, as he watched Louisa speaking to Hannah's parents. He seemed confused. Frustrated at her unwillingness to help.

And now he ignores her, meeting my gaze. "She's right," he says. "This is risky. If this doesn't work out, things could get ugly. But you offered to help, Cass. And if you want to, maybe you should."

"And if you were the Witch," Louisa murmurs, "you could do so much more."

I grit my teeth.

Both of them are watching me. If I want to change my mind, now is the time. An excuse will be made; Louisa is good at that. Maybe it will be *nothing we did revealed anything helpful*, or *our magic isn't strong enough.* If I choose not to do this, she'll make it okay.

Maybe they'll find Hannah without me. Maybe they won't.

You're not the Witch, Merich said. *Nothing you do will be enough.*

But it's never been that simple.

If I were the Witch, I'd be the magical authority in Fallow Creek. Maybe I *could* help Hannah. If I wanted to try, Louisa wouldn't stop me.

And if I were the Witch, I'd also be responsible for everything supernatural within the borders of the town. It would be my job to maintain those borders, to hunt those monsters in the dark. Sure, I'd be more powerful, but only as long as I stayed here. And that's assuming I pass the rite. That's assuming I don't end up like my mother, choking out her last breaths alone on some forest floor.

If I become the Witch, I'm never getting out of this town.

You could do so much more.

But the price is too high.

"I'm going to help them," I say. "My way."

Louisa's face goes blank, and she sits back in her chair, silent.

"Alright," says Will. "At least you know where to start."

I tear my eyes away from Louisa. "I do?"

He raises an eyebrow, as if surprised I haven't already worked it out. "Isn't it obvious? You've got to go back to where you found the shoe."

5

I SPEND MOST OF THE NIGHT AWAKE, STARING AT THE ceiling. Every murmur of wind seems to carry the creak of iron, and not even a pillow pressed over my head dampens the sound. Even without the phantom noise, my anxiety runs rampant.

If I'm wrong, and nothing in the woods leads us to Hannah… what then?

And Louisa is so against this. She's always been overprotective, eager to keep us out of trouble, but this reaction is extreme even for her. She barely spoke to me after I decided to help the Hendricks, and dinner last night was so profoundly uncomfortable that even Pen kept her mouth shut. I'd have gone into the woods then, just to escape the awkwardness, if Theo hadn't pointed out that waiting until the next morning would allow me to avoid the search teams.

I don't understand it. This can't be as terrible as Louisa is making it seem—I'm trying to find a missing child, after all. Yet with all her talk of keeping us safe, she won't admit this isn't as simple as a kid lost in the woods. Something is wrong. The knowledge sits in my bones like dread, humming through my nerves like the promise of danger. Something is wrong.

And it starts with that gate.

Still, that doesn't stop me from staring out the kitchen window the following morning, hoping a small child will wander out of the woods to prove me wrong.

I drink my coffee.

No small child appears.

"Shit," I say glumly.

"Good morning to you, too."

I jump, hissing as I throw hot coffee over my hand. Will has managed to make his way into the house without me noticing, and he looks bright-eyed and fluffy-tailed and far too full of positive energy for six in the morning.

A small foreboding feeling strikes me. Or maybe it's the caffeine.

"Hi," I say warily. "Aren't you working today?"

Drawn by our voices, Pen enters the room, her slippers slapping the floorboards. She ignores me completely, moving to hover hopefully beside Will.

"You expected me to work knowing what you were doing today?" Will passes Pen a paper bag, and she beams, skipping into the kitchen. "I took the day off."

I notice too late that he's dressed warmly. In hiking boots.

My small foreboding feeling grows into a slightly larger foreboding feeling.

"Oh no. *Hell* no."

"Hell *yes*," he counters.

Pen snorts, pulling a muffin out of the paper bag. "If you take him anywhere near that gate, he'll get his soul sucked out or something," she says.

"Which is exactly why he's not coming," I reply.

Will glares at me. "I'm not letting you wander alone in the woods where people keep going missing! And face it, you can't stop me from going with you."

He's right. I can't stop him, not unless I trap him in the bathroom and barricade the door, but I can't bring myself to be annoyed. He has no magic. He can't fight. He doesn't have a ruthless bone in his body—I've seen him apologise to inanimate objects after bumping into them. Yet he's absolutely serious about accompanying me, like *he* could protect *me*.

I'd be offended if I wasn't so touched.

"I'm not a child," I say, already aware I'm fighting a losing battle. "I won't go missing."

"Maybe not, but you take unnecessary risks when you're alone." Louisa swans into the room, brushing past me, and I feel a surge of bitterness as she avoids my eye. "It's a good thing your brother is going with you."

"*What?*"

She shrugs. "He's got a much wider education in magical theory. It can't hurt."

Theo appears in the doorway, looking as if he's just rolled out of bed, and anger burns to life in my stomach. I know what this is. Louisa's made it perfectly clear she doesn't approve of me doing this, and I've made it perfectly clear I'm going to do it anyway. But if she sends Theo with me, if she puts *him* in charge, she still manages to assert some control over the situation.

Theo raises an eyebrow. "Don't look so annoyed. It's not like I *want* to go trudging through the woods."

"So don't come," I reply, my teeth gritted.

"I'm sure we can handle it ourselves," Will adds, looking warily between us.

"If Theo's not going, can I?" Pen asks. "I never get to do anything."

"You're not going, and Theo is." Louisa levels the room with a glare that puts Will's to shame. "If you insist on going ahead with this, you'll do so as safely as possible, or at least in a way that won't result in multiple deaths."

I work my jaw, searching for a response, but nothing comes. Will zips up his jacket, giving me a sympathetic look. Everyone is ready. There's no reason to delay. "Fine," I snap. "Let's go."

"And be *careful*," Louisa says.

Theo flaps a hand in acknowledgement, heading out the back door, and Will follows, shooting me a worried glance. Only once they're gone does Louisa turn to me, her voice lowering.

"I know you're trying to help, but don't be reckless out there," she says.

She's just worried, I tell myself. It doesn't make me less angry. "We'll be fine."

"Remember, you're the one who wanted to go through with this. Will and Theo—"

Of course. She's not worried about *me*. "Yes," I say bitterly. "I know. If anything happens to them, it's my fault. I get it."

She looks stricken, but doesn't stop me as I duck around her, fleeing out the door.

Will and Theo are waiting in the backyard, the two of them looking up as I approach. Will's eyes crease, as if he can tell what happened from my expression, and I feel myself flush. He already knows Louisa and I argue a lot, but it doesn't make it less embarrassing when it happens in front of him.

I don't meet his gaze, marching straight to the garden gate.

"So," he says mildly. "Into the creepy woods."

"Yeah." The gate closes behind us with a *clunk*.

"And what are we looking for?"

I don't see any point in lying to him. "I found Hannah's shoe near a gate," I say.

"A gate?"

"Like a normal gate, but evil. We're trying to find it again."

"Ah," he says. He does not entirely hide his confusion.

"Lead on, then," says Theo.

I shoot him a look over my shoulder, but he seems sincere. Or maybe he's mocking me. "Louisa probably wants *you* to be in charge," I say tautly. "That's why she made you come with me."

He blinks. "Made me come? Cass, I volunteered."

He strides past me, and then the woods swallow us.

It's peaceful under the canopy. Birds are trilling, leaves rustling. Moss climbs the tree trunks in shades of deep emerald and burnt yellow, melting into a tangle of shadows and withering brown undergrowth. Everything glitters with dew, hazy in the cold morning light.

"It's actually not so bad in here," says Will.

"Right," I mutter. "If it weren't for all those vanishing children, we could have a picnic."

"You're the one who thinks there's an evil gate in here." Theo looks around, his nose wrinkling. He's always been happiest in the comfort of his bedroom, preferring to be surrounded by books than by nature. It makes the idea of him volunteering to accompany me all the more bizarre. "We could simply be dealing with a serial killer, you know."

"Don't you think people might have noticed a serial killer?"

"Not necessarily. People are dense."

"Well, I still think it's nice," says Will, picking his way through a cluster of fallen branches. "We should get moving, though. The search teams are trying another part of the woods today, but I'd rather not run into them."

As he moves ahead, I edge closer to Theo. "You didn't actually volunteer, did you?" I ask.

He frowns. "Yes. Why did you think I came?"

"I thought Louisa sent you. To make sure I didn't do anything stupid."

"She didn't want *you* to do this," he points out. "Why would she send me along too?"

I hadn't considered that. The last of my anger dissipates, leaving me embarrassed. "Right. Sorry."

"I didn't really give her the option to say no," he adds. "I just told her I was going with you."

"I imagine she was thrilled," I say. "So… why *did* you want to come? Don't you think this is a bad idea?"

He sighs, dragging a hand through his hair. "Maybe. But you're not the only one sick of sitting around while bad things happen. I'm so tired of being *useless.* But I don't want to be the Witch, either. So I guess we try things your way."

I feel oddly thrown. Theo so rarely agrees with me—the fact he's actually willing to follow my lead is startling. "Well," I reply, clearing my throat. "We'd better not screw this up, then."

He gives me a small, awkward smile, and we start after Will.

The three of us walk for half an hour. I take the lead, following a path I only vaguely recall, but even with my blurred memory it's impossible to miss the strange feeling in the air. Autumn hangs heavy in this part of the forest. There's a stillness in the trees, an eerie silence where there should be birdsong, and it spreads as we move deeper into the woods. Like we're on the right track.

Something black moves at the edge of my vision, and my head snaps around. Nothing. Probably a bird, startled into flight by our passing. But my skin prickles.

"I hope you know I have no idea what we're doing," Will announces.

His voice breaks the tension, and Theo sighs. "Looking for a gate."

"Yes, I know. But where are we going?"

I roll my eyes, stepping over a ridge of gnarled roots. "You're the one who wanted to come."

"Yes, so you didn't get lost in the woods! I didn't want *all of us* to get lost instead!"

"We're not lost!" At least, I hope we're not. "And we're looking for weird shit, okay? Like the gate. So tell us if you see anything weird."

"Hey," says Theo. "Is *this* weird?"

I turn. He's fallen behind, paused beside a tree Will and I walked past a few moments ago. I paid no attention to it—it appeared to be a tree like any other.

From the back, I see the trunk is cratered, a gash burrowing through the bark and into the wood below. The hole travels up from the base of the tree, reaching the height of Theo's thigh, and everything within the wound is black and crumbling, as if scorched by fire.

"What the hell is that?" demands Will.

"Could be a lightning strike," Theo says, sounding unconvinced.

"And when did it last storm, exactly?" I crouch beside the tree, peering at the hole. Weaving through the ashy surface are veins of thick black sludge, glistening like oil.

Theo peers over my shoulder, a line of worry between his eyebrows. "It's eating away at the wood," he murmurs. "Like it's growing."

"Not a lightning strike, then."

"No. But this can't be natural. A fungus or a disease wouldn't present this way. And can you smell that?"

Will frowns, and I sniff. There's not much of note: damp earth, autumn air. But below it…

Rotten fruit. Rot and burning, like an electrical fire.

A chill crawls down my spine. "This is magic."

"*Bad* magic," Theo says. "Cass, how close are we to this gate of yours?"

"It's not *mine*," I mutter, but I look around, trying to judge. "I think we're heading in the right direction."

"We keep going, then."

Will watches us nervously. "This isn't normal, right?"

"No," I reply. "This is very not normal."

Leaves drift down around us, unhurried by wind. It's strangely still under the canopy, the air stagnant, but there must be a rogue breeze, something to stir movement in the nearby trees.

The dark shape is gone before I can make it out, but my unease doesn't lift.

We continue more slowly, in a tighter group than before. We're deep in the woods now, and the branches overhead weave together, little sunlight piercing through. Everything is dim, as if we've left the day behind us, and the ground underfoot is slick with rotting leaves.

There are more trees like the one Theo found. Some are less damaged, only blackened near the roots. Others have darkness spreading up their trunks, until on some trees the crumbling wounds nearly reach my waist.

"I don't understand this," Theo whispers. "It's like necrosis."

"Don't use that word near me," Will mutters, shuddering.

I don't know why our voices are lowered, but it feels appropriate. We must be nearing the gate, and the woods are utterly silent. I can't recall when I last heard a bird.

"What's causing it, though?" Theo continues. "It's not every tree, so it must be from physical contact with something."

"Poison?" Will suggests. "Some kind of tree vampire?"

Theo waves him off. "Vampires stick with blood, and there aren't any in this area."

"What—*I was joking*!"

"You know witches are real. Why should vampires surprise you?"

Will recoils, looking horrified, and I glower at Theo. "It wasn't vampires."

"But whatever it is, it's killing the trees," Will says, somewhat more nervously. "What if it spreads? If we don't know what caused it, how do we stop it? How far could it go?"

"Not beyond Fallow Creek." Theo stops beside the nearest tree, frowning at the oozing wood. "Even if it does spread, it won't move beyond this town. There's a border. A magical boundary marking the territory held by the witches in this area. It keeps evil out, and in."

I watch him, remaining silent. Because that's not true. The territory isn't held by the witches, but by *the* Witch. The stronger the Witch, the stronger the border, and the absence of a Witch may have whittled our borders down to nothing. There's no way to know if they'll keep this sickness in at all.

He meets my eyes, and I know he's as aware of that as I am. "If this has a magical cause, it can't spread past the boundary," he says calmly.

"But we don't know what's causing it," Will counters, oblivious to our concern. "You just *think* it's magic."

"We can find out."

My attention returns to Theo. "How?"

"There's a spell I know. It can show you the history of an object. I'm not sure if it works on living material, though."

"I've never heard of it," I admit.

"You never read."

"I'm a *tactile learner*," I say defensively. "What's this spell, then?"

"If it works, it could tell us what happened to these trees."

He looks at me expectantly, and I realise he's waiting for me to approve. Merich's voice echoes in my memory. *Don't use any magic. They notice that.* But there's already dark magic at work here. We can't ignore it, and it's not like there's a better option.

"Do it," I say.

Theo nods, turning to the diseased tree. "I'm not totally sure how this works in practice."

"That's what happens when you learn out of books," I mutter.

"Shut up. Give me a second."

As he mumbles to himself, Will steps closer to me. "This is safe, right?" he asks.

"Probably."

"How convincing."

I shoot him a smile, hoping my worry doesn't show on my face. "We'll be fine, Will."

Then Theo touches the blackened tree, and the world turns inside-out.

Will gasps, and the breath leaves my lungs. Magic ripples out around us, sparking across my skin, and then—

The woods turn yellow, the sepia haze of an old photo, and they *move*. The darkness creeping up the trees shrinks back into the roots, and bark grows over the empty space. Bugs shudder back to life, uncurling and crawling backward up the reviving trunk. Leaves drift upward. Night falls, day dawns, and it repeats once more—

And stops. The leaves hang in the air, motionless.

Then they fall to the earth.

Theo lifts his head, and something appears among the trees.

The girl is hazy in the golden tones around us, but I can see her clearly. She's small. Blonde. No more than six. Too young to be alone in the woods, but she walks with unfaltering surety, facing straight ahead as she picks her way across the uneven ground.

She wears purple shoes with pink laces.

Her foot slides on a patch of slick leaves, but she doesn't pause, continuing onward. Will steps away from me, leaving a gap, and the phantom girl passes between us. She's close enough to touch, for every detail of her face to be visible.

Her eyes are empty. As blank as those of a corpse.

She's not thinking. The realisation turns me cold. *She's not even awake in there—*

Theo hisses, and I tear my eyes off the girl.

As she passes, a black bloom appears at the base of the tree trunk. And it grows. And grows. And grows.

The spell breaks.

The scene vanishes, the woods erupting into colour. I gasp, blinking at the brilliant greens, the rich browns, the bursts of yellow and velvet shadows and the impossible darkness of the thing slinking through the trees. It's so *bright,* shocking after what we just witnessed.

Will spins in place, and Theo releases a long breath.

"Holy shit, Theo," I croak.

"Was that real?" Will asks, in a distinctly higher voice than usual.

"Holy shit," I repeat. "That was Hannah fucking Hendricks."

"Yep." Theo rests his head against the tree trunk, closing his eyes. Sweat beads his forehead, and his skin is grey and clammy.

Will is still turning in circles. "I thought you were looking at the history of the tree."

"I was," says Theo. "I did."

I can still picture the ghostly Hannah. The black blooming in her wake like plague flowers.

Will stops moving. "She did that?"

"She can't have done," I splutter. "She's *six.*"

Theo opens his eyes. "She went that way," he says heavily.

Dread sits in my stomach like a stone. I hardly need to turn. I already know what I'll see.

Hannah Hendricks walked into the woods, heading straight toward the gate.

We're silent for several moments.

"It might not mean anything," Theo offers. "Maybe she was just walking."

"Toward the gate," I reply.

He doesn't respond.

I remember Hannah's face. The blankness in her eyes. "We need to go." My pulse thunders in my ears, my chest tight. "We need to see if she's there."

"You know she's not there. She wasn't there when you found her shoe—"

"Guys."

Will speaks so softly I almost don't hear him. He stares into the trees over my shoulder, his face grey, and a cold feeling settles over me. I follow his gaze.

And I see the rabbit.

It stands among the roots, watching us from a few trees away. It's the closest I've ever been to a rabbit without it bolting, but that's not what frightens me.

The rabbit is dead. The rabbit *should* be dead. The fur on its side is gone, the flesh below torn until ribs are visible, glaringly white among the red.

But it's not all red. Some of the flesh is turning dark, not in the usual manner of decay, but like the crumbling trees around us.

Its eyes are black. Blood streaks its face.

It doesn't blink.

"Cass," Theo murmurs. "I think we should go home now."

I keep looking at the rabbit, too afraid to breathe. We're so close to the gate. I glance up, searching the trees as if I might spot it.

I do so in time to see the long, black hand curled around a trunk, the fingers sharp and spindling.

As I watch, my thoughts silent with terror, it slowly slides out of sight.

"Cass?"

I close my eyes. Swallow hard.

When I open them there's nothing there. I can almost pretend I imagined it.

"Yes," I whisper. "Let's go."

Will tugs at my sleeve, and I let him draw me away. The rabbit's tattered sides jerk with each heartbeat, but otherwise it doesn't stir.

It watches us go, blood leaking from its eyes.

•••

Theo takes the lead on the way out. Will is right behind him, pausing only to make sure I'm following, but there's no chance of me lagging behind. We move at a pace slightly below a run, and although fear strangles me into silence, my thoughts are screaming. I try counting back from ten, but the numbers vanish in my panic. There is no room in my head for anything but that terrible hand.

It didn't belong to anything human.

So what was it?

Finally we stagger to a halt, and Theo collapses at the base of a tree, wheezing. Will drags his hands down his face. "Oh man," he pants. "I can never tell Steph about this."

I try to imagine Stephanie's reaction to what we saw, or the reaction of *any* regular churchgoer. To hell with finding the kids, they'd burn down the whole forest.

"No," I rasp, my heart slamming in my chest. "In fact, don't tell anyone."

"Oh, I won't." He takes a deep breath. "So, uh, that seemed bad."

I almost laugh, until I remember those glistening black fingers, slipping out of sight. Instead I choke back the urge to be sick.

Bad is an understatement.

"I'm sorry I didn't believe you, Cass." Theo watches me, his cheeks pale. His spell might have shown us some answers, but it took a lot out of him. "Something weird is going on here. Beyond weird, this is scary shit."

"What *is* going on here?" Will demands. "We all saw Hannah, right? She turned those trees black. Is she possessed or something?"

I start to shoot the idea down, then hesitate.

Will looks appalled.

"She's not possessed," Theo scoffs. "It's not demons."

"*It kind of looked like demons—*"

Will's voice is rising rapidly. I don't blame him for freaking out. I'm on the brink of a breakdown myself, but there's no time for one now.

"Will," I start.

He cuts himself off, turning to me. His expression is pleading, like he's desperate for me to give him a sane explanation for all this.

There is no sane explanation. But I can't lie to him, either.

"There are things I haven't told you," I say carefully. "Something happened a few months ago. Something magical. And bad."

He swallows. "Right."

I press my thumbnail against my finger, the pressure keeping me focused. "I think it involves the gate I found. And those missing kids."

"The first kid went missing a few months ago." He frowns. "But those trees, the rabbit…"

"I think they're connected," I say. "Whatever happened, I think it set something loose in the woods."

"You didn't tell me this earlier."

"I wasn't sure what was happening. I didn't want you to worry."

Will shoots me an incredulous look. "Well, I'm worried *now*."

"You should be," says Theo. "Whatever is happening, I think it's safe to say it's very, very evil."

Will is quiet for a moment. I wait, the painful bite of my thumbnail reminding me to breathe. Maybe this will be too much for him. After what we saw, it wouldn't surprise me; we went looking for missing children, not semi-dead animals. I expect him to walk away.

Instead he squares his jaw and says, "So. What do we do?"

And he looks at me.

I blink. Then I look at Theo.

He cocks an eyebrow, as if to say, *Well?*

"We're going to try and fix it," I say. Firmly. Like I know what I'm doing. "We're going to find out what's going on, and we're going to stop it."

It seems like such a weak way to address what we just learned, to ease the terror we all seem to feel. But something relaxes in Will's face, and his steady blue eyes meet mine.

"Alright," he says. "Let's do it."

Theo hauls himself to his feet, groaning. "I guess we're saving the day, then. But for now, can we please get out of here?"

I glance around. No dark shapes slink between the trees, but still my skin crawls. "Sure. Let's go."

We make our way through the woods, and the air slowly starts to lighten. Sunshine filters through the branches, and at the first sound of birdsong some of my fear eases. As the treeline appears Theo speeds up, and Will trails behind him, appearing lost in thought.

A figure moves at the edge of my vision.

I freeze, my hand flexing in preparation for a spell, but no bleeding-eyed beast leaps out of the shadows. Instead when I look over, my heart pounding, I find a face peering out of the trees.

Merich gives me a hard stare, then slips back out of sight.

I bite my lip. Will and Theo have continued on, too preoccupied to notice I've fallen behind. The house is almost visible. It should be safe.

I follow Merich.

The shadows off the main path are deep and cold, casting everything into a glorious green gloom. I pause, adjusting to the dim light.

"Didn't I tell you to stay out of the woods?"

I jump. Leaning against a tree, Merich raises an eyebrow, and my gut twists at the sight of his eyes. *Not like the rabbit's,* I tell myself. *Not blank, or dead.*

Yet still so very, very black.

"I didn't have much choice," I hiss, embarrassed by my fear. "What are you doing, stalking me?"

He scoffs. "You aren't that interesting. Are you aware you're being followed?"

"What?"

His head tilts. In the low light his hair gleams like polished wood. There's no sign of his sword, but surrounded by darkness and creeping vines, he looks more dangerous and less human than ever. "It appears your adventure the other night disturbed a creature best left unantagonized."

The hideous black hand. The flitting shadows. "I thought you said the monsters were invisible."

"I assure you this one is quite noticeable." Merich sounds unbothered, as calm as if he's talking about the weather. "It's a Hound."

"A dog?"

"They're creatures that feed off this world. They drain emotion, power, sucking the life out of everything they can, as there's no life where they come from. They slip between realms more easily than other monsters. I suppose a hole in the world would make their passage easier still."

My chest tightens. "You think it came through the gap you talked about."

"I do."

"And one is following me?"

"You're a source of power. All witches are, as are the Fae. It'll track you wherever you go—*that's* why it's called a Hound. Hence why I told you to stay out of the woods. And to avoid using magic."

He gives me a pointed look. At least, I think it's pointed. It's hard to tell with his eyes, but I still feel a flush of guilt. "I can't stay out of the woods," I say. "Merich, one of the missing children went toward that gate I saw."

"And?"

I stare at him. "Well, they're obviously connected. We can't ignore it."

"It would be the easiest option."

"I'm not abandoning a small child because it's convenient for you," I say coldly.

Merich frowns at me, appearing puzzled. "You *are* aware you can't save everyone, right?"

His matter-of-fact tone strikes a nerve, and I storm forward through the undergrowth. "You and everyone else seem to think I should do nothing," I snap. "At least I'm trying to save someone! Have you seen what's going on in these woods—those trees, and the animals? You really think this will stop on its own? Someone has to fix this, and I don't see anyone else volunteering!"

I don't realise it's true until I say it. Until today I thought this was about Hannah, a problem as simple as finding a missing girl. But something else is at work here, something dark. No cop will be able to fix this, and no amount of search parties will help.

Magical problems call for magical solutions. And if something evil is growing in these woods, I'm going to stop it.

"You really think you can do it," Merich says wonderingly.

"You don't get an opinion on what I can or can't do," I snap.

He looks down at me, his expression unreadable, and I notice we're now standing almost chest to chest. "Fine," he says. "Do what you like. I simply thought you'd want to know about the creature following you. The Hound will pursue you, and a house full of witches will stick out like a neon sign."

I hide the rush of fear that goes through me. "So we'll fight it off."

"It's not from this world. I doubt it will be so easy."

"I'm sure we can deal with *one* unholy abomination." I watch him, thinking, and realise what's bothering me. Merich gives off the impression he couldn't care less about this, but if he doesn't care, why bother warning me?

"That event you mentioned," I say. "The magical disturbance."

He inclines his head.

"It happened around the same time the first of those children went missing."

I don't know what reaction I'm looking for until I see it. Merich stiffens, taking a sharp breath in, and I know he's having the same realisation I did: the gate, the missing children, the monsters in the woods. All connected. All leading back to that moment when the world shook.

I was right.

"They can't be connected," Merich says, but there's doubt in his voice. "Nothing from beyond the gap should be strong enough to interact with humans."

My feeling of triumph vanishes. "What do you mean, *interact*? You think something could be taking them?"

"I think this is more serious than I thought." He looks at me. "You shouldn't get involved. I'm staying out of this."

I gape. "But… it's your *job* to guard the woods!"

"Not from this. Go home. This isn't a problem you're equipped to handle."

My teeth click together, cutting off my response. I don't know why I expected anything different. I barely know him, so why should I expect his help? And why do I feel so disappointed? "Fine." I spin on my heel, starting back the way I came. "Thanks for the warning, Merich."

His hand closes around my arm.

"Cassandra," he says. "It's not a problem *I'm* equipped to handle, either."

Maybe it's his gentle tone, or the way he said my name. Whatever it is, I find myself turning back toward him.

Merich's eyes stay fixed on me. "Whatever is happening in these woods is more dangerous than I thought," he continues. "It is infinitely worse than you can imagine. I understand you want to help, but this is unlike anything you or I have ever experienced. Even if something did take those children, this is *out of our league.*"

He sounds almost sorry to be telling me this. I can't think of a response.

"I know what happens to people who meddle in things like this," he says. "It would be unfortunate if it were to happen to you. Please, stay out of the woods, and leave it alone."

His fingers tighten on my arm, and I wonder if he can feel my pulse fluttering.

"I can't," I whisper.

From nearby, a voice calls my name.

After several seconds, Merich nods. He releases me, stepping away. "I see. Then I hope for your sake things aren't as bad as I fear. Guard your house; that Hound will come for you. You're lucky there's only one. They can be bloodthirsty."

His voice is flat, all kindness gone. Maybe I imagined it altogether. It doesn't matter, it *shouldn't* matter, but I suddenly feel as if I've done the wrong thing.

"Merich—" I start.

"*Cass?*"

I look over my shoulder. Theo's shape is coming through the trees.

From behind me I hear a low, "Farewell."

When I look back Merich is gone, leaving only the faint smell of greenery and woodsmoke.

6

THE NEWS OF BLACKENED TREES AND BUNNIES WITH bleeding eyes does a significant amount to convince Louisa something horrible is happening in the woods. It's also possible she simply trusts Theo's judgement over mine, which would sting more if he weren't backing me up.

Unfortunately, this means for the rest of the day she insists on repeatedly going over everything we've learned. She even overlooks my meeting with Merich. Instead of berating me for it, she makes me recount every word he said, in detail.

"One more time," she says.

Night has fallen, darkness pressing against the windows. While Louisa washes dishes, the rest of us sprawl across the couches, digesting dinner and being interrogated.

I groan. "I already told you everything!"

"Tell me again."

Will gives me a sympathetic smile from the other side of the couch. He's been hanging around since we returned from the woods, and I don't blame him for it. If I were him, I'd be determined to avoid my overly religious fiancée after what we saw. I'm sure undead wildlife will haunt my dreams tonight. How can he go home and pretend everything is fine?

"The first time I met Merich, he said that a couple of months ago the world shook," I say. Again. "He thought it was caused by some sort of magical disturbance."

"And none of you felt anything," Louisa interrupts, shooting us a suspicious look.

Draped across the other couch beside Theo, Pen rolls her eyes. "Yes, we actually *all* felt the giant magical earthquake. We just didn't tell you."

"Sarcasm is unbecoming, Penelope."

"He said," I continue, "he thinks the disturbance caused a gap to open in our world, which opened a pathway for… things. And now those things are in the woods."

"This… man," Will interjects. "He said one of those *things* is following you?"

"He called it a Hound."

I push away visions of dark shapes moving through the trees. Black hands clawing at the windows.

"And he's not a man," Pen says. "He's one of the Fae, he's immortal, and he's gorgeous. Keep up."

Will's worried expression doesn't ease. I had intended to keep Merich's nature quiet; Will only just found out about vampires, and discovering two types of immortal beings seemed like a lot for one day. My efforts only lasted until Pen got involved, of course.

I try to regain control of the conversation. "Merich said—well, insinuated—that one of those creatures could be involved with Hannah's disappearance."

"So there's a chance she's still in the woods," Theo murmurs.

I nod. "But if something took Hannah…"

"Maybe it took the other kids, too."

A chilly silence falls.

Louisa sighs, paddling her fingers in the dishwater. "That doesn't help us decide what to do next."

I bite back a sarcastic response. "We have to find those kids, obviously."

"We could put up wards in the woods," Theo suggests. "To alert us if a human goes past."

"Search parties go through there every day," Will replies. "They'd set them off all the time."

"There's locator spells." I gnaw my lip, thinking. "But those need something personal from whoever you're trying to find."

"Oh, good luck explaining *that* to the grieving parents," Pen mutters.

I glare at her. "You can leave if you're not going to be helpful!"

"You need *someone* with a brain here."

"Don't bicker," Louisa chides. "Anyway, there's nothing we can do tonight. If Merich's warning can be trusted, we may be in danger. The house is well warded, so we'll be safe here, but we should stay out of the woods as much as possible. Especially you, Cass."

I nod gloomily.

The water drains out of the sink with a gurgle, and Louisa leaves the kitchen. "I'm going to bed early. Will, are you staying overnight? I can make up the spare room."

Pen sits up, her eyes narrowing. “That’s *Helen’s* room.”

“Your sister doesn’t live here anymore,” Louisa icily replies.

I instinctively lean back as Pen bristles, but Louisa ignores her, returning her attention to Will. “You’re welcome to stay. I know it was a big day.”

“Oh, no.” Will seems as uncomfortable as I feel, desperately trying to avoid Pen’s stare. “Steph is expecting me.”

Louisa says goodnight, heading upstairs. Pen immediately follows, as if she’s expecting her to meddle with the unused bedroom anyway, and we wait, listening for an explosion of rage.

Nothing comes.

Will gives me a pained look. “Sorry.”

“Don’t worry about it,” I sigh, already anticipating several days of Helen-related animosity. Pen has never gotten over our sister’s sudden departure. Neither has Louisa, but for different reasons. The easiest way to ruin a day is to mention Helen’s name.

But Theo hardly seems to have noticed their exit. Instead he stares out the window, frowning deeply.

I prod him with my foot. “What’s wrong with you?”

He lifts his head, watching me. His expression is troubled, and I get the feeling he’s deciding whether or not to speak.

“The things Merich told you,” he says finally. “About the world shaking, and a gap opening. It sounds… familiar.”

“Familiar?” Will echoes.

“How can it sound familiar?” I ask. “*I* barely understood what he meant.”

Theo’s not even listening. “He told me about something like this,” he murmurs distractedly. “But it can’t really be…”

I poke him again. "*Who* told you? We don't know anyone with magic!"

He doesn't answer, instead searching through the clutter on the coffee table until he finds a scrap of paper and a pencil. Will shoots me a questioning look, and I shrug, watching as Theo starts to write. "All this talk about a gap," he mutters, as I try to read upside-down. "I'm sure he mentioned..."

He finishes writing, scrawling five marks around the paper, then snaps his fingers. A small flame bursts to life, and he performs an elaborate hand gesture. The marks flare.

And the note vanishes.

Will's jaw drops.

"Cool trick," I say, as if I'm not wild with jealousy. "So, this friend of yours. Why didn't you mention him earlier?"

Theo's mouth twists. "Some of Louisa's beliefs about other magic-users are outdated."

"There are other magic-users?" Will asks.

"Sure," I say slowly. Theo didn't say *witches*, he said *magic-users*. And when I try to recall the last time Louisa voiced any beliefs about magic-users, only one occasion comes to mind. "You didn't freak out when I met Merich in the woods," I realise.

Theo blushes.

I gasp. "*No.*"

"It's really not a big deal—"

I point at the empty spot on the table. "Who did you send that note to?"

"A friend!"

"A friend, or a *friend*?" Will asks, catching on.

"Shut up," Theo hisses.

"Oh my God." I close my eyes, savouring the moment. "The golden child has a Fae boyfriend."

"Shut up!"

"Wait, there are more of them?" asks Will. "Are you saying there's a bunch of immortal people wandering around? Is dating them *allowed*?"

"I'm not dating one," Theo snarls. "Look, do you remember when I left town for a bit? Went to California?"

"Yes."

Will and I answer in unison. It's hard to forget: Theo was unbearably pretentious when he came back, when he wasn't moping in his bedroom. It also started his short-lived campaign to move out, which was swiftly stamped out of existence by Louisa. And though I never admitted it, I was desperate to copy him, to leave Fallow Creek and travel somewhere new.

"Well, I got mugged. And this guy stopped it. He took me under his wing, I guess."

I cup my chin in my hands and beam at him. "What an adorable way to find a boyfriend."

Will looks uneasy. "Was it a *real* wing, or a metaphorical wing?"

"No, not a real wing!" snaps Theo, his cheeks scarlet. "Anyway, it wasn't like that! I mean, we're still friends, but Mosi is—"

He cuts off as a ball of fire appears over the table, and a piece of paper emerges from the flames. It's not the same one he sent away. This is thicker, as if it's been torn from a book. Theo snatches it out of the air, shaking off embers.

"Love note?" I ask

"Hilarious," he replies, but his heart isn't in it. He scans the paper, the divot between his eyebrows deepening every moment, and my amusement slides away.

"What is it?"

He says nothing, passing me the note. The handwriting is elegant, but uneven and sloping, as though written in a hurry.

Theseus—

I know what caused this, but I didn't expect the effects to reach so far. A few months ago the veil slipped. The threat has been dealt with, but if a gap has appeared, you are in immediate danger while it remains open. Creatures will come through, and they will be drawn to your family.

I can't help you; I'm not even in the country. Ward your home in the ways I taught you. If possible, close the gap. If not, secure it well, and hope that will be enough.

Keep me posted, and keep safe.

M.

"Not a love note," I say, my stomach sinking.

"No." Theo slumps back.

I scan the note once more, Will peering over my shoulder. "Creatures will come through…"

"And be drawn to us. Merich said the same thing."

The paper trembles in my hand. Seeing the words there, written with such obvious haste, makes this real, and it sets my heart racing. "This guy—"

"Mosi," Theo murmurs.

"Whoever he is! Does he know what he's talking about? How well do you know him?"

He called him Theseus, my mind whispers. *Theo doesn't let anyone call him Theseus.*

"Well enough," Theo says. "I trust him."

"But he knew about this veil slip and didn't tell you?" I shake the note at him.

Theo yanks it out of my hand. "He's like that! And if he says it's been dealt with, I believe him. This gap we're dealing with is obviously a lingering issue from the veil slip. We're lucky it's not worse."

"Okay," says Will. "That's good. What's the veil?"

Theo looks at me expectantly. I say nothing, privately glad I wasn't the one who had to ask.

He sighs. "Don't you ever read?"

"No," I admit. "I prefer *hands-on* learning—"

"Yes, we all remember when you almost summoned an Old Creature in the backyard," Theo snaps. He takes a deep breath. "The veil is… imagine a curtain. On this side, there's our world. It's nice and normal and everything is as it should be."

Will looks wary. "And on the other side?"

"It's full of homicidal monsters."

"Oh," I say glumly.

"Wait." The colour has drained from Will's face. "Are you talking about *Hell*?"

"No." Theo grimaces, his hands waving as he searches for words. "More like another dimension. Our world overlaps with others. Sometimes, a gap appears between them. When it does, it leaves an opening for entities to come through."

"That's what Merich said about the Hound," I recall. "He said they could slip between realms, and a hole in the world would make it easier."

"He's right," Theo says. "Physical forms can't exist on that side of the veil, so the monsters there can't be seen by normal people. But if they come through a gap and take on a physical body, or if they find a way to interact with humans..."

"I assume they become more dangerous," Will murmurs.

"Yes."

I stare at the note in Theo's hand. What he's saying is horrible, and the implications are terrifying. But it doesn't sound unfamiliar. "How do you know all this?" I ask.

"The Fae have always known more about this sort of thing than the rest of us. They're older. More in tune with it." He smiles wanly. "Perks of knowing one of them, I guess. You learn stuff."

"Then Merich..."

"He probably knows too."

There's a strange swooping sensation in my stomach, like I've missed a step. Merich tried to warn me away from this. Is this why? Did he know how deep this danger ran? Did he suspect?

This is out of our league.

"If the veil between worlds slipped enough to cause this, we're lucky we weren't all killed immediately," Theo says. "But even a gap in the veil is dangerous. If there's one open in the woods, we have to close it."

That shakes me out of my thoughts. "We have to find Hannah."

Theo frowns at me. "Cass, if there's a gap, it's an access point for *literal monsters.* That takes priority!"

"And it wastes time we should spend looking for Hannah!" I argue. "We don't even know where this gap is!"

"The gate."

Will is staring at the floor between his feet. He looks up as our attention turns to him, his jaw clenched.

"It's where Hannah was going, isn't it?" he asks. "Toward the gate you found."

"Yeah," I say slowly.

"Well, if there's a gap… doesn't it make sense it would be there?"

I open my mouth. Close it. Theo goes white.

"It's literally a gate," Will continues. "Isn't it obvious?"

And it is, now he's said it. So obvious. My skin ripples into goosebumps. "But if that's where Hannah went…"

"Where is she now?" Theo finishes.

Nobody answers. I don't know if it's because nobody wants to speculate, or if the ideas entering their heads are as awful as the ones in mine.

I knew the gate was connected. I didn't know *how* connected.

"What do we do?" I whisper.

I suppose I'm hoping Theo will take the lead. He's older. Smarter. More suited to dealing with this in every possible way.

Instead he simply looks at me, saying nothing.

"Well," says Will. "It's late. I'm off."

My head snaps toward him. He doesn't meet my gaze as he gets to his feet, shrugging on his jacket. The terrible tension lifts, but this change leaves me shaken. Will's voice is mild and even, as if he hasn't heard anything we've said.

"Fine." Theo leans back into the couch, his eyes closing. "Nice facing the nightmares in the woods with you, Will."

Will doesn't respond, striding out of the room. I gather my wits and chase him into the dim hallway, catching him by the front door.

"Will. *Will.*"

As I touch his shoulder he twitches, then turns to face me. The faint light falling through the frosted glass in the door reveals glimpses of his face: bone pale, rigid with fear.

My chest tightens. If *I'm* worried by what we just learned, how must he feel?

"It's alright to be scared," I say softly. "I am too. If you want to stay out of this, it's okay. It's probably safer."

I find myself hoping he'll agree. That he'll decide this isn't worth it.

Instead he croaks, "You think I'm scared for *me*?"

My heart feels like a small, hard lump. "Will—"

"You think I'm scared for *my* safety?" He laughs, quiet and hysterical. "There are *monsters* after you. There's a portal to Hell in the fucking woods!"

"Not Hell," I correct.

"It might as well be! I don't know what to do, Cass! You're supposed to fix this, and I can't help you, can't protect you—what am I good for?"

"I don't need you to protect me," I say. "I can protect myself."

"I know," he whispers. "But from this?"

In my head I see fleeting shadows, the deliberate curl of a blackened hand, vanishing around the curve of a tree. My throat closes as my fear returns.

"I don't know," I whisper. With Will, I can admit what I'm afraid to tell anyone in my family, the things that will make them believe they were right to doubt me. "I don't know if I can handle this."

He sighs, leaning his shoulder against the wall beside me. "You can," he murmurs. "Well, maybe you can't. We'll find out together."

"That's encouraging," I mutter.

"I'm all out of supportive comments for the day. Try again tomorrow."

I snort. He huffs in response, and for a moment we stand in silence. From here I can smell the lingering scent of coffee and pastry clinging to his jacket. It's so familiar, so normal, I can almost ignore my growing dread.

A shriek splits the air.

Will flinches, and I turn to see Theo appear in the doorway. "Was that—"

"The wards," he says.

Pen hurtles down the stairs. "What did I miss *now*?"

Theo strides back into the main room, and Pen races over to the kitchen window, pressing her nose to the glass. I push Will up the hallway. "Go. Get home, now."

He rolls his eyes at me. "I'm not going to abandon you—"

The light falling through the front door vanishes.

He goes silent, and I clutch at his jacket, my breath catching. Together we watch as a shadow moves past the door, slow and sinuous. There's a *thud*.

Then another.

Something slowly climbs the outside wall.

I drag Will back into the light of the main room. Theo watches us stumble in. "Merich said the Hound would follow you," he says.

I stare at him, and it's only then I remember what else Merich said.

Guard your house.

There's a dull scratching on the roof.

"Seal the house," Theo rasps, and he runs out of the room. Pen watches him go, gaping, before she scrambles up onto the kitchen counter, skimming her hand over the top of the windowsill. Wards bloom to life in the wood, the carved symbols releasing a soft white light.

"Will these hold?" she asks.

I move to the back door, slamming my hands against the doorframe. More wards light up. They're always there, waiting and ready, but they need to be powered to protect the house from intrusion, and I feel the energy bleed out of me as I wake them.

"They should," I respond.

But the ones outside didn't.

Will watches me ward the front window. "Monsters?"

"Yep." I count back from ten, wrestling with my fear. "I wanted you to make a run for your car."

"Too late." Theo returns, a gentle glow emitting from the hallway behind him. He glances at Will, and I know what he sees: pale, human, useless. I can't imagine we're much better. "You can't go outside with that thing out there."

"Ah," says Will. "So we're locked in."

"Fish in a barrel," I mutter.

Theo looks at me, his expression softening. "It's only an animal, Cass." I realise his soothing tone is for my benefit, and for a second I'm outraged, until I understand why. I'm the one the Hound is hunting. I'm the one who should be panicking. "Just an animal. Like a raccoon."

Images of slinking shapes fill my head, and some of that panic finally appears. "It's not a raccoon, Theo!"

"It's as good as," he says calmly. "And we can deal with one raccoon."

As my thoughts howl about the inaccuracy of what he's saying, footsteps thunder down the stairs. Louisa appears, pausing on the small landing to glare at us. "What the hell is going on?"

Her hair is wet, and she's wearing a pink bathrobe. I experience a brief moment of hilarity at the idea of her relaxing in the shower as a monster descends upon us, and then claws screech across glass.

"There's something on the porch!" Pen shrieks.

Theo whirls. "Get away from the window!"

"I'm going to set it on fire!"

"Pen—"

The wall shudders under the weight of a body. There's scrabbling on the roof. Then—

Upstairs there is an unmistakeable crash of breaking glass.

My heart stops. "It's in the house."

She might be half-naked and late to the party, but Louisa reacts like a war-time general. "Theo, you protect the others," she barks. "I'll—"

Pen screams, and I look up in time to see a black hand appear on the topmost stair.

My blood turns cold. Theo freezes, his eyes widening, and Louisa—

Louisa.

There's no time for her to react. Only a few feet separate her from a monster, and even as she looks over her shoulder the hand tenses on the step, as if the creature is preparing to leap.

I clench my fist and wrench, the air rippling. As Louisa ducks the stairs shudder, splinters lancing up like spears, and the hand whips back, disappearing from view.

There's a chilling hiss.

"Well done, Cass," Louisa croaks. She waves her hand and there's a fleshy *thunk*. "I'll deal with this. Stay down there!"

She charges back up the stairs while I'm too shocked to protest, and Theo turns to us, a grim look on his ashen face. "The bathroom," he says. "It's defensible. This thing is after you, Cass. Take Will and hide."

Will balks. I'm not surprised; the downstairs bathroom is little more than a box under the stairs. It's less *defensible* and more of a death trap.

I hesitate. "But Louisa—"

"*I'll* help Louisa," Theo says. "Now go!"

He gives me a shove, and I lead Will into the hallway. Theo bounds up the stairs, and Pen hovers nervously behind us, as if unsure whether to follow.

Glass breaks.

I stop.

A window sits at the end of the hall, the sill glowing with wards. The hallway itself is only long enough to accommodate the stairs and the front door, so the window is a small thing, barely serving to shed light into the narrow space.

Right now there's no light. Just darkness, and the glint of glass on the floor.

An icy finger runs down my spine. *There was only one. Merich said there was only one Hound.*

But.

An arm comes first. Long. Groping. Spindling fingers feel their way down the inside wall, claws dragging with a skin-crawling *scrape.* Then comes the second arm, sliding through the narrow gap with the glistening squirm of a worm, and the body follows.

The torso is mottled black, like rotting flesh. It looks like a man's, then an animal's, and then it doesn't matter, because the Hound is in the hallway with us, and it looks like nothing that exists in this world.

I step back into Will. His hand closes around my arm, his fingers trembling.

The Hound doesn't have a face. Or maybe it does, and my mind rejects it.

Somehow, I know it's looking at me.

"*Cass*!" screams Pen.

I don't respond. My words are trapped in my throat. I lift my hand, but I can't think of a single spell.

The Hound approaches. It doesn't walk so much as climb, arms and legs pushing off the walls, so it surges toward us with the terrible speed of a spider emerging from a hole.

"Cass?"

Will's voice is a croak. He's still there. And Pen, behind him.

And the only thing between them and the Hound is me.

Stop. I claw my hands, feeling my feet root to the floor, and watch the floorboards shiver and warp, snagging at the Hound's feet. It slows, but not enough, so I slam my palms flat against the air, forming a wall between us and it.

My lungs turn solid, but the Hound stops. It makes a slow clicking sound, like the clatter of mandibles.

I shove at the wall, and it takes a step back. But only one step. A questing talon tests the wall, and the air shivers at the place of contact.

Panic crawls through my veins. The price for manipulating air is simple—I can only hold this wall for as long as I can hold my breath. Once it falls, the Hound will leap.

And my lungs are burning.

Behind me I can dimly hear Pen shrieking, Will's breaths rasping over my shoulder. For a moment I can feel their blood on my hands, hear the strangled gasps of their lacerated throats, torn by those black claws. I see their bodies lying on the floor, the image so stark it's as though their deaths have already happened.

No. I throw my mind out in search of a spell, of an anchor-point that might save us. I can't create magic from nothing. There must be something to work with, wood or flesh or bone, but my pulse pounds in my ears and nothing appears, and I can't think—

Pen's blood seeps into the floorboards. Will's chest heaves as he fights for air—

There.

A dark spot in the universe. Normal magic specks the world like tiny stars, all anchor-points for spells, rooted in the physical world. This is like a hole, negative space, thudding like a disembodied heart. It's strange, *wrong*. My mind recoils from it.

The Hound presses one finger through the wall of air, and my chest seizes.

There's no choice.

I drop the wall.

The Hound surges forward in a mass of limbs. Pen screams, and as I gasp for breath I reach for that dark spot and *yank*.

The Hound stops.

No. It staggers, a guttural sound emerging from its throat.

I twist my hand, the muscles in my arm cramping, and the sound becomes a high screech. The creature bends back on itself, claws gouging the walls as it scrabbles away.

Away from *me*.

I chase after it, wrenching my wrist, and the Hound howls. The air shudders and I flinch, but the beast keeps retreating, limbs crackling and snapping until it reaches the window it came through. Its arms buckle inward as it slithers out, slick flesh sliding past the shattered glass as it forces its way out into the night.

And it disappears.

I wait, but nothing moves. It doesn't come back. Almost without noticing I drop the spell, my hand trembling.

"Oh my God," says Pen.

"All clear," Louisa calls from upstairs.

"Cass?"

I blink, turning. Will watches me carefully, his face grey, and my eyes catch on the curling scar in his throat.

"Oh my God," Pen repeats. "That was so fucking cool."

Will is still waiting. I'm supposed to speak.

"It was definitely something," I croak.

Pen laughs, and Will gives me a relieved smile. Footsteps thunder down the stairs as Louisa and Theo return, and voices collide in the narrow hallway.

I hardly notice.

It was definitely something. Certainly magic.

But despite the effect it had on the Hound, that magic cost me nothing at all.

7

MORNING ARRIVES, AND I CAN'T STOP LOOKING AT MY hands.

Magic always has a price. I've known that since I was old enough to realise compelling butterflies to fly in circles made me dizzy, and that if I healed the cut on Will's knee, it would likely appear on my own. It's simply a fact. There must be a balance.

So what kind of magic exacts no price at all? What kind of magic wounds monsters?

Bad magic, my mind whispers. *Unnatural magic.*

I clench my fists, biting down on my lip so hard I taste blood.

This can't be happening again.

"Hey." Pen leans through the doorway, a sour look on her face. "Were you planning on helping, or are you too busy revelling in your victory?"

After last night's invasion, Louisa decided the wards protecting the house weren't strong enough. This morning has been spent reinforcing every symbol laid into every possible entry point, then adding more for good measure. Midmorning sunlight floods my bedroom, almost glaringly bright, but the glow from the wards in my windowsill is still visible, and as I power each new symbol my weariness deepens.

Nobody mentions how the Hound crawled through the downstairs window without any hesitation, paying the wards so little mind it was as though they weren't there at all. Nobody mentions how there were two of them, even though I only expected one.

Nobody mentions what I did.

I should be finishing the upstairs windows, but the movement of my fingers distracted me. Why should laying wards, a passive magic that drains energy with each symbol, require a higher price than fighting a monster? More than that, all magic has some link to the physical world. With wards, the magic is bound to whatever surface they're carved into. Last night I manipulated the air in the hallway. But when I hurt the Hound…

Nothing. There was nothing. I didn't find an anchor; I found some kind of *void*.

"Or ignore me," says Pen. "That's fine too."

"Sorry," I say guiltily, but she's already gone, returning to her own bedroom. "Sorry, Pen."

"Whatever."

Overhead I hear muffled thumps as Theo climbs around on the roof, checking for points of entry. For the tenth time this morning, I glance at my silent phone.

Will has never seen a monster before. He's never seen me use magic like that before. I haven't heard from him since he left, white-faced and quiet, and with each minute of silence it feels more like this is what will drive him over the edge, and he'll finally realise he should have joined the rest of the town and left the witches alone.

"Hey," Pen calls. "There's a hot guy in the garden."

I blink, looking up. My bedroom window overlooks the backyard, as does Pen's. Even from here I can see him, a tall figure standing on the other side of the fence.

Merich waves.

"Oh, for God's sake," I mutter.

Pen peers out of her bedroom as I pass, her expression hopeful. "If you don't want to talk to him, I'll do it."

"No." I start downstairs.

She sniffs. "Buzzkill."

There's no sign of Louisa as I move through the kitchen, striding out the back door. Merich watches me cross the garden, idly swinging the gate with a finger. "Your wards are down," he says.

"I know." I pause a few feet away from him. Even with the fence between us, it feels too close. Something about Merich seems to make me act stupid. "Why are you here?"

"A bored man can't come by to talk to his local witches?"

"You are not here because you're *bored*," I scoff. "Besides, our last conversation gave me the impression you wanted nothing to do with us."

"Maybe I've changed my mind."

"Or maybe you're here to make my life more difficult."

"You're a shockingly cynical woman." He leans up against the fence, resting his forearms between the pickets, and the wards stay silent and dead. In the sunlight Merich's hair is like polished bronze, the black of his eyes specked with gold. With a start, I notice only his irises are black today. In his old jeans and a scuffed leather jacket, he could almost pass for a human, albeit a ridiculously attractive one.

For some reason the idea makes me uncomfortable. "No sword today?" I ask finally.

"It tends to scare the mortals." He gives me a thoughtful look. "What happened here last night?"

I scowl at him. "I have better things to do than entertain you, you know."

He sighs. "Indulge me."

My first instinct is to refuse, but it seems childish at this point. "We were attacked by Hounds."

"Hounds."

"Two of them," I confirm, and then, snottily, "*You* said there was only one."

"I was only aware of one."

"Well, you were wrong. And they got through our wards. *That's* why they're down."

Merich's fingers drum out a slow rhythm against the fence, his eyes fixed on me. "And yet you're not dead."

My palms tingle, and I flex my hands. I notice too late how he follows the movement, and I flush, shoving them into my pockets where they can't draw more attention to me.

But instead of commenting, Merich says, "I spent *my* night observing the gate you mentioned."

I start, all thought of my hands forgotten. "*What?*"

He shrugs. "You made me curious. I thought it doubtful that a gate could be as dramatic as you implied."

"Stop admiring the sound of your own voice and get on with it!" I snap.

His mouth quirks. I wish I hadn't noticed. "You were right. That thing certainly isn't normal. And last night, it wasn't quite as inactive as I might have hoped."

Without noticing I've drifted forward, and now I grasp the fence as if it might steady me. "What are you talking about?"

"Something emerged from the gate last night. Not a physical presence, but some kind of power, reaching into the woods."

My heart stutters. "Then the gap in the world…"

"It exists, and it's appearing as that nasty little gate of yours," Merich finishes. "Correct."

The gap is the gate, and the gate is the gap. Will was right. And yet I don't feel any better for knowing this.

"I made myself scarce, obviously," says Merich. "Whatever that thing was, I didn't want it setting its sights on me. But I think it was searching for something. And it was doing so while a certain family of witches was otherwise occupied."

He taps one finger against the silent fence.

"You think the Hounds were a distraction?" I ask incredulously.

"Intended or coincidental. But yes."

My grip tightens on the fence, the wooden pickets biting into my hands. Monsters are one thing—monsters working together are something else entirely. And—

Ice slithers through my veins. "You said something emerged from the gate. As in… it was *inside* it?"

"I thought that was implied."

I don't reply. If something emerged from inside the gate and took Hannah, then where is she now?

"I can see this is thrilling news," Merich says drily.

"Why are you here?" I ask. My stomach has become a hollow pit. "I seem to remember you telling me to leave this alone. I thought it was out of our league."

"It is," he says. "But as you said, I am a Warden of the Woods. This is my job."

He smiles slightly. I can't bring myself to return it.

"Whatever reached out from the gap," I say, hoping my fear doesn't show in my voice. "Can we fight it?"

"I doubt it. I doubt you could even fight the Hounds." I start to respond, and Merich shakes his head. "It's not a slight against you, so try to control your wounded indignation. Creatures of their nature just don't seem to respond to magic. You didn't wonder why your wards did nothing?"

In my mind I see the Hound in the hallway, pressing forward against everything I threw at it. Until…

"Why not?" I ask softly.

"They're not from this world. They're not bound by normal rules—even their bodies are made from a different kind of magic, so why should anything in this world have an impact on them? Your magic might have *some* effect, but not enough to deter them."

"You didn't mention that when you warned me about them."

"Would it have changed anything?"

Of course, I start to say, but I bite the words back. It wouldn't be true. The wards would still have done nothing. The Hound would still have found me. I would still have fought it.

I should feel angry. Instead all I feel is dread.

I choose my next words carefully. "But if that's true, if normal magic can't hurt them… what can?"

Merich watches me, his expression unreadable. *And yet you're not dead,* he said. I remember how his eyes followed my hands, as if he were searching for something.

He can't know. Surely he can't. It's not like he can *sense* magic.

Can he?

"I don't know," he says. "You tell me."

My breath catches. He gives me a long look, opening his mouth to speak—

"*Kiss him or come inside*!" Pen screams.

I pull away from the fence, heat flooding my cheeks, and Merich straightens, his face blank but for the slightest twist of his mouth. I can't tell what it means. Maybe amusement at the idea. Maybe disgust.

"Thank you for telling me about the gate," I say stiffly. "I know you didn't want anything to do with this."

"It appears I have little choice," he replies. "But you're welcome. Your manners are improving, by the way."

The awkwardness vanishes. I scowl at him, turning toward the house, and pull a rude gesture at Pen where she hangs out the upstairs window.

"Cassandra."

I glance back.

Merich raises an eyebrow. "Be careful."

A small chill runs through me, and I flee inside.

•••

The screen door slams shut behind me, and Louisa turns away from the kitchen window, looking expectant. The scent of burning wood hangs in the air: for some reason she's warding the kitchen more heavily than anywhere else in the house, as if she believes otherworldly entities might be drawn to the smell of her cooking.

In fairness, she might be right.

"What was that about?" she asks. Her voice is cool, but not quite disapproving. I'm still in her good graces after fighting off the Hound last night, and Merich seems to grow slightly less intolerable with every useful piece of information he provides. But somehow, I don't think this news will be well-received.

Panic builds in my chest. If magic doesn't stop the Hounds, what good are wards? If magic doesn't stop them, what exactly did I do last night?

Something unnatural. Something I thought was gone. Something that should have been left in the woods all those years ago.

"Cass? What is it?"

I stare at Louisa, paralysed by indecision. I so rarely seem to do anything right in her eyes. God knows what she'll think if I tell her this, yet who else can I tell? She fought off a Hound too, she must know *something*. Maybe Merich has it all wrong, and I'm worrying for nothing.

"Merich says our magic shouldn't have any effect on the Hounds," I start.

Louisa doesn't look surprised. "No. I noticed that last night."

My insides turn cold. "But you fought one off."

She pulls a face, brushing a loose curl out of her eyes. "Not exactly. It would be more accurate to say I threw magic and a few lamps at it until it decided I wasn't worth the effort." She tries a tentative smile. "Why?"

My palms itch. I wonder if I'll look down and find them black, a glaring sign there's something wrong with me. Louisa has coached us through the rules of magic for as long as I've been alive. Everything I know, I learned from her. So for this, magic even Merich thinks shouldn't be possible, to spring from nowhere...

But I have to tell *someone*.

"I did," I whisper. "I fought it off. Not like you did."

Louisa's smile fades. "What do you mean?"

I press my fingernails into my palms, trying to focus. "I tried throwing magic at it. It didn't work. I couldn't stop it, and I wasn't hurting it, and I thought it was going to kill us. And then I felt... something. Like an anchor-point for a spell, but... it was darkness. A void." I take a deep breath. "So I used it."

Louisa looks wary, but not angry. Not yet anyway. "And?"

"It hurt it," I say. "And the more power I poured into it, the better it worked. I drove the Hound off, but the magic didn't cost me anything, Louisa! I felt *nothing*. Merich says none of our magic should have worked, so what did I do?" I drag a hand through my hair, biting my lip. "Is there something wrong with me?"

"No." Louisa crosses the distance between us, folding me into her arms. For a moment I stand motionless, stunned, and then I cling to her like I'm a child. She smells like lavender and magic, and tears prick my eyes. "No, sweetheart, there's nothing wrong with you."

"But I shouldn't have been able to do it." I whisper it into her shoulder, letting my fear swallow me. "The last time I used that magic was when—it's not *normal*, Louisa."

"No," she agrees. She pulls back, giving me a sad, weary look. "It's not normal magic, but it *is* magic. It's in your blood." Her voice grows so low I'm not even sure she's talking to me anymore. "Your mother was always powerful. And your father—he could do things like this too. See things, feel things that weren't there for other people. I suppose you're more like them than I thought."

I forget how to breathe.

Louisa rarely talks about my mother. I was eight when she died, but she'd been out of our lives long before then. I have only scraps of memories: her long dark hair, a barking laugh. Some things I learned from Theo, or Helen, but the thing I learned first was that my mother wasn't made for parenthood. We weren't planned children; we were simply the result of a string of romantic affairs. None of us share a father, and none of us interested our mother for any longer than a year. One by one she left us in Louisa's care, and she rarely returned.

But if Louisa doesn't talk about my mother, she has never, *ever* mentioned my father.

He could do things like this too.

"Louisa." The world seems to have tilted beneath me. "Were my parents—was my father—"

"Do you guys know Theo is on the roof?"

I whirl.

Will stands in the doorway, looking concerned. He gestures upward. "Because he's up there," he continues. "He's cursing a *lot*."

"Will." All trace of emotion vanishes from Louisa's voice as she releases me, sweeping over to him. "How nice to see you. Let me take this."

He lets her remove the cardboard box from his hands, and she strides back into the kitchen, the wafting smell of apple pie trailing in her wake. Will follows her, pausing beside me, and my relief at his appearance wars with my frustration over his timing.

"Everything okay?" he asks, his eyes flicking to Louisa.

"Fine." I look him over, searching for signs of last night. He wasn't hurt. The colour has returned to his cheeks, and he doesn't look uncomfortable being here. Being around me.

The knot of fear in my chest loosens. "I wasn't sure you'd come back," I admit.

He frowns. "What?"

"You *were* attacked by a monster from another world. For most people, that's a good reason to stay away."

"Well, maybe those people just can't handle some excitement." He takes a seat at the kitchen table, glancing at the wards shining in the windowsill, and I wonder if he's remembering the way the Hound stepped over them as if they didn't even exist.

For a moment I want to tell him to leave. To go home, where he can stay safe, unharmed, *alive*.

Then he looks back at me, his expression weary, and the moment is gone.

I sit down beside him. "What's going on?"

Louisa disappears out the back door. I can't tell if she's giving us privacy, or if she's simply glad she doesn't have to answer any parent-related questions. Will traces a dent in the table with his finger, his jaw working.

"Steph was waiting up last night," he says quietly.

Thank God. I shouldn't be so relieved to be confronted with normal, human drama, but I am. "Was she angry?"

"Worried, more like."

I have to hide my scepticism. I don't tell Will how intensely I dislike Stephanie, though she makes no attempt to hide the fact she thinks I'm an abomination. I'm sure she has some good qualities, or

Will wouldn't be interested in her, but I've never seen them, so the concept of her worrying about him is hard to imagine.

"Is it because you told her you were with me?" I ask. "You could have said you were with a search party."

Will shakes his head. "Other stuff was going on."

"What other stuff? Don't tell me the wedding venue cancelled on you or something, because I don't think she's going to like getting married in the diner."

Will looks at me, and I freeze. I know this face. This is how he looks when he's withholding bad news, biting it back between his teeth.

I prepare myself. "What is it?"

"Max Elbridge."

Unexpected. "Who?"

"Max Elbridge." Will leans back in his chair, closing his eyes. He looks tired. Resigned. "He's the kid who went missing last night."

8

MAX ELBRIDGE IS SEVEN YEARS OLD. HIS PARENTS KNEW about the missing children, but they considered it a distant threat. Such disappearances only happen to other people. They certainly didn't believe *their* family was in danger.

They were so sure of it that they went ahead with their regular date night, leaving their children at home. The Elbridge boys spent the evening playing outside, racing toy cars around an elaborate route stretching from the back of the house down to the woods.

The youngest boy tripped over as he ran and started to bawl. The second looked back. And Max, triumphant, took his car to the end of the track, ducked around the tree marking the turning point, and disappeared.

Will weaves the story like a newsreader, his bland tone dampening the awfulness of what he's saying. We gather around the kitchen table to listen, Pen with her arms crossed, Theo staring out the window. Louisa sits like a statue, her eyes down, and I stand, gripping the back of a chair until my knuckles turn white.

There's a long pause once Will finally falls silent.

Theo speaks first. "It has to be connected to Hannah."

"We can't know for sure," Louisa says softly.

"We can." I release my grip on the chair. "Merich told me something happened at the gate last night, while the Hounds were here. Like we were a distraction."

Will blinks, straightening. "Then... I was right?"

"The gate I found and the gap in the veil are the same thing," I confirm. "Whatever took Hannah has to be in that area; it's where I found her shoe. Merich saw something last night, and now Max is missing. This isn't a coincidence."

"You're speculating," says Louisa.

"And she's probably right!" Pen exclaims. "Is it really likely there's another reason for kids to be going missing?"

"There's a way to find out." Theo turns away from the window. "The search parties will be out this morning. They've got two missing kids now, everyone will be looking for them. But they don't know what they're looking for."

"And we do?" Will asks.

"Not yet. But this is our chance." Theo looks at me. "Remember the spell I used in the woods?"

I remember the ghostly Hannah, drifting through the trees, and my breath catches. "You can do it again."

He nods. "We still don't know what happened to Hannah. But if the same thing happened to Max, there must be *something* for us to see. Something nobody else will be able to find."

"And then we'll know what kind of monster we're dealing with," I murmur.

Will throws his hands up. "Well, we *have* to go, right? This is our chance! Fresh evidence!"

Pen snorts. "What are you going to do, jump the fence and dig around in their backyard?"

"I was planning on knocking first—"

"I think you would be making a mistake."

The conversation dies, and my shoulders sag. Despite everything, I'm disappointed. It was stupid to think Louisa's feelings might have changed after this morning's conversation, where we *finally* seemed to get along, yet the words still sting.

"Let me guess," I say. "You think we're being reckless."

"On the contrary, it's a solid plan." I frown at her, and Louisa shrugs. "It's the logical next step. But you need to consider that there's a good chance people now know you agreed to help find Hannah Hendricks."

"And?"

"You haven't found her. And another child is now missing."

"That's not her fault," Pen protests.

"No," Louisa agrees. "But the mood in town will be getting ugly. Do you think it's a good idea to go waltzing up to the front door of the people whose son just vanished? If you're out of sight, you're out of mind. And they don't start wondering why you're so eager to be involved."

I gape at her. "You're saying they'll think *I* had something to do with it?"

"It's possible."

"No, it's not," Theo says firmly. "Nobody genuinely thinks we had anything to do with these disappearances. This isn't the Middle Ages, people don't accuse witches of everything."

"It's better to be safe than sorry."

Safety. Again. Does she ever worry about anything else? "What exactly are we keeping ourselves safe from?" I demand. "Should we expect mobs with flaming torches? Bricks through the front window? Dangerous levels of excitement?"

Louisa looks at me, and for the briefest moment a shadow crosses her face. Her mouth jerks, as if she's about to speak.

But she says nothing.

"Max's parents are out looking for him," Will says. I reluctantly tear my eyes away from Louisa, turning my attention back to the conversation. "I saw them at the diner this morning. Their house will be empty."

Theo extends his hands, his point made. "See? No danger. We'll go over while they're out, and we'll be back before they even know we were there."

"I'll drive," says Will, sweeping up his car keys.

"Great!" Pen claps her hands. "Let's go."

"Absolutely not," says Louisa.

I wince. Will edges his chair backward.

Pen turns in her seat, glaring. "I want to go!"

"You're underage." Louisa meets Pen's stare without blinking, facing her down with will-withering steadiness. "And I don't believe you have any previously undiscovered skills making your presence crucial to their success. You're not going."

There's a hint of smoke in the air as Pen lunges to her feet. "It's not *fair*!"

"Life's not fair."

"I never get to do anything!" Pen shrieks. She hurls her chair aside and stomps out of the room, her footsteps thundering up the stairs. A few seconds later her bedroom door slams shut, the windows rattling in sympathy.

There's a pause. One of the framed photographs on the wall swings back and forth, then falls down.

"Well," Theo says sourly. "That was fun. Shall we go?"

Will practically hurls himself at the front door, and Louisa sighs, her attention returning to me. "I hope you realise what you might face out there."

"Can't be any worse than that was," I mutter.

She gives me a tired look, suddenly seeming much older. "People will always look for a scapegoat, Cass," she says. "Just make sure it's not you."

•••

The Elbridge family live on the other side of Fallow Creek. To get there, we have to drive through town.

After this morning's news, I expected a grim scene. It's always like that in movies: an overcast day, people silently walking the streets, a general feeling of oppressive misery.

But the day is sunny and clear. Several buildings are freshly painted in bright colours. The church steeple is almost blindingly white, piercing a cloudless sky. People are going about their business like there's nothing wrong in the world, though I suppose for them, maybe it's true.

In fact, the only indication something is wrong comes when people glance at the car and see me looking back at them. We only get brief glimpses of each other, but it's enough for them to recognise me, and enough for me to see their expressions change. Their faces close over, noses wrinkling, and they look at the car like it carries a plague victim.

I never expected to be treated like a hero if I found Hannah, but I didn't expect outright animosity for *trying* to find her, either. Even the sight of me seems to provoke disgust.

They tolerate us if we're helpful when they need us, and if they don't see us any more than necessary. Louisa's words. I've always thought her warnings were exaggerated. Fallow Creek is a small town—it revolves around church and gossip and weddings and funerals, and most of the time, nothing remotely interesting happens. Yet Louisa has always maintained that the only way to protect ourselves is to stay isolated, to fly under the radar at all times.

I remember that moment earlier, the shadow crossing her face. *What exactly are we keeping ourselves safe from?* I asked.

It's never occurred to me she might have a reason for all these years of caution, a reason to be so sure of some looming threat. But as another person sneers at the car, a sudden chill runs down my spine.

The Elbridge house sits away from the bustle of town, backing onto the woods. Before long we leave the buildings behind, and Will takes us down a quiet road, the trees rising tall around us. I don't let my gaze linger on the shadows beneath the canopy.

"There shouldn't be anyone home." It's the first time anybody has spoken for a while, and Will's voice seems deliberately light. "If

Max's parents are out searching for him, I doubt they left the other boys home alone."

"At least we don't have to skulk around like thieves," Theo says.

Will turns down a half-hidden driveway. "It should be easy enough to sneak around to the back of the house."

The trees fall away. My jaw drops.

"Oh," Theo says dully. "They're *those* Elbridges."

Those Elbridges. The ones on the town council and the school PTA, as well as every important committee. They don't just run, but *sponsor* the school sport teams, along with multiple art groups. They're new money, and every hard-earned dollar of it shows in their house. Immaculate lawns roll up to a building formed from buttery yellow stone, topped with a red tile roof. Climbing roses wind up white trellises, and two stone columns frame a beautiful, ink-black door. It's a fairy-tale cottage on steroids.

"We're going to get shot for trespassing," Theo says.

I don't disagree.

"We'll be fine." Will stops the car in the circular driveway, next to a central sculpture featuring a flock of winged, chubby babies. "Nobody's here."

Theo laughs humourlessly. "I hate to tell you this, but you're wrong."

He points at the house. A figure stands in one of the downstairs windows, framed by gauzy white curtains. They're watching us.

Louisa was right. This *is* a bad idea. We're going to get arrested. Or shot.

"Oh." Will hesitates. "Well, we're here now."

He gets out of the car.

In the back seat, Theo sighs. "Cass, you need smarter friends."

"You don't even *have* friends," I mutter defensively, and follow Will out of the car.

The figure is gone by the time we reach the doorstep—paved, of course, in luxurious, honey-coloured stone. My shoes seem appallingly worn by comparison.

"We could still try sneaking around back," I say hopefully.

"You're just trying to avoid human interaction," says Theo.

"God, yes."

Will scoffs, leaning forward to knock. "Stop worrying so much!"

The door flies open before his knuckles make contact.

Will recoils, clutching his hand to his chest, but I'm too nervous to laugh. A girl stands in the doorway. She's tall, perhaps a few years younger than I am, with striking features and a mass of dark gold curls.

And she's looking right at me.

"Oh," Will squeaks. He flushes, clearing his throat. "Ah, hi. Are you—"

"Fleur Elbridge." Her startlingly blue eyes don't leave my face, and I shuffle, flustered. "You're the ones they call witches."

"Yes!" Will pauses. "Well, I'm not."

"They call us lots of things," Theo says easily. "I'm Theo Reilly. That's Cassandra."

She doesn't even look at him. It's surprising—most girls at least take the time to admire Theo, if in a resentful kind of way. "What do you want?"

Will coughs again. "I don't know if you've heard, but Cass—"

"You're supposed to be looking for Hannah Hendricks." She looks away, and I sag with relief as she examines Will and Theo, frowning suspiciously. "Why are you here? Because don't you dare think you're going to pass on a message from the beyond or something—"

Well, this is a good start. I step forward. "Max's disappearance could be related to Hannah's."

Fleur cuts herself off, a flicker of emotion crossing her face. I wait for her to start screaming at us, wondering how fast I can make it back to the car.

"So, what?" she asks. "You're looking for clues? A lead?"

"Something like that," I agree. "Do you mind if we come in?"

"We don't want to invade your privacy," Will adds. "Just to see the spot where he disappeared."

A moment passes. Fleur looks over each of us, and I wonder if she's going to call the police. Frankly, after the reactions in town, I'm surprised we got this far.

Finally she pulls the door open, stepping aside for us to enter. I hesitate, then follow her.

Despite its rustic storybook appearance, the interior of the house is bizarrely clean. With three young boys around I'd expect some chaos, but the wooden floors are shining, there are numerous breakable ornaments at elbow-height, and the entire house smells like orange-scented cleaner. At first I think someone is stress-cleaning, and then I realise there's no sign of children at all. No toys. No shoes. Nothing.

"So," Will says delicately. "You're Max's…"

"Sister." Fleur's voice is cold.

"I didn't realise—"

"They don't talk about me much. I was the accidental baby." She says it without emotion, as if it's a fact she's known for years. Even

Theo looks taken aback. "I was fourteen when Max was born. Fifteen for George. Simon was a year later. I've always been the babysitter."

I turn my gaze to the wall, trying to hide my discomfort. Something in this house seems *off*. Maybe it's the oddness of the situation; I haven't been in a stranger's house for years.

Then I notice the photos.

Family photos are scattered throughout our house. One of us is usually taking the picture, so we're never all in the same shot. In a few Pen is missing her eyebrows after burning them off. I refused to be photographed between the ages of thirteen and fifteen. For a while Helen's hair was blue, but even after the argument, after she left, her photos stayed up. Sometimes we're covered in dirt, or paint, or flour. The pictures are chaotic, but fitting.

The photos in the hallway of the Elbridge house are the opposite. All of them are staged. The boys are immediately identifiable, blond and solemn. Fleur is featured far more rarely, and while her brothers hold trophies and certificates, her hands are always empty. The only family photo is large and elaborately framed. The three boys are arranged like toy soldiers in starched shirts, while Mr. and Mrs. Elbridge are dressed to the nines, their expressions aloof. Only Fleur has any character at all, her hand fisted in her modest black skirt as she glares at the camera.

It makes me like her.

"Good lord," Theo murmurs. "I thought people were only like this in movies."

"My parents are big on image." I jump. Fleur has materialised beside us, eyeing the photos disdainfully. "They want us to excel. They figure if they have money and we do every extracurricular in existence, we're sure to get into the good schools."

"Did that work?" asks Theo.

"Well, I'm gay, I got suspended for fighting, I didn't go to college, and they don't talk about me in public," she says drily. "You do the math."

"And the clothes?" I ask. "Is that part of the, uh, school application thing?"

"No." The corner of her mouth twitches. "They just have no taste."

We continue through the rest of the house, past a gleaming kitchen and a painfully stark living room. A pair of glass doors open on to the backyard, and Fleur leads us outside.

Despite the sunlight, a chill goes through me.

It's a beautiful day, but the garden bears signs of a terrible night. The racetrack is marked out with a collection of shoes and toys, winding between bare flowerbeds and down to the edge of the woods. The toy cars are scattered. Mud smears the patio pavers, and deep gouges mar the perfect grass, carved up by running feet.

"What happened, exactly?" I ask softly.

"It was getting dark, but they wanted to play outside," Fleur replies, her voice equally quiet. "Our parents don't like them playing in the dirt, but y'know, they're boys. And I was the one babysitting." She shrugs. "Everything was fine. Then Simon fell over, and I heard him crying. I came out in time to see Max run into the trees. I thought maybe he'd pushed Simon, then run off to hide. But by the time I'd sorted the other two out, he hadn't come back."

"And there was no sign of him?" asks Will.

Fleur shakes her head. "I searched the woods. Then I called my parents, and they looked too. There was nothing."

There was no trace of Hannah, either. Not until I found her shoe. But I don't say that.

"I doubt you'll find anything, but you can look," Fleur continues. She pauses, her eyes on the trees. "They blame me, you know."

I start. "Your parents blame *you*?"

"They needed to blame someone. I was there. I was the babysitter."

Louisa's words echo in my head again. *People will always look for a scapegoat.*

There's a clatter behind us, and two boys—Simon and George, I assume—stop in the doorway, staring at us. I stiffen, eyeing them warily. They don't look inclined to move on, and I'm pretty sure performing magic in front of small children isn't the best way to remain inconspicuous.

"Did you find Max?" one of them asks.

A tiny shudder runs across Fleur's shoulders, and Theo shoots me a panicked glance.

But Will simply smiles, sinking into a crouch. "Hey. No, we haven't found him yet. I heard you two were playing together before he went missing. Can you tell me about it?"

Behind his back, he gestures frantically toward the woods.

"How about we stay here and let the nice people do their work?" Fleur asks calmly. She herds Will and the boys inside without looking back, then closes the door behind her.

And Theo and I are alone.

"Do you suddenly feel like our upbringing wasn't so bad?" he asks.

"I have a new appreciation for it," I admit. "At least Louisa never made us wear uniforms."

He snorts.

I start across the backyard, stepping delicately over the gouges in the grass. The homemade racetrack runs all the way down to the treeline, curving around the roots of a particularly large oak before disappearing from view.

I take a deep breath, then enter the woods.

I don't bother looking for signs of a disappearance. Anything obvious will have already been found, and it's not the obvious we're here for. There are no scuffs in the dirt, no scraps of clothing caught on twigs. The forest looks exactly as it should: quiet and shady, carpeted in bronze leaves.

Once we're sheltered by the branches, Theo peers back at the house. "Are they watching?"

"Will's distracting them."

He grimaces, placing his hand on the tree. "Well, let's hope he's good at it. Ready?"

I nod.

A second passes. Another.

Then the world turns inside-out.

Even though I'm ready for it, the shock staggers me. Magic ripples across the ground, scattering the leaves. Wind hisses through the trees, and birds swoop past us, their flights reversed. Day fades into dawn, then into night, and fades once more into the blur of evening, the light soft and dim.

The movement stops.

And Max Elbridge, hazed in the yellow of magic, steps into the woods.

I immediately search his face, but unlike the phantom Hannah, Max's expression is alive. He wears a green jacket, zipped up to his throat, and his cheeks are flushed. One hand holds a plastic car, and the other slaps the tree trunk, marking his turning point.

He looks back. I wonder if he's hearing his brother's wails.

Then he turns, facing out into the trees, and goes perfectly still.

The warmth leaves my blood. Whatever he's looking at, it must be the same thing Hannah saw. My head fills with visions of monstrous creatures, beasts with black teeth and claws, things to rival the Hounds.

But… Max doesn't look *scared*. He looks almost confused.

So what is he seeing?

I swallow, my throat tight, and follow his gaze.

There is no monster. No looming terror.

Instead there is only a shadow.

It moves with the fluidity of water, sliding over the ground like a black fog. As we watch it rises, forming a shape. It looks like a woman, then a man, then an animal, then like nothing recognisable at all.

I glance at Max. His confusion disappears, and his eyes widen, his expression brightening as if he's seen someone familiar. His mouth opens—

A high whine pierces the air. The leaves shiver.

And as if a switch has been flipped, the emotion drains from Max's face, leaving only the deadened look I've seen once before.

The shadow withdraws, retreating into the brush, and Max steps away from the house and follows.

The spell breaks.

I suck in a lungful of clean morning air, squeezing my eyes closed. The shadow is not there. The shadow is *not* there. There is nothing behind me, lurking like something from a nightmare.

It takes a few seconds before I feel brave enough to peek between my lashes, though.

The woods are empty.

Theo leans against the tree, his face pale and clammy.

"Well," I croak. "That was unexpected."

He barely seems to hear me. "You saw the way he looked at it, right?"

I glance at the spot where the shadow stood. Now, in daylight, there is no proof it was ever there. I nod.

Theo's mouth twists. "I don't think he saw the same thing we did."

Understanding slithers through me, bringing with it a sickly feeling. "He saw something else." I remember the moment when Max's face lit up. "Something he wanted to follow."

"It lured him in. It affected his mind. That's strong magic; there wasn't even a physical creature here, but he followed it willingly." Theo scans the woods as if he expects them to unfurl, revealing their secrets. "But where is it luring him *to*?"

Something emerged from the gate last night. Not a physical presence, but some kind of power, reaching into the woods.

I think it was searching for something.

I didn't catch it when Merich first said it. *Not a physical presence.* I've been picturing a monster, leaving a trail of blackened trees through the forest, slipping out of its lair to steal children. But it never left the lair at all.

An anglerfish leads prey in with a light. They don't even see the teeth.

Why should a monster leave the lair when it can lure in children with some lovely vision?

I want to be sick.

"You know where he went," I say softly.

Theo looks at me, silent.

The pieces come together in my head, forming a terrible picture. "This is what happened to Hannah. I found her shoe at the gate; the gate and the gap are the same thing." I take a deep breath, my fingernails biting into my palms. *I will not panic. I will not.* "You *know* where Max is. I bet if we went deeper into the woods, eventually we'd find some black trees and undead animals."

"Cass," he rasps. "If you're right, it means—"

Before he can finish there's a shrill whistle from the house. Will.

"Let's go," I say.

Theo straightens. "We need to talk about this."

"There's nothing to talk about." I leave the shade of the woods, starting back toward the house. Sunlight glares down into the empty backyard, gleaming off the plastic bodies of toy cars.

Theo catches up to me. "There's no way to be sure that's where Max went! And the further this goes, the more dangerous it gets! If you're right, this changes *everything*. We need to talk about how far we're willing to—"

"It changes nothing!" I halt, turning to face him. "I always said this was connected to the gate, and now we know I'm right! I said I would try to find Hannah, and now we know where she is—where Max is!"

"You're not thinking this through," he hisses. "You're being reckless, Cass!"

I recoil. "Reckless."

"What do you think happens if they're *inside* the gate? What do you plan to do then?"

My throat tightens. Does everyone think I'm an irresponsible fool, incapable of making a single good decision? "If you're too afraid to help anymore, that's fine, Theo," I snap. "But I know I'm right, and I'm not backing out now!"

His expression darkens, and he storms past me, marching into the house. I scowl at his back and follow.

We find Fleur waiting in the immaculate living room. I try to look less angry, but I'm not sure I manage. "Did Will leave without us?"

"He's waiting in the car. The boys are upstairs." There's a dullness to Fleur's voice that wasn't there before, though her face is blank. "I think he got intimidated when they started asking him if Max was dead."

Theo's breath catches, and my own heart skips a beat. "Fleur," I start. "It's still—I don't think—"

What am I supposed to say? *It's still early*, or *I don't think Max is dead*? The first won't comfort her, and I can't prove the second. How did Louisa manage to sound sincere when she was trying to comfort Hannah's parents? What can I possibly say without sounding like an idiot?

Nothing. The answer is obvious. Nothing I say will sound genuine. Max is either alive or dead; nothing I say will change that. It all comes down to what I can do.

I steady my nerves. "Thank you for letting us into your home," I say. "We appreciate it."

Fleur looks up. I'm distantly aware of Theo disappearing down the hallway, probably to distance himself from me, but I feel pinned in place by her gaze

"Are you really witches?" she asks.

I freeze. “Uh.”

“People call you witches,” she continues. “But people say a lot of things. Just tell me. I need to know if there was a point to this. If you’re useless to me or not.”

That should make me angry. Indignant, at least.

Instead I understand her completely.

We live in a small town. It’s still early, and we’re likely the first people here since the disappearance, but news spreads fast. In the next few hours Fleur’s family will be subjected to a deluge of compassionate, useless support. People will bring food. Max’s schoolmates will probably send handmade cards. Church ladies will descend in flocks, with their conservative dresses and lowered voices, assuring them Max will be found.

Then they’ll say they’ll pray for him.

Then, finally, they’ll whip out the tried-and-true ‘*maybe this is just God’s plan.*’

It’s the way it’s gone with every other missing child. All of it is well-meant, and none of it is helpful. None of it has the slightest chance of bringing Max back. Either I am useful to Fleur, or I’m simply another person who can do nothing.

And I get the sense she, like me, is sick of people doing nothing.

I strike my thumb across my fingers, and light blooms in my hand.

Fleur gasps. She looks incredibly young as she stares at the light, her eyes turned silver by the glow. “Is it real?” she whispers.

“Yes.” I release the spell and the light vanishes. “It’s basic magic.”

“Basic.” She looks away from my empty palm. “So you can do other magic, too? *Bigger* magic?”

“You catch on fast.”

"Tell my parents that." She gathers herself. "Then… is there magic you can use to find Max?"

This is where I should be sensible. It definitely isn't the time to make promises I can't keep. But—

"Yes," I say. "I think there is."

Fleur's eyes close, and she nods, once and stiffly. She says nothing else as we walk to the front door.

The cold glares of the people in town return to my mind, and I realise I may have been stupid.

"Fleur," I say awkwardly. "I'd appreciate it if you didn't tell anyone what I just did. Most people think we're frauds, and as long as they think that… it's easier to work in the background, y'know?"

She shrugs. "I understand. I suppose you don't want to end up on TV, either."

"Or on a pyre," I mutter.

We pause by the door, and Fleur finally looks at me. A crack appears in her expression, some desperate emotion piercing her careful calm.

"Please find him," she whispers. "My parents will never forgive me if he's gone. *I'll* never forgive me."

I don't know what to say. "Fleur—"

"I know. They didn't find the others. But please. Try."

It's what I've already promised to do. Yet somehow it feels more binding when I say, "I'll try."

She shuts the door behind me, and I try not to run to the car, throwing myself into the safety of the front seat. Theo waits in the back, Will behind the wheel, and as the door closes he looks eagerly between us.

"So? Did it work? Did you find anything?"

"Max was taken," I say shortly.

Will lets out a whistle of air through his teeth. "*Shit*. So you saw the monster? Does this mean we can track them through the woods?"

"He's not in the woods."

"We don't know that yet," Theo murmurs.

"Yes, we do." I fix my eyes on the dashboard, digging my fingernails into my palms. The pain is immediate, but it's a distraction from the panic pressing in at me from all directions. "The monster isn't in the woods. It's inside the gate itself."

9

OUR NEWS DOES NOT GO DOWN WELL.

While we manage to make it home without running into any angry mobs, we then have to tell Louisa what we've learned. It doesn't seem too bad at first, but when she ascends to a new level of icy calm and brews some extremely strong coffee, radiating the kind of menace that should send all self-respecting monsters slinking off home, I know an argument is coming.

Still, it doesn't start until we're seated in the kitchen with some freshly baked cookies. Because the woods may be full of nightmares, but heaven forbid we look uncivilised.

"We're closing it," says Theo.

"We're not," I reply.

I could really use some reinforcements right now, but my options are limited. I have Will, of course—he sits beside me, shooting me a reassuring smile every so often, but I know he's nervous. Pen has entered a sulk of gargantuan proportions, barely deigning to acknowledge our presence.

And Theo has completely turned on me.

Across the kitchen table, he takes a deep breath. "Cass," he says. Calmly, as if he's trying to reason with a particularly stupid child. "Whatever presence emerged from the gap got all the way to the Elbridge house. It's getting stronger."

"I figured that out for myself," I snap. "I'm not a total idiot."

"Then we need to close the gap *now*."

Maybe it's ridiculous to feel betrayed by his change of heart. I know his idea is the safest one; if we close the gap, no more children go missing. Yet I can't bring myself to agree.

I suppose having him support me—my brother, supporting me, for the first time ever—meant more than I thought. Having him believe I was doing the right thing gave me more confidence than I've had in years.

Maybe that's why I can't look at him without a surge of anger. And why I feel like throwing my coffee mug at him.

"Theo is right," says Louisa. "The longer the gap stays open, the more danger we're in."

I tighten my grip on my mug. "We're not closing it if there's a chance those kids are inside."

The worst thing is I know they're right. The shadow was strong enough to reach Max's backyard, on the other side of town. Did it choose him randomly, or did it pick the easiest target? What does it want children for? Why not some other prey? Closing the gap is the safest option if we can figure out how to do so. But if Max and Hannah are in the monster's lair, we'd be abandoning them.

"Cass is right," Will says loyally. "We have to try to find Max and Hannah."

Theo shoots him a glare. "How long do you think it will be before that monster decides it likes it better on this side of the gap? How long until it gets out? Who do you think it's going to come after first, Will?"

Us. I realise it immediately. Merich already told me creatures like the Hounds are drawn to power. What if the monster is drawn here? Our magic doesn't work on entities from beyond the gap. We'd be sitting ducks. And Will—

Will can't use magic. Will is only a harmless human, here because he wants to help me.

I look at him, filled with sudden fear. His eyes are fixed on Theo, an argumentative set to his jaw. He's always been there for me. I know him almost as well as I know myself. I can't imagine life without him.

And if I get him killed?

My insides go cold.

"We can't abandon little kids," Will says evenly.

Theo sits back, exasperated. "We don't even know where they are. Not for sure."

I give him a withering look. "You think they vanished off the face of the earth and *haven't* gone into the creepy gate?"

"In which case, they're probably dead! You can't have it both ways!"

"You don't know that!"

"I know physical forms can't exist on the other side of the veil, Cassandra! If they *did* go through that gap, what do you think will be left of them?"

I recoil, the words conjuring images so jarring I can't bring myself to respond.

If I'm right, and the children are inside the gate, they're probably dead. If Theo is right, they're almost *definitely* dead. Am I putting us in danger for nothing?

Will watches me, his eyes worried. "There must be some way to find out. It can't all be guesswork."

There's a groan from one of the couches. Pen has been ignoring us, lying with one arm draped theatrically over her eyes, but now she lets it fall.

"*Oh my God,* why is this so complicated? If you want to know whether those kids are inside the gate, just scry and find out. Jesus."

Nobody responds.

She sits up to find us staring at her. "What?" she demands. "Nobody else was suggesting it!"

"That's not a bad idea," I say slowly.

Will looks suspicious. "*What* isn't a bad idea?"

"Scrying," I reply. "When you perform a scrying spell, your body stays in one place, but you send your mind out to look for something. Or someone."

"It also requires extreme precision and has absolutely no room for error," Theo says.

"It could work," I insist.

"Unfortunately not." Louisa pours herself more coffee, her expression suggesting she'd really prefer something stronger. "Scrying only works when you have something belonging to the person you're trying to find."

Will delves into the pocket of his jacket and brings out a toy car. Dirt is still lodged in the little plastic wheels. "Would this do?"

I look at it, then at him. He flushes.

"*William*," says Pen, sounding impressed. "Did you rob a crime scene?"

"No!" He goes red. "When I was talking to Max's brothers, they said this was his car. They found it at the edge of the woods. You said you could do locator spells, so I just..."

"Stole it," Pen says.

"*Borrowed* it!"

"Why didn't *I* think of that?" I complain.

"You were otherwise occupied," Will says. "Well? Could you use this?"

"We could," Louisa says reluctantly. "Max only went missing last night, so it would give us a strong connection. If he's alive, it should lead us to him. But..."

I'm so tired of excuses. "But *what*?"

"But it's *dangerous*!" Theo exclaims, slamming down his coffee cup. "It's all well and good to ditch your body and take your mind on a walk, but there's no telling what will happen if you accidentally walk it into another world!"

"If scrying leads us to the gate, we'll know the kids are inside the gap," I argue. "If it doesn't, then we can close the stupid thing!"

"I'm sure *that* will be nice and easy," Pen mutters.

Louisa lets out a long breath, folding her hands on the table before meeting my eyes. "You realise even if scrying leads you to the gate, it would be far too dangerous to go inside," she says. "Entering the gap is equivalent to entering another world. It could totally sever your mind's connection to your body. No amount of magic would be able to save you."

Will looks uneasy. "She'd be a ghost?"

"Her body would still function. But her mind, her personality… they'll be gone."

"The wheel will be turning, but the hamster will be dead," Pen says, more succinctly.

"So it's risky, but not impossible," I say. "It's not like anyone *wants* to go through the gap. We'll be sensible. If the spell does lead to the gate, whoever is scrying will just come back."

"Oh no," replies Louisa. "*You're* doing it. This whole thing was your idea. I'm not making Theo do it, and Pen is underage. I need to run the spell. That leaves you."

"Ah," I say lamely.

She's right, of course. I'd simply expected that as the most experienced witch, Louisa would be the one scrying. I've never participated in a spell like this before, and it's not the kind of thing you can practice beforehand.

I suddenly feel a lot less confident.

She notices my hesitation, and one golden eyebrow lifts. "You wanted to know if those kids were inside the gap. This is your chance. There are other options."

Other options. Like giving up, leaving those children to their fate. Or giving up everything, and becoming the Witch, like Louisa wants.

Theo stares angrily at the wall, saying nothing.

"No," I say. "I'll do it."

Louisa looks out the window, judging the height of the sun. "Midnight, then. That's when it works best. Pen, you'll help me set up. We'll do it on Cass's floor."

"I always get the boring jobs," Pen complains, but she rolls off the couch and flounces out of the room.

"Fine." Theo shoves his chair back. "I'm going to work out how to *close* this gap once you finally decide to do it. If any of us are alive by then."

He stalks out after Pen, and my gut twists. I don't know if it's from anger or guilt.

Louisa is the last to leave, sighing deeply as she rises. "I hope you know what you're doing, Cass."

"Yeah," I reply. "Me too."

Then she's gone, and it's just me and Will with a pot of cooling coffee for company.

Will turns to face me. "This scrying thing. It's not that dangerous, is it?" There's a crease of worry between his brows, and he holds his mug slightly too tightly.

"It's probably fine," I assure him. "You know Louisa. If she'd really been against it, there's no way she'd allow us to do it, let alone actually help."

"She said you could lose your mind. *Literally.* It would be gone."

"But I won't. Because I will be sensible."

The anxiety doesn't leave his face. "I don't like how everything is falling on you," he says. "You're only one person. There must be something I can do to help you."

My heart thumps unevenly, and I press my thumbnail into my finger, focusing on the ache. "You got us Max's car. We wouldn't have gotten this far without you."

"That's not what I meant." He pauses. "You'll tell me if there's something I can do, right?"

He only wants to help. It's all he ever wants. And the more he tries to help, the more danger he's in. If he gets hurt, it'll be my fault. His blood will be on my hands.

My gaze moves to the scar on his throat. That wicked little twist.

"Of course," I lie. "You know I will."

It's almost concerning how smoothly the words come out, but Will's face falls. He doesn't believe me.

"You can trust me, you know." His voice is so low I barely make it out. "I know I don't have magic. I can't do much. But you don't have to do everything on your own, either."

It feels like a kick to the stomach. "I know." I try a smile, but it feels weak and wavering. "Why don't you go home? Stephanie probably wants to see you at least once this week. And you should show your face at the diner before they fire you for not turning up."

He scoffs. "They can't fire me. You're right about Steph, though."

"Otherwise she'll turn up here, and it'll get ugly." Inspiration strikes, and I add, "You could bring us breakfast, though. It'll be a long night. It would be nice to have something to look forward to."

Will's face softens, and the knot of tension in my gut eases. "Alright. Then I'll do that. You'll call if you need me though, right?"

"Of course."

Another lie.

We drift toward the front door, and as he leaves Will pauses, giving me a half-hearted smile. "Good luck, Cass."

The door shuts behind him. He's safe, for tonight. I'm sure I did the right thing.

But all I feel is guilt.

•••

There's nothing I can do until midnight, but that just makes the passage of time slower, until the minutes seem to last hours. Louisa doesn't cook, telling us to fend for ourselves while she and Pen prepare the scrying spell, but I can't bring myself to eat.

In the space of a day I've improved my relationship with Louisa, ruined my weird new friendship with Theo, and agreed to find another missing child. It's suddenly striking me that the last of these things might not be achievable, and it gives me a sick, seedy feeling. If I sit for too long my anxiety threatens to overwhelm me, and I end up pacing the house, trying to outwalk my worries. If scrying doesn't work, what do I do next? What if I *can't* find Hannah, or Max? What if Louisa's right, and I end up facing an angry mob of townspeople, set on blaming me for these disappearances?

I could go live in the woods, I suppose. If it weren't for the undead animals.

As I cross the dark upstairs landing there's a sizzling sound, then a whiff of smoke.

I pause outside Theo's room, nudging the door open.

He sits huddled over his desk, scribbling feverishly across different pieces of paper. Every so often one bursts into flame and vanishes, only to be replaced a few seconds later by a scrap appearing from empty air.

I watch for a moment, wondering what's so wrong with texting.

"I'm busy," Theo says tightly. "Get on with it."

"What are you doing?"

"Trying to figure out what kind of monster we're dealing with. Trying to figure out how to close the gap." Flames crackle, and a note vanishes. "Mosi's helping."

I step tentatively into the room. "And… are you having any luck?"

A sizzle. Paper appears, and Theo seizes it out of the air. "Not yet."

He doesn't look in my direction, his shoulders hunched. I

remember our brief argument in Fleur's backyard and wince, the words sounding so much harsher in hindsight. Theo has always hated confrontation, and when I think of the fear I felt seeing that shadow… well, why *wouldn't* he be reluctant to continue down this path? His worries were justified. And I bit his head off, after we were finally working as a team.

"Theo, I'm sorry. For what I said before." I pick at my fingernails, searching for a way to continue. "I know you're right. I know how dangerous this could get; I'm not oblivious. I know the gap needs to be closed. I just can't give up on finding those kids without at least *trying*."

Maybe I'm imagining it, but some of the tension in his back seems to ease. "Don't worry about it," he says quietly. "I know the pressure you must be feeling. I'm sorry I panicked."

A burst of flame. A note disappears.

"It's more pressure than I expected," I admit. I take a few steps deeper into his room, glancing around. His bed is unmade, his twin computers powered down. His bookshelf sags under the weight of its contents, and his desk is covered in scraps of paper and smears of soot. "So. Does Mosi think the gap can be closed?"

Theo shrugs. "He thinks there's a way. It's just complicated. Not helped by him being on a different continent. It all comes down to wards, though, power. I think we'll figure something out."

His voice changes as he speaks, becoming less curt. I suppose this is familiar ground to him: wards and languages and writing. Maybe there's something comforting in it.

Another scrap of paper appears in the air, adding to the smell of burning.

I try a lighter subject. "Well, at least you're having a good talk with your boyfriend."

"Don't call him that."

I falter. Theo has snapped at me in the past. It'd be a miracle if he hadn't. But I've never heard *that* tone before.

"Sorry," I say carefully. "I didn't mean to offend you."

I'm not sure if it's the right thing to say, but after a long moment Theo sighs. "You didn't. I wasn't lying earlier, though. Mosi's not my boyfriend. He's a friend. That's all."

"Oh." I perch on the end of Theo's bed. "It's just, the way you reacted when you first mentioned him… you were never together?"

"No."

There's a pinch around his mouth. A strain around his eyes.

Oh. "But you wanted to be," I realise.

Theo's jaw works, and finally, he nods.

I hesitate, perplexed. "You've never dated anyone, though."

"We're shut-ins," he snaps. "We're social outcasts with no idea how to relate to other people, in a town where they view us as freaks. Does it really surprise you that we might not be capable of normal relationships?"

The question comes out sharp and angry, striking like a slap, and I immediately regret prying. This is something he's thought about. A lot.

And so have I. Most people my age have normal relationships: platonic, romantic, whatever. I have a grand total of one friend and the social skills of a hermit who has lived in a cave for twenty years. Even if someone managed to ignore the whole *witch* thing, I wouldn't know how to date someone. I barely even know how to interact with a stranger.

Louisa might have thought we were safer isolated, but it's turned us into hollow humans, without a clue how to face other people. In a small, religious town that views us with suspicion, all we have is each other.

And God, does it get lonely.

I pick at the bedspread, suddenly feeling wildly out of my depth. "Is that the reason nothing happened between you, then?" I ask softly. "Because you're a witch?"

I'm almost afraid to know the answer.

"No." Theo closes his eyes, tipping his head back. "He was one of the Fae, why would my magic bother him? He taught me a lot, actually. I suppose I was almost like an apprentice for a while. And he was lovely. I felt *normal* with him. But it never turned into anything. He knew how I felt, but we both knew I wouldn't be in California for long, and there was such an age difference. And I always suspected he had feelings for someone else. Still." He smiles bitterly. "You can't change how you feel."

I stare at him, lost for words, and wonder if I'll ever feel anything like the sad yearning in his voice. "You never mentioned him. Once you came home."

"What would have been the point? It wouldn't have made me feel better. I just locked myself in my room and waited for the sting to fade. It did. A bit."

"I'm sorry," I say. Then, because I can't leave things alone, I continue, "It still bothers you? After this long?"

For a moment I think he won't answer. He doesn't move, and I ready myself to slip out and pretend this conversation never happened.

"Have you ever met someone who made you feel seen?" he asks quietly. "When nobody else did?"

Will, I want to say. Will has always understood me.

Except he hasn't. And he sees what he wants to see. And today I lied to keep him out of the way.

"No," I whisper.

Theo nods. "Once you do, it's hard not to get attached." He straightens, turning back to his desk without meeting my gaze. "We'll work this out. Between us, Mosi and I will figure out what to do."

It's a clear dismissal, and I'm almost relieved the conversation is over. But I find myself pausing at the door.

"You never think of leaving?" I ask. "Getting out of this town and going somewhere you're actually happy?"

"Do you?"

I go still.

Thankfully, Theo doesn't wait for an answer. "Sometimes I do," he murmurs. "I think of leaving. Never having to think about becoming the Witch. But it would mean leaving all of you behind. And Louisa must have her reasons for making us live like this. She must."

I frown, looking over my shoulder. "You don't wonder what that reason is?"

Theo glances up, and the dim light from his desk lamp turns his eyes the colour of a sea in storm. "I try not to," he says. "I'm not sure I want to find out."

•••

Scrying is a dangerous form of magic.

The price for the spell is always energy, but it's not paid by the person scrying. Their only job is to find who they're looking for, and to try not to disconnect their mind from their body along the way.

The price is paid by the people watching over the scry: the controllers. They remain linked to the spell, powering it until the person scrying returns to their body. As long as they remain linked, the controllers are slowly drained of energy. If they break the spell first, the person scrying will be severed from their body.

It's a risky balance. If the person scrying is useless, they might take too long and kill their controllers. If the controllers aren't strong enough, and they're unable to maintain the spell, they'll kill the person scrying. You need skill, speed, and a lot of trust in the other people involved.

So I'm not thrilled to learn the controllers will be Louisa and Pen.

"You said Pen was underage!" I protest.

"Too underage to scry," says Louisa. "She's the perfect age to get some hands-on experience with this form of magic."

Pen grins at me, kneeling on my bedroom floor. Midnight is approaching, and my room has been transformed. The furniture has been pushed against the walls, the rug shoved aside, and a circle has been traced on the floorboards in chalk. The line is dotted with several smaller circles, each containing an unlit candle: another energy source. It's the centrepiece of a large, confusing map of lines and symbols, all of which are apparently necessary to ensure my body won't be possessed by something evil while I'm not in it.

I was perfectly happy to remain unaware of this possibility.

"*I* don't have any experience with this form of magic!" I say.

"I promise not to kill you," Pen says sweetly.

"That's not funny," Louisa snaps. Pen's smile vanishes. "This is *extremely* dangerous magic. If this goes wrong your sister could die."

"Only technically!"

"Technically dead is still pretty dead, Penelope!" I snarl. "Can't Theo do this?"

"Oh, God no," Theo says, peering in through the doorway. "I'm not touching this shitshow."

"You have more experience!"

"I learned out of *books*," he replies. "What happened to being a *tactile learner*?"

"You're a traitor and I hate you," I declare, turning back to Louisa. "Are you and Pen going to be enough?"

"We could call Helen," Pen mutters.

"We are *not* calling your sister." Louisa sighs. "Go to the bathroom. Once we get started you're not leaving this room. And you, Theo, go away. At this point you're a distraction."

They both leave the room, Theo giving me a final wave as he trudges downstairs. Louisa looks at me.

"Are you *sure* you'll be enough?" I whisper. My heart is trying to beat free of my ribcage, and counting backward from ten is utterly failing to calm my anxiety. This seemed like a good idea. Now I'm certain I'm going to die.

Louisa raises her eyebrows. "I hope you're not questioning my abilities."

"No! But—"

Her expression softens, and she touches my cheek. "I *have* done this before. One person can control a scrying spell on their own. With Pen, it will be easy."

I wrangle my words, trying to voice the fear creeping through me. "And with *me*? With what we talked about, the magic I did... is it safe for me to do this?"

"I don't see why it should be any different for you than anyone else. Just... be careful."

"I peed!" Pen charges back into the room, her arms spread expectantly. "Are we doing this?"

Louisa lets out a long breath. "Alright. Let's begin."

She and Pen kneel, and as they light the candles I step through the web of lines, entering the central circle. The space is empty but for Max's little toy car.

"I'm safe in here," I ask. "Right?"

"Nothing evil can breach the circle as long as the lines remain intact," Louisa says. "All you have to worry about is getting your mind back to your body."

I nod, kneeling. My pulse hammers in my throat, and my hands tremble.

Louisa watches me. "You know what you're doing?"

"I'm looking for Max Elbridge."

"And?"

"And if he's inside the gate, I'm turning around and coming back," I say obediently.

"Good." She pauses. "Things will be strange, once the spell starts. It will take you a moment to adjust. Try not to get distracted."

One of my legs twitches with the urge to run. “Alright,” I croak. “How will I know where I’m going?”

“You’ll know,” says Louisa. It’s not a reassuring answer, but she’s already looking at Pen. “Ready?”

Pen nods, her eyes enormous and dark. Every trace of amusement has left her features, and I’m not sure if her obvious fear makes me feel better or worse.

“Okay,” Louisa says. “Then like I taught you.”

The two of them raise their hands, the candles flaring, and the world goes black.

10

I OPEN MY EYES.

The world is there… and also not. Louisa and Pen still kneel in front of me, but they're faded grey shapes, almost ghostly, their movements as slow as if they're underwater. And while I haven't moved, everything is murky, like my bedroom is filled with fog.

I slowly get to my feet. Something feels wrong. I seem to be moving normally, and at a normal speed. The spell is obviously working. Yet something isn't quite right.

I glance at Louisa. She continues her drifting gestures without appearing to see me.

"Huh," I say uneasily. I turn.

I'm kneeling in the centre of the circle.

I flinch back, hissing with fright. I am here, standing. I am there, kneeling: hands on my thighs, eyes closed, motionless.

An involuntary shudder runs through me, though the body in the circle doesn't move. It's not like I didn't know this was coming. I knew I'd be separating my mind, my consciousness, from the rest of me.

I just didn't expect an out-of-body experience to be so… literal.

I press my fingers to the inside of my wrist, then my throat. There's no pulse, no throb of a heartbeat. There's no sound in my ears when I swallow, and though my chest moves when I inhale, there's no rush of air. This is what felt wrong. I'm basically dead.

"Mm, no." My voice comes out weak and panicky, but at least I can hear it. "Nope. This is not cool."

Nobody replies, obviously. Neither Pen nor Louisa look up, and inside the circle, my body doesn't speak. So I'm talking to myself, but since the sound of my own voice is the only thing convincing me I'm not a ghost, I don't feel bad about it.

I tear my eyes away from my body, unable to stomach the sight any longer, and look around. Like Pen and Louisa, the furniture in the room is hazy and grey, as if covered in a layer of dust. Only one thing has colour: a small, red toy car, sitting in the scrying circle near my feet.

I frown at it, then remember. "Max."

Max Elbridge. That's why I'm here.

And as I think it, the chalk lines forming the scrying circle, previously as faded as everything else, flood to red.

I take a step back, watching as the web of lines darkens and spreads, like ink in water. The marks seethe over the floorboards, drifting like searching tentacles, until they pause, writhing in place for a moment. Then they straighten.

All of them lead toward the bedroom window.

You'll know, *Louisa said.*

Well, this seems like a pretty obvious sign. She never told me I'd be following blood-coloured lines, though. This is the kind of thing that gets people killed in horror movies.

I stare at the vague shape of the window, and from somewhere outside I feel a faint, insistent tug.

"Oh, this is bullshit,*" I mumble. Then, with a final glance back at Pen and Louisa and my empty body, I follow the lines.*

The bedroom wall looms before me, but even in this state, it looks pretty solid. The lines go straight through it, leading outside. Am I supposed to jump out the window?

I think about heading back to the stairs, but first I reach for the wall—

And I'm outside.

I blink.

I'm outside. In the backyard. The grass is grey and motionless, the fence standing before me. The house is behind me, my bedroom upstairs, yet I appeared down here as if I teleported.

It's not totally *horrible, I suppose, but it's still pretty weird.*

The lines pass through the picket fence, red as veins, and lead into the woods. The trees stand tall and empty, like columns of pale marble, their branches indistinct shapes. Somehow it's even creepier than usual.

I sigh, then follow the lines.

The ghost-woods are eerily silent: no birds singing, no leaves rustling. My footsteps are soundless, and nothing, nothing *moves. The undergrowth is an unshifting tangle of grey, the earth blank but for roots, twisting across the path like fat white worms.*

The red lines run through it all, uninterrupted, and I follow them like they're strings in a labyrinth. The tug I feel earlier repeats itself, stronger this time, but I don't need encouragement now. My anticipation outweighs my fear, and I keep my eyes down, concentrating.

It takes me a moment to notice I'm no longer alone.

It passes in slow-motion: a long black shape, blurred through the pale trees. It must be something in the real world, but though I can follow its passage, I can't make sense of what I'm seeing. Whatever the strange thing is, it stands out like a smear on an empty page, an aberration in this silent space.

I watch it go, bewildered, and then it vanishes, heading in the direction I came from.

Toward the house.

I feel a flicker of worry. I could go back. I could at least warn someone.

But I'm the one scrying. My job is to find Max.

A second shape moves through the woods, following the first, and I turn away.

I don't know how long I walk for. It could be minutes or hours. After a while I stop trying to keep track, too focused on the lines at my feet as I walk deeper and deeper into the woods.

And then, suddenly, they stop.

I look up.

Before me stands the gate.

I halt at the edge of the ghostly clearing. The red lines continue forward before stretching outward, flowing across the pale earth until they form a circle around the gate.

If I had a pulse, it would be racing. The gate is exactly as I first saw it. Exactly. *The rest of the world exists in a weird fog, but the gate is as stark and real as I am. It's black iron, formed from bars and bold curlicues. It stands slightly ajar, no taller than my hip.*

And one single scarlet line has branched off from the others, leading directly inside.

Max.

Fear tightens my chest. I'm not exactly breathing, but I still feel the air catch in my lungs as I step forward.

The red line stops at the foot of the gate. I crouch, peering cautiously through the iron bars. The line doesn't pass through to the other side. It simply stops, as abruptly as if it were cut.

The scry has undeniably led me here. If I can't see anything outside the gate, what I'm looking for must be inside. Yet there doesn't appear to be *an inside.*

"Max?" My voice sounds painfully loud, and I grimace. "Hannah?"

No answer comes.

I reluctantly creep closer to the gleaming iron bars, half expecting them to move. I feel an urge to reach out, to see if they're as cold as they look, to stick my hand into the space where they sit ajar.

Entering the gap is equivalent to entering another world. It could totally sever your mind's connection to your body. No amount of magic would be able to save you.

I imagine my body sitting empty, and I shiver.

I can't stick my hand in, and I can't go in myself, so only one option is left. I lean in as close as I dare, and call, "Max?"

Silence.

And then. Maybe. Soft as a whisper on a breeze.

A faint reply.

I reel back, letting out a wild laugh. The sound shatters the silence, but I don't care.

He's inside the gate. He's inside the gate, and he's alive. Hannah must be in there too—maybe all five of the missing children are in there. And if they're alive, there must be a way to get them out.

I have to go back. I have to tell Louisa and Theo.

I turn to follow the lines home, and the creature strikes me in the chest, knocking me back into the gate.

☙ 11 ❧

"IS SHE DEAD?"

"Of course she's not dead," Louisa snaps. "Don't be ridiculous."

She may not be dead, but Cassandra doesn't look totally *alive,* either. She kneels in the circle with her head tilted back, her eyes closed. Her pulse flutters in her throat like a moth trapped beneath her skin. All seems well.

Pen sighs. "How long do we do this for?"

"Until she gets back, or we run out of energy."

Louisa's youngest niece shoots her a narrow look, her dark eyes sharp. For an instant she looks startlingly like her mother, and Louisa resists the urge to recoil. "Don't we die if we run out of energy?"

"Eventually," Louisa replies. "But it takes a lot to get to that point. We'd have to be here for hours. Besides, look." She nods at the candles, placed carefully around the circle. Their flames burn with a faint green tinge. "Those are our markers. If they start going out, the scry is taking too long and the spell is starting to draw energy from the fire. That's when we get concerned."

"And if Cass isn't back in time? Do we drop the spell? Then *she'll* die."

Louisa takes a moment to wish Pen were slightly less intelligent. Or at least less questioning. Oh, she's a bright girl and a brilliant student, but there are some questions Louisa would really rather not answer. "With luck," she says carefully, "it won't come to that point."

Pen's mouth opens.

"*Louisa?*"

Feeling tremendously grateful for well-timed distractions, Louisa springs to her feet. "I'll be back. Keep going."

Pen goes pale. "You're leaving me alone?"

"Keep doing what you're doing. Channel your energy in, keep up the hand motions, and don't break the spell. Call me if anything changes before I get back."

Pen looks stricken, but Louisa turns and strides downstairs. Theo waits in the kitchen, staring out the window. He doesn't look over as she enters the room.

"What?" she asks. "We're in the middle of the spell."

"I know," he replies, and she notices the grim set to his face. He nods toward the window, and she moves across to join him, following his gaze.

There are few lights on in the house tonight. Only the moon illuminates the world outside, but the sky is wreathed with thick cloud, casting the backyard into patches of silver and shadow. She sees the pale shape of the fence. The spindling forms of the treetops.

The faint movement just beyond the backyard.

Her heart skips a beat. "It could be an animal."

"It could," Theo agrees.

Neither of them believe it.

Pen gives an indignant shout from upstairs. Flustered, Louisa says, "Keep an eye on it. Unless it—"

There's a sound like the scream of a thousand birds, and they both flinch. She looks out the window in time to see a sinuous shadow slip over the fence, vanishing into the darkness of the backyard.

Cold sinks into her bones. "They're back."

Theo's eyes are wide. "Those wards were *new*."

And Louisa remembers what Cass said earlier, the conversation forgotten in the business of the day. *Merich says our magic shouldn't have any effect on the Hounds.*

"Wards won't work," she says softly.

Theo blinks at her, confused. He doesn't understand, so this dread is hers alone, and she closes her eyes, letting it wash through her.

It's one thing to know magic can't protect you. It's another to realise it when the monsters are already at your door. And now it's too late to run.

"The wards mean nothing to them," she continues. "Our magic can't hurt them. We can't fight them, and we can't keep them out."

A dark shape rushes across the back porch. They scramble away from the window, and there's a dull scrabbling sound, a *crack* of tearing wood.

"It's trying to get into the house," Theo hisses.

Leaves scrape against the windows on the far side of the room and Louisa whirls, seeing the bushes in the front yard sway.

"There's more than one," she says.

Theo looks at her. "What do we do?"

What is there to do? The roof moans under the weight of something heavy, the beast stepping slowly, deliberately, searching for a way down. She imagines herself as a rabbit in a burrow, listening to the fox overhead, just before it starts to dig.

"*Louisa*?"

"We'll do what we did last time." The words sound clumsy on her tongue. Unconvincing. "If we hold them off—"

"Until *when*?" Theo demands. "We don't exactly have reinforcements on the way!"

Despair takes root in Louisa's chest. He's right. They're on their own. It's only the two of them, with Cass and Pen oblivious upstairs—

The blood leaves her face. "Oh God," she whispers. "The scry."

Then she turns, sprinting for the stairs, and Theo is alone.

There's a shriek as claws rake across the front window, and he jumps, his heart thundering. The noise is shrill, drawn-out, almost as if the Hound is trying to get his attention. When he looks over he sees four silver lines marring the glass.

The blood pounding in his ears is almost loud enough to drown his terror. If magic doesn't bother the Hounds, what the hell is he supposed to do? Nobody is coming to save them. It's not like there are any other witches around.

Well, there's *one*.

"Now would be good, Helen," he mutters. But even if she could somehow hear him, she couldn't help. Magic is useless here, and Helen left to avoid death, not to dabble in life-threatening situations.

The back door shudders in its frame, and Theo instinctively throws out one hand, then hesitates. What spell can he use? What's the point of a spell if it's not going to help him?

The kitchen window explodes inward, and he buries his face in his arm, shielding his eyes from the flying glass. Before he can think his feet carry him sideways, and he drops down behind the kitchen counter as the ring of glass subsides.

Nothing happens. All is quiet.

His breath emerging in rasps, Theo peers over the top of the counter.

Two long, dark arms reach in through the broken window. The Hound's skin is black, mottled in places with ugly violet and inky blue, until it looks like the skin of a bruised, bloated corpse. Claws scrape across the counter with a sound that raises the hair on his arms, and in a rush, the Hound slithers inside.

Theo ducks, smothering his mouth with his fist. The Hound pauses on the other side of the counter, and he forces himself to be absolutely still.

There's a slow, thoughtful clicking, like talons on tiles.

Theo waits for it to exit the kitchen. Maybe it won't see him. Maybe it will climb back out the window.

But his skin prickles, and he looks up in time to see bony fingers curl over the top of the counter as the Hound appears above him.

He hurls himself away, colliding with the kitchen table, and chairs go flying as the Hound swipes down at him, claws shining in the low light. He throws a fireball, not bothering to aim, and it sails past the Hound to explode against the kitchen ceiling. The beast recoils with a hiss, but he has no time for relief.

The back door flies open with a thunderous *bang*, and a second Hound bounds inside. It moves like murder made flesh, and as Theo scrambles to his feet, it lunges for his throat.

He seizes a chair and hits the Hound in the face.

It's not a dignified approach, or a tidy one. But the monster reels, claws gouging at the floorboards as it stumbles back, and as it flounders over the threshold Theo slams the door shut behind it.

Theo has never been interested in fighting monsters. It was different when he was a kid—who *didn't* dream of wild adventures, of saving the day, of being the hero? But it's hard to imagine those things when you actually have magic. You can't dream of battling werewolves when you know they're simply regular people, trying to get on with their lives. And most of the time, nobody needs a magical hero. Besides, even among witches there are nerds, and he's comfortable in the knowledge he is one. Why fight monsters when you can read about them in the safety of your bedroom?

Unfortunately, that strategy has left him woefully unprepared for this.

The front window shatters in a spray of glass, and he lifts his hands, hardening the air to protect himself from the shards. Hounds pour in like wasps from a hive, all skittering movements and grasping limbs. One clambers in upside-down, hanging from the ceiling, another slinking low through the gloom. The beast lurking in the kitchen scuttles over to join them.

The last creature, the largest, enters with the confidence of a predator, stalking toward him, and Theo freezes as he looks the Hound in the face.

He sees a slick, lupine skull, darkness streaming from it like water. A mouth full of teeth and shadow. White eyes, like the death of the world.

Theo's blood turns cold. Ice runs through his bones.

There is only one light on in the room, and now it flickers and brightens, shining like a captive sun, before it explodes. The surge and sudden blackness blind him, and in his panic Theo hurls a fireball.

Instead of searing orange, this one is a dull yellow. It fades further as he watches, as if the Hounds are draining the power from it, but it still illuminates the roiling mass of monsters on the ceiling, their white eyes fixed on him.

The breath leaves him in a gasp—

And the back door bursts inward.

•••

Not for the first time, Pen contemplates her bad luck.

It's bad enough being the youngest. The others have already done everything: Theo is the golden boy, Cass is the black sheep, and Helen was perfection personified, until she abandoned them. What's left for her to do?

And *because* she's the youngest, she gets the worst jobs. Like watching Cass, who may or may not be dead.

Downstairs glass shatters. There's an interesting *crash*.

Basically, everyone is having fun but her. Again.

Footsteps race up the stairs—*finally*, she thinks sourly, *they remember I exist*—and Louisa hurtles into the room. "Are you alright?" she asks breathlessly.

"I'm fine," Pen snaps. "Where have you been? I've been waiting for you!"

"They're back."

"What?"

Louisa's eyes widen, and before Pen can turn the bedroom erupts. She shrieks, her cheeks stinging as glass strikes her face, and realises the window has shattered. The candles flare, a cold breeze surging in as the curtains are torn aside, and something huge and dark appears in the empty window frame.

Two grasping hands reach inside, and the Hound pulls itself into the room.

It makes a sound. Pen can't name it. Her mind bends away from the noise, trying to reassemble it into something she can understand. It's the moan of a ship, breaking on the waves. The groan of a plague victim, dying in agony. The echoing proclamation of a monster, announcing that there is no escape, no mercy, only death.

And then it turns to her.

"*Here*!" Louisa's voice shrieks, and a moment later a lamp strikes the beast in the head. *Does it have a head?* Pen wonders. *Does it even have eyes?* If it does they vanish from her memory, blurring out like something too hideous to recall, but the Hound looks away from her, prowling toward the door.

Louisa backs out of the room, light blooming in her hands. "Don't drop the spell," she rasps. "We'll deal with this."

The Hound springs, and Louisa runs.

Cass still hasn't moved. Pen looks anxiously from the broken window to the empty doorway, horrific crashes and the gentle *whump* of magic echoing up from downstairs. How is Cass not hearing this? Maybe she died without Pen noticing.

She peers suspiciously at her.

Down the hall there's a short scream, then a series of rapid thumps. Glass rattles. The dresser jolts.

One of the candles around the scrying circle tips over.

"Oh crap," Pen hisses. She reaches for the candle with one hand, maintaining the spell with the other. The candle rolls, wax puddling on the floor, until it strikes the wall, the magical flame still flickering cheerfully.

It touches the fallen curtain, hanging lopsidedly across the window.

And it catches.

And burns.

And burns.

•••

The creature strikes me in the chest, and ice blooms under my skin, the force of the blow sending me flying. I reel backward, one step, another—

Into the gate.

A scream rips from my throat, and I throw out one hand. My fingers catch iron, cold enough to burn, and I jerk to a halt.

Safe.

From the corner of my eye I see movement, and I hurl myself away, landing near the red lines of the scry. Only once there's some distance between me and the gate do I turn.

The creature stands horribly still, frozen mid-step. One foot is lifted, its bone-white hands raised like a monster in a children's book. Only its face moves, features jittering and sliding, its skin as pale as a new corpse. I see a gaping mouth. Eyes as empty as an abandoned grave.

It shrieks, lunging.

I skitter backward, trying to keep the gate in sight. Falling inside would be disastrous, and this thing tried to push me in. Did it know it could kill me? How can it even see me, or touch me? Technically I'm only a wandering mind, so what does that make this thing?

Physical forms can't exist on that side of the veil.

The creature moves, faster than I can follow, and white fingers scrape across my ribs. Agony erupts in their wake, and I buckle at the knees, gasping as I stumble back. I might not have a body, but the pain is perfectly real, and the unnatural cold sinks into my muscles, turning them to stone.

If physical forms can't exist beyond the veil, maybe this thing doesn't exist in the real world. But we're not in the real world, and I don't have a physical form either. Maybe it can't kill me here, but if it gets me inside the gate…

The creature darts forward, joints jerking, and I throw out my hand, summoning a fireball—

Nothing comes.

Panic chokes me. No body, no magic. I'm going to have to run.

I risk a glance down, searching for the lines that will lead me home. But as I find them, red as veins against the pale landscape, they flicker.

As if they're fading.

And cold fingers close around my throat.

12

FOR A MOMENT THEO CAN ONLY STARE, SHOCKED.

The door slams against the wall, and in walks a figure as beautiful and terrible as an avenging angel. The spluttering light of the failed fireball illuminates knifelike cheekbones and hair the colour of darkest bronze. A narrow gash marks the man's forehead, slicking his face in blood, and his eyes—

His eyes are black from rim to rim, and they burn.

The stranger doesn't falter. As the Hound on the ceiling leaps he flicks his hand, and the shadows surge around him like waves up a cliff. The Hound is thrown backward, tumbling out the broken window, and it lands in the front yard with a muffled *thump*.

"Oh my God," says Theo.

"You're welcome." The stranger wipes a smear of blood off his cheek. "You know, for a house full of witches, you really do *not* have a handle on things. Behind you."

Theo spins, seizing another kitchen chair and striking a second Hound in the face. It gives up, deciding to try for easier prey, and springs at the newcomer.

There's a flash of pale blue, and the beast wails, crumpling. Black blood splatters the floorboards.

The stranger is holding a sword.

"You're Merich," Theo croaks.

"Well done," Merich says sourly.

A shadow looms in the doorway behind him, and Theo returns to his senses. A fireball crackles to life in his hand, and he hurls it past Merich. The Hound flinches away from the flames, and Merich whirls, his sword lancing out.

There's a high shriek, and he kicks the door closed. "Where are the others?"

As if on cue there's a scream, and then Louisa tumbles down the stairs, landing in a heap. A Hound dives after her, claws gleaming.

Merich waves his hand once more, and the shadows flash. The beast goes flying, slamming into the ceiling before falling to crunch against the stairs. It doesn't move again, and then it vanishes, as if it were never there.

"You're hurting them." Theo rasps. "You're actually hurting them."

"I'm not even touching them." Merich plunges his sword into the Hound writhing on the floor, and it too disappears, leaving only a spray of gently sizzling blood. "I'm manipulating what's around them. The sword hurts them. Magic might not do much, but nothing enjoys being stabbed. Or having all of its bones broken."

Indeed, the room is suddenly remarkably empty of monsters, the survivors slipping away while the two of them were distracted. Theo looks at the shattered remnants of the chair in his hands, and Merich starts up the stairs, pausing to peer at Louisa's motionless form.

"Alive," he announces. "Where's Cassandra?"

"Upstairs," Theo replies.

Merich nods, gesturing at Louisa. "Get her down there with you. What are you people *doing* here?"

"What?"

Merich shoots him an irritated look. "Someone is using magic. A *lot* of magic. You're leading the Hounds straight to you."

"Oh God," says Theo. "The scrying spell."

Merich's expression darkens, and he charges up the stairs.

•••

Pen has been ignoring it so far, but she can no longer deny the truth.

The bedroom is *definitely* on fire.

Flames ripple up the curtains, reflecting in the glass jutting from the shattered window. Embers smoulder on the woven rug, burning black spots into the floor.

And as the fire grows, it creeps closer to the careful lines marking out the scrying spell.

If Pen had her hands free, she could tear moisture out of the air to drown the flames. If she were closer, she could pull the curtains down and throw them out the window.

If someone were *listening*, they could bring her *actual water* and solve this problem before she burns to death.

"Fucking ridiculous," she mutters, moving her hands the way Louisa taught her.

In the centre of the circle, Cass shudders.

Pen stares at her.

She does it again.

Panic prickles up Pen's spine, and then Cass bends *backward*, her throat rising toward the ceiling as if she's being dragged by a noose. She twitches, flinching as though she's been struck, and makes a low rattling sound.

"Oh shit," says Pen, and as the rug on the floor finally ignites, fire crawling toward the trailing bed linens, "Oh, *shit*!"

Footsteps thunder toward her, and her heart stops as she looks to the doorway, preparing to be devoured by whatever monsters are apparently killing everyone downstairs. Instead, a man appears.

She gapes. "*Merich*?"

"Younger sister," he replies, which would sting more if she weren't so glad to see him. His eyes fix on Cass. "What's going on here?"

"We're scrying."

"Well, stop! You're drawing the Hounds here!"

"Seriously?" she squeaks.

He doesn't have time to answer. Cass jolts again, more violently this time, the cords in her throat standing out like strings on a harp. Merich curses, stepping toward the circle.

"Stop!" Pen shrieks. "You can't!"

He glares at her. "What?"

"You can't enter the circle while she's scrying! I… uh. I think." It occurs to Pen that Louisa wasn't clear on this matter. Then again, she probably didn't expect this. "She might die."

"Not to criticise your methods or anything," he snaps, "but she doesn't look like she's doing too well anyway."

He's not wrong. As he says it Cass jerks, her back bowing like the curve of a bridge, and Pen's mind goes blank with terror. Surely if she bends any further, she'll break...

"The circle keeps evil things away while she's not in her body," Pen says faintly.

Merich's mouth twists. "Luckily, I'm not evil."

He steps into the circle.

The candles flare, their green flames a strange counterpart to the fire raging around the room. As Pen watches Merich sinks to one knee, the movement as elegant as a gentleman's bow, and he curls himself around Cass. Her head rests on his shoulder, his arm braced against her back to release her from that awful bend.

It is, Pen thinks, possibly the most romantic thing she's ever seen.

"Cassandra," Merich calls. Pen shivers. His voice is... different. It's the rumble of thunder on the horizon, the hollow *boom* of old trees turning in the wind. It's the horn that calls armies to war.

The sound thrums through her bones, and she realises this is a different kind of magic. Merich is not a man—he's something older, and stranger, and infinitely more powerful.

He ducks his head, his mouth almost brushing Cass's ear. "You need to come back now, Cassandra."

•••

Pale fingers bite into my throat, and my body screams.

I've never known cold like this. It races through my veins, sending shocks through my heart. This is the kind of cold that freezes people to death, and I gasp for air, feeling my muscles lock so tightly they threaten to shatter.

And as the paralysis grips me, the creature drags me toward the gate.

I'm going to die. *The thought comes to me with stunning clarity. How long has it been outside the scry? Surely long enough for those candles to be burning low, for Pen and Louisa to feel the energy seeping out of them. Will they break off the spell and let me die? Or will this thing kill me first?*

What happens if it pulls me through the gate?

I'm supposed to be a witch. I'm supposed to be better than this, but I have no magic here.

So do something else.

Maybe dying clears your thoughts. But I'm not interested in dying today.

I pull back against the creature's grip, choking as those sharp fingers dig into my throat. The monster looks back at me, empty eyes as dark as the void, its mouth gaping wider—

I punch it right in its demon face.

My fist connects with a sound like ice cracking, and there's a high, muffled scream. The creature tumbles backward, hand ripped away from my neck.

I turn and run, following the red lines as they flicker and sway. Now that I've found Max, the urge to return to my body overwhelms everything else. I hardly feel the pain as I sprint through the woods, a faint shriek echoing behind me. Trees blur past like pale shadows.

Is the creature following me? Is it faster than me?

What happens if it gets to my body first?

The image of my body, unguarded and empty, springs into my head, and I force myself to go faster. The house looms before me, the window a ghostly shape above, and—

"—back now, Cassandra."

The world floods into colour, and I heave in a breath.

Pen shrieks, leaping to her feet. I watch dazedly as she runs past me to the window, where the curtains are—

On fire?

Arms tighten around me, and I realise my cheek is pressed into a muscular shoulder. I blink, then look up into glittering black eyes. After the empty sockets of the creature I faced, they're impossibly beautiful.

"*Merich*?" I croak.

He smiles. I probably imagine the relief that crosses his face. "Cassandra. Always a pleasure."

Then he flicks his hand, and the Hound creeping through the doorway is thrown backward.

I struggle upright, trying not to notice how I use his torso for leverage, or how he's still holding me to his chest. Blood slicks his face, seeping from a gash in his forehead.

"What—"

"You're under attack," he says.

"It would be good to get some *help* over here!" Pen screams.

"It would also be a good time to get up," adds Merich.

He gets to his feet in one smooth movement, lifting me with him as if I weigh nothing. I let out a dismayed squawk.

My bedroom is on fire. Flames devour the curtains, spreading across the room, and smoke clouds the ceiling. Pen coughs as she throws her hands up, releasing a spray of water, and patches of curtain sizzle pathetically.

"I didn't do all this just to burn to death!" she screeches.

A dark shape appears at the window.

"*Pen*!"

I barely have time to scream before she's leaping away, landing on the bed as the Hound crawls through the window, heedless of the jagged glass sticking out of the frame. A final shower of water evaporates in the hot air, and Merich drags me back as the Hound clambers up the wall. It halts on the ceiling, eyeing us.

Deciding who to kill first.

Merich's arm tightens around me. "Cass," he murmurs. I sway, my head pounding as the world rocks sickeningly. "These things were drawn to your magic. If you *happen* to know a way to drive them back, you could finish this."

He knows. Of course he knows. I can't seem to hide anything from him, so why can't he see how useless I am in this situation? If he weren't holding me up, I'd be in a pile on the floor.

But the Hound is still looking at me. At Pen.

At him.

Merich's breath catches, and the Hound prepares to leap.

I find the web that makes up the world. I see the anchor-points like stars around me, linking to the air, the fire. To Merich.

And there, at the heart of the Hound, a small point of darkness.

The beast jumps.

I pour my magic into the black spot, and I tear it to pieces.

The room explodes. Air ripples out from the place where I stand, and the candles fall over, the curtains billowing outward. The flames are extinguished, smoke flooding the room, and downstairs I hear faint shrieks.

But my attention stays on the Hound, where it hangs in mid-air. It twists and writhes—

And bursts apart at the seams.

I expect blood and gore. A wave of viscera.

All that lands on the floor is a fine grey dust.

Finally, everything goes silent.

Pen slowly sits up on the bed, her eyes wide. I stare at the drifting dust, my vision blurring. Glass tinkles.

Then a hand touches my back, as warm as sunlight.

"Cassandra?"

"Holy shit," Pen whispers. "You blew it up."

"Cassandra," Merich murmurs. "Breathe."

Have I breathed yet? My lungs ache. I search my body, trying to find the right function, and finally take a gasping breath.

My vision goes black, my knees buckling. The last thing I'm aware of is a pair of arms closing around me, gently lowering me to the floor.

13

I WAKE THE NEXT MORNING IN HELEN'S OLD ROOM.

For a few minutes I remain motionless, staring at the unfamiliar ceiling. After Helen left in a storm of righteous fury, making it exceptionally clear she wasn't coming back, Louisa kept her bedroom as it was for a few years. Out of hope, I suppose. Or maybe she was in denial. I assume she thought Helen would change her mind one day. But eventually the posters came down, and the few things left behind were packed up in boxes. They're gathering dust in the closet, because when Louisa finally tried to throw them out, Pen went ballistic.

The room is still painted buttercup yellow, though. A couple of Helen's sketches hang framed on the wall. There are marks on the ceiling where she once stuck glow-in-the-dark stars.

The sight sends a pang through my chest, and I close my eyes.

Slowly, the memories come back to me. Last night. The scry. Max.

The children are alive, or Max is, at least. And they're inside the gap, where no physical forms are meant to exist. Presumably they're guarded by terrifying monsters, like the one that attacked me while I was scrying.

And then I blew up one of those monsters, using my strange magic.

I flex my hands, the bedsheets soft against my palms. Knowing I'm capable of such things makes me deeply uneasy, but if it can kill monsters, I suppose this magic can't be evil. And Louisa said it was in my blood. I'd be able to call it natural if it weren't linked to monsters from another world, but every time I've accessed it, it was because someone else was in danger: Pen, Will, Merich.

Merich.

I cover my face with my hands, overwhelmed with embarrassment. To top off a bad evening, I *literally* fainted in Merich's arms. Not only is it the most pathetic thing I could possibly have done, but I now have to thank him for not dropping me on the floor.

If I survive the next few days, of course.

I drag myself out of bed and hobble into the shower, hoping to wash away the reek of smoke. Unfortunately, when I emerge the smell is as strong as ever. All of the upstairs windows are open, but the whole floor stinks. While I can't bring myself to check the damage to my bedroom, Louisa has apparently ventured in with the goal of putting my clothing through a brutally thorough laundry cycle, which explains the clean clothes I found waiting in the bathroom.

The rest of the house is quiet, so I make my way downstairs.

I appear to arrive in an alternate dimension.

Every window in the main room is broken, glittering glass covering almost every surface. There are scorch marks on the ceiling, and patches of black blood on the floor. The kitchen table has been knocked out of place, and half the chairs have been reduced to sad wooden splinters. After last night I expected Louisa to be waiting to Discuss What Happened, likely over a fortifying breakfast, but there's no food and no coffee.

Also, Merich is standing in the kitchen, his sleeves rolled up to his elbows as he attempts to cover the shattered window.

I stare at him until he looks over. His eyes are fully black today, not human at all, but after last night they no longer frighten me.

"Good morning," he says calmly.

"Good morning," I echo, wondering if I'm still asleep.

He turns back to the window, trying to position a thick sheet of plastic over the empty frame. "Your aunt put me to work," he explains. "She's out getting more supplies."

Well, at least I don't have to worry about Louisa's reaction when she finds one of the Fae in her house. "The others?"

"Asleep."

"And you're… fixing windows," I say. Because that's normal. One of the Fae, covering our windows after a monster attack. "Did you sleep here?"

"I napped on your porch." Merich tucks a hammer under his arm and tries to pick up a nail, then hisses, his teeth bared. "Iron," he says, inserting a massive amount of loathing into the word. "Do you mind giving me a hand here? This is a two-person job."

It seems like the only reasonable thing to do. I make my way over. "You don't like iron?"

"Silver burns vampires, iron burns the Fae. Go on then."

I help position the plastic and hold a nail to the corner, trying not to cringe as he twirls the hammer. "Don't you dare hit me."

"Wouldn't dream of it," he says airily, and delivers a stunningly fast blow. He strikes the nail with perfect accuracy before I have time to flinch, then hammers it in as I withdraw my hand.

This is as good a time as any. "Thank you," I say. "For what you did last night. I think we owe you our lives."

Merich shrugs, gesturing for me to place another nail. "It seemed rude to watch you all die."

"How did you know we were in trouble?"

He points at the gash on his forehead. It's far smaller than it was last night, as though it's had several days to heal. "A Hound ran into me. I put it down, then thought I'd see if its friends were going where I suspected they were going."

"Good deduction."

"I *am* brilliant. But you're welcome. You do seem determined to ignore that whole *don't use magic* thing I mentioned, though."

"We didn't have a choice!" I say indignantly. "And I didn't realise you meant *no magic at all.* I thought you meant not to use it in the woods!"

"Yet you performed an immensely powerful spell anyway." He sighs. "You must have a death wish."

"Says the man who stepped into a scrying spell without knowing what would happen."

"I was reasonably certain I wouldn't die."

"*Reasonably* certain?"

He meets my eyes, the corner of his mouth twitching. "I found the risk worth the reward."

The blood rushes to my cheeks, and I fix my gaze on the plastic sheet.

I help Merich hammer several more nails into place before he speaks again, and by then I've managed to regain control over my expression. "Your spell," he says. "It was to find those missing children?"

"Yes."

"It worked?"

"It did." I touch my throat, where I can still feel the phantom grip of cold fingers. There are no visible marks, no trace of the fight against the monster, yet the chill remains. "They're inside the gate."

Merich's face darkens. "Ah. Dead, then."

"No."

The hammer pauses mid-fall. "*No?*"

"I heard the voice of the boy who went missing yesterday, and he responded when I called out to him. He was definitely inside the gate, though." I fiddle with a nail, struggling to voice my thoughts. "My brother says the Fae know more about magic and the veil than most people."

"We do."

"Is it possible the place beyond the veil isn't as bad as everyone thinks?"

"No," Merich says instantly. "It's bad. And if those children are in there, they should definitely be dead."

We're both quiet as he hammers in the final two nails, and I consider his words. If physical forms can't survive beyond the veil, what happens when something living enters the gap? Does it still exist in some way, or is it just... gone? Theo seemed convinced that entering the gap would be a death sentence. Is he wrong, or does something make this situation different?

"My brother found out the veil slipped," I say.

Merich's head whips around. "Slipped?"

"Apparently it was dealt with. The gap in the woods is a leftover issue."

I watch as he frowns, glaring at the hammer in his hand like it's withholding answers. "It would make sense," he murmurs to himself. "The slip must have been enormous to cause such widespread damage. It could have torn the world open. But if it didn't slip *enough*…"

He seems to have forgotten I'm here. I tap his shoulder. "What does that mean?"

Merich turns to face me. "Think of the veil slipping as a door opening. If it slips all the way, the door is wide open. Anything can come through. If the veil is stable, the door is closed. Nothing comes through at all."

"But you said—"

"If it doesn't slip *enough*—well, maybe some kind of monster has a foot stuck in the proverbial door. It might not be capable of pushing all the way through. Not yet, anyway. It's possible it's created itself some kind of middle ground, like a pocket space between our world and theirs. If it can't survive here yet, and we can't survive there, it might be a neutral zone."

My pulse quickens. "A place where everything could survive."

"Temporarily," Merich adds. "I assume the environment is… hostile. It would explain why your missing children appear to be alive. But whatever creature lurks in that space, it's only there while it gathers the strength to push through the door. To exit the gap."

It makes sense. It also gives me a horrible little idea. "Why wait, though?"

Merich's voice is very quiet. "Why does it take children?"

The question is like being doused with cold water. "To build its strength."

Of course. Merich must be right: Max is alive, therefore his theory about a neutral zone must be true. But why would a monster need a neutral zone unless it wants to keep its prey alive?

"Maybe it eats them," Merich says. "Maybe it drains them for sustenance. Most creatures of that ilk work along those lines. There's no life on the other side of the veil, so they steal it from here, like leeches. The more powerful a creature is, the more work it takes to exit a gap. But sooner or later, this monster *will* get out."

And then it won't need to lure children. It'll just take what it wants.

It took so much effort to kill a Hound. What would it take to kill something like this?

"So we have to close the gap before it escapes," I say softly.

"That would be preferable."

The pieces are coming together. I'm getting the answers I wanted, but they're so much worse than I thought they'd be. "What if we got the children back?"

"The monster would have no way to strengthen itself. Until it finds new prey, at least." Merich glances at me. "As long as the gap remains open, nobody near it will be safe. Closing it should be the priority."

I shoot him a glare. "The *children* are my priority. If I have to kill a few monsters to get them back, I will, but I'm not closing the gap with them inside. If you don't like it, don't help."

Merich says nothing, instead turning away to gather up the shards of glass littering the kitchen counter. Wonderful—he saves my life, I bite his head off. But I'm too embarrassed to apologise for my tone, and I'm not willing to apologise for the words. Instead I silently join him, and we pick up the pieces one by one.

Once they're wrapped in newspaper and the kitchen is mostly glass-free, Merich speaks again. "I'm sorry," he says, his voice low. "I didn't intend to sound like I'm telling you what to do. You've accomplished more than I thought possible. I have no right to insert my opinion."

The apology saps away the last of my irritation. "You did save my life last night," I admit. "I suppose you have some right."

"Yes, but I thought it would be obnoxious to point that out."

I snort, sagging against the kitchen counter. "The gap has to be dealt with. But…" I pause, reluctant to continue. It feels strange to voice my thoughts to Merich of all people, but he listens with a quiet patience that makes it seem okay. So I talk. "This is a lot more than I bargained for. I thought some human creep was to blame for this, and instead I got a monster from another world. I don't know how to handle this."

"You've been doing well so far."

"We nearly died last night."

"Well, that's true." He leans up beside me, giving me an easy smile, and my heart stutters. "But it seems I'm helping you now, so you've got that going for you."

I stare at him, struck silent. I should be thanking him. I should be asking him about the magic I used last night. He didn't seem surprised at what I did; in fact, he seemed to expect it, as if he knew what I was capable of. Maybe he can sense something. Maybe he knows something I don't.

But instead of doing either, I meet his perfectly black eyes, and all I can think of is the moment I returned from the scry to find his arms around me, his face so very close to mine.

A voice cracks the silence, and footsteps race through the house. "*Cass*? Are you alright? I saw the broken windows—"

Will. "Fix your eyes!" I hiss, hoping Merich can control his appearance, and I whirl as Will stumbles into the room.

He stops in the doorway, a covered dish clutched to his chest, and relief floods his face. "Oh, thank God. I saw the glass and I thought…"

I stay perfectly still, hoping this situation will go away if I ignore it. But Will has already trailed off, blinking with surprise as he notices Merich.

No. Not just Merich. The two of us, standing hip to hip.

"Oh. Uh. Sorry." Will gathers himself. "I didn't know you had, uh, company."

"Ah," I say weakly. "Yeah."

I risk a glance at Merich. He appears human, the darkness of his eyes now restricted to his irises, but he watches Will with a predatory scrutiny. Will looks at me, as if searching for a clue about how he should feel, before returning Merich's stare. I don't know if they're sizing each other up or if they're about to start hitting each other with the remaining kitchen chairs.

Manners win out. "Hi," Will says slowly. "I'm Will."

"Merich."

Will flinches, some of the colour leaving his cheeks. I can only assume he's recalling where he knows that name from and is realising what he's looking at. He recovers admirably, giving Merich a tight nod, but he looks wary.

That's not what makes me so uneasy.

There's a birdlike tilt to Merich's head, his face blank as he studies Will. There's something unnerving about the intensity of his focus. He doesn't even blink.

He looks almost as wary as Will.

This situation needs defusing. I start toward Will, and his attention turns to me, though his expression remains strained. "You're okay?" he asks.

"Fine." I point at the dish in his hands. "What have you got there?"

"You asked me to bring breakfast. Cass, what the hell happened? This place is a warzone!"

I gently remove the dish from his hands, my stomach growling as I catch a whiff of bacon and pastry, and set it down on the table, on top of more broken glass. "The Hounds came back. There were more of them."

"You got rid of them, though? You're not hurt?"

The worry in Will's voice tightens my chest. "I'm fine," I say softly. "Everyone is fine. Well, Pen set fire to my bedroom, but nobody was hurt."

He nods, taking a deep breath. "Right. Okay. So, your scrying thing. Did you find anything?"

I'm aware of Merich behind me, watching us in silence. "Yes," I say. "I know where the kids are."

Will looks resigned. "It's some magical shit, isn't it?"

"They're inside the gate."

He sighs.

"I think I can get them out." I try to sound confident. Calm. Like I don't need his help.

"You know how to do it?"

"Not yet. But I think you should—"

He gives me a hard look. "Do you *think* you can get them out, or do you *hope* you can?"

I falter. "Maybe a bit of both."

"Well, it sounds like you need a plan." He removes his jacket, draping it over a chair. "I can tell this will be a bastard of a day. Give me a few minutes, then we'll get started."

"Get started," I echo.

Will raises his eyebrows. "You think I'll let you do this alone?"

So loyal. So kind. So damn breakable. Panic takes root in my gut, like a tremor running through me. I can't let him stay involved in this. He'll wind up dead. There's a good chance we'll all wind up dead, of course, but I can't risk Will. I can't have his blood on my hands. Not again.

I swallow. "Will—"

"You can't argue with me on this," he says brightly. "Whatever you're doing, I'm doing it with you."

His jaw has the obstinate set I know so well. I'd have more luck reversing the path of the sun than changing his mind. Maybe that's why tears sting my eyes. "Okay," I whisper.

Will smiles crookedly, pulling me into a hug. He smells like coffee and fresh bread, and, as always, damp, dark earth. "Don't get upset about it," he murmurs. "You don't have to do everything on your own. There's no getting rid of me."

I rest my cheek on his shoulder. "I know."

"Good." He releases me, casting a final glance at Merich. "I'm going to the bathroom, and then I'll check if I've got anything useful in the car. We're going to need to clean this mess up."

I nod mutely, and with a final smile he leaves the room. It's not until I hear the bathroom door close that I turn back to Merich.

He looks at me, his expression unreadable.

"So," Merich says quietly. "What the hell is he?"

14

THIS IS THE STORY.

Two children walk alone in the woods.

The first is a boy. He is taller, but barely. His hair is a dusty brown, his cheeks freckled from the summer sun. His eyes are a stunning shade of blue. He's the type of boy mothers coo over. If you believe them, he'll be a heartbreaker one day.

The second is a girl. Her hair is black, the kind of messy that implies an ongoing battle over the importance of a hairbrush. Her knees are stained with dirt. Her eyes are beautiful but eerie, a strange pale grey. The girl herself is eerie. There is something odd about her, something other.

She is the type of girl who makes mothers nervous.

"I'm pretty sure I could do magic," the boy announces. "If someone taught me."

The girl scowls at his back, following him through the trees. This has the feel of a conversation gone over many times and never resolved. "No, you couldn't," she says grumpily. "It has to be in your blood."

"Maybe it *is* in my blood."

"You can't do magic."

"Can so." The boy turns, leaping into a duelling position, and points a stick at her. "*Abracadabra*."

The girl looks thoroughly unimpressed. "You're stupid."

He grins, waiting for her to catch up. "You're just jealous because Helen can change her face."

"*That's* stupid," she replies, with considerably more heat. "Why would anyone want to change their face? What if you forget what your *actual* face is like? What if you get stuck and you're, like, really ugly or something?"

"I think it's cool. She's like a superhero."

"She is not!"

The boy shrugs. "You do something cool, then."

The woods are deep and growing dark. Clouds are gathering overhead, and things stir in the trees.

"I don't have to do something cool," the girl says, sounding wounded. "At least I can do magic. *You* can't."

"But *I* can bake," the boy says, in a tone implying this is a much more impressive skill, and therefore worthy of some admiration. "What were we looking for again?"

"Mushrooms," the girl replies. "Louisa said you can do magic with some toadstools and mushrooms. Heal people and stuff."

"Can you poison them?" the boy asks hopefully.

She glares at him. "I'll poison *you*."

"Hey, you asked me to help!" He stops. "What was that?"

The girl pauses beside him, listening. The boughs above them link like the bars of a cage, a veil of leaves covering the sky. Shadows fall thick among the tree trunks, and the undergrowth swells around them, like the arms of a trap drawing closed.

In the brush, something moves.

There is a slow, heavy step. Heavier than any deer the girl has ever heard, a low *thump* that seems to echo through her bones. It's followed by a rasping slither.

And another step.

So slow. So careful.

The sound of something stalking.

The brush crackles and sways, and the stink of rotting meat comes over the wind.

The boy's face has gone pale. The girl reaches for his wrist, her heart thundering in her chest. Her older sister always tells her there are monsters in these woods, and the girl always laughs at her.

It doesn't seem so funny now.

"Let's go back," the boy whispers.

She opens her mouth to agree, those grey eyes fixed on the bushes.

Before she can speak, the creature lunges.

The pair do not wait to see what appears. As the foliage parts and something huge and dark and reeking surges toward them they run, sprinting deeper into the woods. Roots tangle around their feet, the ground rough with stones, but they run, hand in hand, as those dreadful footsteps follow. Thunder booms, the first raindrops striking the leaves with a hiss.

The boy falls first.

As they dive through some thick, thorn-riddled bushes, the ground opens up before them. He is in the lead, dragging the girl with him, and his feet find empty air. Both of them fall, their hands torn apart as they tumble down a slope studded with rocks. The girl squeezes her eyes closed, resisting the urge to shriek as sticks and stones gouge her skin, and then she hits the bottom of the mud-slick trench with a *crack*.

She bites her lip so hard she tastes blood, but she doesn't scream.

Above them, behind the wall of thorns, there's a growl. Slow footsteps prowl up and down, and she hears the rasping breath of something much, much larger than her. She waits for it to spring, to find and devour them both.

The footsteps pace and pace.

And then they begin to fade.

After a moment they're gone completely.

The girl allows herself to breathe, then slowly pushes up to her knees. One wrist aches, and it looks wrong. She has some idea about healing magic, but Louisa knows best. She can fix it, and she can heal all the cuts from the sticks and rocks, too.

"Will?" she whispers. "Will, I think it's gone."

There is no reply. Only a wet gurgle.

The girl looks around, and this time she does scream.

The boy is on his back, one hand clawing at his throat. A thick, gnarled stick protrudes between his fingers, and blood pools around it, a bright, shining red.

She scrambles over, the pain in her wrist forgotten. "It's okay," she gasps. The words come out high and shrill, but it's what Louisa says whenever she gets hurt, and it's always true, so it must work here, it must. "It's okay!"

The boy's blue eyes find hers, wide and full of terror. He tries to speak, but blood spurts from his mouth.

The girl recoils. "I'll go and get help!"

He snatches her wrist, the panic in his eyes growing, and she hesitates. Then she throws her arms around him, holding him in her lap like it will help.

"Someone will find us," she whispers. "It's okay."

But the woods are dark and deep, and she is very, very lost. In her arms the boy chokes and splutters, blood pouring over him, over her. His chest heaves as he tries to breathe and fails. His lips turn blue.

He'll catch his breath, though. If she counts back from ten, it will be alright. He'll catch his breath, and everything will be fine.

When she reaches the number six the boy's hand falls from his throat.

And Will dies.

"*No,*" the girl sobs. "No, no, no—"

Louisa would know how to fix this. If she goes and finds Louisa, they can heal Will. But what if she can't find her way out of the woods? What if she can, but doesn't remember the way back to this spot?

There's not enough time. Will's blood is growing sticky on her hands. If you want to heal someone, you have to do it quickly, right?

She can do magic. She told him so herself.

First she draws the stick out of his throat. She retches as she yanks it, and then it's in her hand, like the shattered end of a spear. She hurls it away, sucking down air that tastes like pennies, and closes her eyes.

Louisa taught her that all spells link to something. If you want to pull down a tree, you find a link in the wood. If you want to heal a broken arm, you find a link in the bone. She wants to heal Will, so she searches Will.

Nothing appears in her mind. There is no sudden sense of knowing. She feels no surge of blood, no gleam of bone, no slowly beating heart. *You can't heal what's dead,* she thinks, then silences the thought and looks harder, her breaths growing panicked. There's nothing, except—

There.

It's small. A dark spot, like a little shadow in his chest, a tiny hole. It grows as she notices it, spreading through his ribs. It's the only thing she can find.

So she seizes it.

Spells don't have words. Louisa taught her that.

Instead she thinks, *live*.

The black spot pauses, pulsing.

And then it recedes. Shrinks.

Vanishes.

She feels one uncertain heartbeat, the slow drift of blood in veins. The shiver of waking nerves.

A fresh burst of blood pours from Will's throat, and he chokes.

"*No*!" She presses her hand to his neck, blood slicking her fingers, but this time she sees them: little points of starlight. *Anchors,* Louisa calls them. Normal magic, *proper* magic. One spot burns brighter than any of the others, so she seizes it with her mind, pouring power into it.

And the wound in Will's throat, gaping, raw, red—it begins to close.

She laughs, the sound half a sob, and as she does the knowledge appears in her mind: a sudden burst of understanding, as certain as prophecy. This is enormous magic, and it demands an enormous cost.

She has saved Will's life, and so, she will be the one to kill him.

All magic has a price. Louisa has drilled that into her since she was a baby. But she's never going to kill Will, not ever. This price doesn't even *count*.

The wound closes. All it leaves behind is a small, twisting scar, like a wicked hook, and as blood surges and heart pumps, Will opens his eyes.

He blinks, then frowns up at her, appalled. "Did I *faint*?"

And Cassandra, young, unaware, *oblivious*, smiles.

☙ 15 ❧

MERICH STARES AT ME. SOME OF THE COLOUR LEAVES HIS face, turning his sun-browned skin sallow as he says, "You brought him back to life."

I nod, unable to meet his eye.

Merich glances toward the bathroom, where the sound of running water is barely audible. "He felt… strange," he says wonderingly. "Not entirely human."

Maybe this explains why Merich seemed to know about my magic. Maybe he sensed it, like he senses this. The thought does nothing to alleviate my guilt.

Not human.

A sick feeling comes over me. "Is he… is he not human anymore?"

"He is." Merich sounds distracted, but my fear eases a little. "But he's… less. There's less to him than to an ordinary human." He pauses. "Does he know?"

I shake my head. "He didn't remember what happened. He thought he fainted. Louisa found us first, so she knows. Everyone else… we said there'd been an accident, and they believed it. They were probably glad it wasn't worse than it looked."

"But it was."

"It was."

On some level, I've always suspected Will's parents knew something odd had happened in the woods. For two children to come out covered in so much blood, but with only minor injuries—well, *something* must have happened. And the new scar on Will's throat proved it. Maybe their relief stopped them from seeking answers, but they must have had an inkling. There were rumours about my family even then.

Before that day, Will's family lived right down the street, and if I wasn't at his house, he was at mine. Afterward they moved into town, closer to the diner and away from the woods, and Will never seemed to be allowed to come over anymore, and there never seemed to be a good time for me to go and see him.

It's been so long since I remembered the details. Since I let myself remember. The days of repetitive showering, yet never feeling clean. The weeks of being afraid of the dark. The months of nightmares. The years of fear, of anxiety that crept into every aspect of my life.

Even now, sometimes when I look at my hands I expect to see blood.

"It wasn't normal magic," I say softly. "I don't know where it came from. I shouldn't have been able to do it, and I never did it again—not until I killed the Hound. It's been gone for all these years. I suppose I hoped it was gone for good."

"Why?"

Merich's voice is far too even. He doesn't understand. "Do you know how many people have been brought back to life by witches?" I ask. "*None*. Nobody should be able to do it! It's against the laws of nature. The dead are the dead. But I brought him back to life. That's huge magic, and it cost me *nothing*. There was no price. But the injury should have killed him. By saving him, healing him…"

Maybe that's why the price was so high. To punish me for using unnatural magic.

I clench my hands tight, my fingernails biting into my skin. My palms are littered with red half-moons, some more faded than others. It's an old habit. It started the day Will and I emerged from the woods. The pain is a distraction, a way to keep my mind in the moment, to stop it from wandering down dark paths. I desperately need it right now.

I can feel Merich's eyes on me, but I can't bring myself to look at him. "Nobody should have been able to fight off those Hounds," he says. "You did that too."

He says it like it should comfort me, but having a bizarre connection to monsters from another world isn't exactly soothing. "I did." I cover my face. "Maybe I'm a freak, even for a witch."

It would make sense. God knows where this magic comes from. Louisa said it was in my blood, but I know next to nothing about my parents. My mother is dead, and my father might as well be, so it's not as if I'll ever find out the truth. Even Louisa can't know for sure. For all I know there's just something rotten inside me, and it's been there from the start.

"No."

Hands cover mine, and Merich gently pulls my fingers away from my face. He watches me carefully, his expression soft.

Like this, I can't remember why I ever found him frightening in the first place.

"You are not a freak," he says. "You brought a boy back to life."

"And made him less," I whisper. "Whatever that means."

"It means you gave his family many more years with him than they would have had otherwise. You have nothing to be ashamed of, Cassandra. Strange magic does not necessarily mean *bad* magic."

He holds my gaze until I nod, the knot of misery in my chest loosening. Only then does he seem to realise he still has my hands cradled between his own, his fingers cool against the pain in my palms.

He releases me. I pretend I'm not disappointed.

"What you said," he says. "About a price."

"All magic we do has a price." I pause. "It's not like that for you?"

Merich looks bemused. "For the Fae, magic is as natural as breathing."

Well, *that's* unfair. "For us, every spell has a price," I tell him. "A witch doesn't choose the price for the magic they use, but it's always balanced. The sacrifice always matches the gain. Sometimes it's obvious. If you want to temporarily heighten one sense, you might temporarily lose another. But sometimes…" I hesitate. "Sometimes you just know. It's like an epiphany. You use the magic, and *then* you know the cost."

His eyes are keen. "And with Will?"

"When it happened, I thought I'd gotten lucky." Our voices are low. I can hear Will rattling around in his car outside, and I block the noise out. "I was a kid. I didn't think I'd ever hurt Will, so it didn't count. But when I got older, I started to understand what

Louisa meant when she said *all magic has a price.* Maybe the price is paid now…"

"Or maybe later," Merich finishes, understanding.

I nod. "I tried to create some distance between us when we were teenagers. I thought if we weren't friends, maybe he'd be safe." My smile feels like a grimace. "That's the thing about Will, though. He's too loyal. He made other friends, but he never gave up on me."

"He cares about you."

"It'll kill him." I shrug, trying to pretend my eyes aren't stinging. "I keep him away from magic. I try not to ask him for help. If I ever do magic for him, I make sure he never pays the price. I take it myself." I flex my hand, the scar from Will's knife shining silver. "I thought it would help, but I know it won't."

Merich's head tilts, bronze curls brushing his cheeks. "You feel guilty."

"Of course I do! I brought him back, and apparently I'll be the one to kill him. That was the price—one day it'll be paid. I'm trying to give him a better chance of staying alive, and this gate *really* isn't helping things." My chest tightens, and I search for a way out of the conversation before I burst into tears. "I'd really rather keep *all* the humans away from the Gate of Unimaginable Evil, to be honest."

"Is that what we're calling it now?" Merich straightens, picking up the discarded hammer. "Seems as good of a name as any. Now we just have to work out what to do about it."

"Yeah," I say lamely. "We do."

And I have a sinking feeling I already know what has to be done.

The next round of hammering rouses Pen and Theo, who trudge downstairs in similarly bleary states. By then Will has commandeered the kitchen and is dividing his attention between making coffee and staring nervously at Merich, while I've moved on to clearing up the vast amount of broken glass in the main room.

Theo collapses onto one of the couches, appearing unsurprised by Merich's presence. Pen's eyes nearly bug out of her head.

"You're still here!"

"Cassandra's younger sister," Merich replies. He's busy examining the black bloodstains on the floor, which appear to be partially eroding the floorboards. "I am indeed still here."

I roll my eyes. "Merich. Since you haven't been properly introduced, this is my younger sister, Penelope. That's my older brother, Theo."

"His name is Theseus," Pen says immediately.

Theo glowers at her.

To his credit, Merich doesn't laugh. "Someone liked their mythology, I see."

"Sure," Theo mutters. "Our mother's favourite things were mythology and abandoning her children."

Pen is already rummaging through the various pastries Will brought with him. It appears he's taken the job of supplying breakfast seriously, since he's also frying bacon and making eggs. Pen sighs wistfully. "You always bring food, Will. Can't you marry me instead of Stephanie?"

"You're too young," he says, without looking away from Merich. "I'm an old grey man. It would never last."

"But I'd be fed."

"This is all very pleasant," Merich says, neatly wrapping a pile of broken glass in newspaper, "but shouldn't we be concerning ourselves with the monster lurking in the woods?"

"Oh, don't be a bitch, Merich," Pen replies, and throws a muffin at his head.

Merich, who I'm assuming has never been called a bitch in his life, blinks. The muffin hits the wall with a depressed *thunk*, and Will clears his throat. "The search parties are back in the woods today."

"They'll find a whole lot of nothing, I assume," says Theo.

"They won't find anything," I reply. I never had the chance to tell my family what I discovered while scrying. After fainting my memories become dark and blurred, largely consisting of a swaying motion as someone carried me to bed. I have an uncomfortable feeling it might have been Merich. "The kids are inside the gate."

Pen pulls a face. Theo sighs.

"Max is still alive," I continue. "And something attacked me while I was scrying. It might have been protecting the gate."

"What kind of something?" Will asks suspiciously.

"Something monster-ish," I admit. "So there's that to think about."

"What are we thinking about?"

Louisa enters the room, carrying several sheets of heavy-duty plastic. Will rushes over to help, and she looks around expectantly. "Well?"

I've come this far. There's no turning back now.

I meet her gaze. "We need to talk about what happens next."

•••

The last of the glass is cleared away, plastic sheets put up to cover the windows facing the street. It turns the light in the house dim and gloomy, lending everyone's skin a greyish cast. I wonder if anyone outside has noticed the shattered windows, or if they care.

Even if they did, they probably wouldn't be able to guess what we're discussing inside.

"I'm not saying I don't believe you," says Louisa, "but are you sure?"

While I'm used to Louisa's doubt by now, I still have to bite back a harsh response. You'd think undergoing an intense magical ritual would persuade her I know what I'm talking about, but apparently she was hurled down a flight of stairs last night, so I try to control my temper. She's healed any major injuries, but she looks bruised and sore.

"The scrying spell proved Max went into the gap," I say. "It also revealed something guarding the gate. It tried to drag me inside."

"Since you're no more brain-dead than usual, I assume it failed," says Pen. She sits on the floor under the window, picking the raisins out of a pastry and lining them up on the coffee table.

"I wonder why it was defending the gate." Theo perches on the couch beside Will, frowning as he thinks. "Maybe it's the monster luring in the kids."

"It's doubtful."

Everyone straightens as Merich speaks, as if his voice carries some unspoken command. He and I are seated on two of the remaining kitchen chairs, both unnervingly wobbly, but he seems entirely relaxed, as though the fragile wood is as good as a throne. I try not to stare at him, still unsettled by our earlier closeness.

"The mere presence of a gap will draw entities," he says. "If any weaker creatures have come through, they'd likely feel compelled to stay close."

"Like animals staying near their dens," Theo muses.

Merich nods. "If Cassandra encountered that creature while she was scrying, it may not even exist in this world. It might be lingering in some in-between place, not quite here, not quite there."

"So it's an otherworldly horror, but not the otherworldly horror we're looking for," Pen says drily.

"Yes."

I lean forward, resting my elbows on my knees. "The gap has to be closed, but I know Max is alive in there. If he is, Hannah could be as well. I'm not closing the gate without getting them out."

"You're thinking about a rescue mission," Louisa says, her brow furrowing.

"Seems like the practical option," Pen says. "If we know a monster is stealing kids, it seems dumb to just, y'know, let it keep doing that."

Will clears his throat. "I know this is a vague area, but when you say *creature* and *monster*... what are we actually dealing with?"

Everyone looks at Merich.

He grimaces. "You're thinking too literally," he says. "These things don't have specific names because we don't know what they are. Creatures like the Hounds adopt a physical form when they slip through the veil, and it's easy to recognise them, as we see them fairly often. They're small, common monsters."

"*Small?*" Pen squawks.

Merich ignores her. "We can't name the creature we're dealing with because we don't know what it is. I can only assume it's like the rest of its kind."

"A leech," I say softly.

His eyes flick to me. "Yes. Some are like tiny parasites; you might never notice them, even if they do reach this side of the veil. They latch on to something like a bird or a bug, suck the life out of them, and die before they can harm anything else. Others are more like an entire plague unto themselves. They can infect people, *things*, with their mere presence."

I remember the rotting trees, the black blooming in the woods as Hannah walked to nowhere. "If something like that ever made it through the veil..."

"We wouldn't be around long enough to give it a name," Theo finishes. He turns to me. "Mosi and I talked last night. As long as the gap stays open, it will act as a power source to any creatures already loose in the woods. If we close it, they'll either weaken and die or vanish entirely. The longer the gap is open, the bigger it will get, and it's more likely something larger will eventually force its way through. If the monster inside gets out, we probably can't stop it."

"Even if it escapes the gap, it can't escape the woods." Louisa has a thin line of worry between her eyes, her fingers tapping out a rhythm on her knee. "The boundaries will stop it. We could deal with it then."

"It *will* escape the woods."

I look at Merich. His demeanour has changed, his face growing serious.

"It will escape the woods," he repeats. "Then it will make its way into this town, killing as it goes. It will find the border of this territory, and it will push through. The Hounds were drawn to the power in this area—to you, to this house. There are more like them, and if they come through the gap, they'll grow tired of being trapped here. They will want your borders to fall. And there's only one way to be sure it happens."

"Which is?" Will asks.

"No border will exist if there are no witches in the area."

My stomach drops. "So whatever that thing inside the gate is, if it gets out..."

"It will kill all of you," Merich says. "Then the borders will fall, and it will go on its way."

Will turns white.

"So we'll kill it first," says Pen.

"You can't kill it. Things like that don't die easily."

"Cass *literally* blew one up!"

"What?" says Will, in perfect unison with Louisa.

"She blew up a little monster," says Merich. I scowl, and he waves placatingly in my direction. "It was impressive, I'll give you that. But whatever is lurking inside the gap, and whatever else it might draw out with it? You can't kill them. Not permanently. That would take power nobody here possesses."

"Even you?" I ask.

He glances at me, and for a moment the tightness around his eyes fades. "Even me."

"So we have two options." A stormy look is growing on Pen's face, a strange contrast to her pink, bunny-covered pyjamas. "Either we close the gate, or we die."

"That pretty much covers it," says Theo.

"There is a third option."

Louisa stares down at her hands, clasped at her knees. I know what she's going to say before she says it. "If one of you were to become the Witch—"

"No," I snarl.

"I'd rather not," Theo mutters.

"Fuck that," says Pen.

Louisa looks up. "It's time to be serious about this," she snaps. "I've been patient. I've waited for you to decide for yourselves. If we'd sorted this out earlier, we might not even be in this situation!"

My blood burns. "You're blaming *us* for this?"

"This territory is a well of power. It needs a Witch to protect it, and it hasn't had one for a long time." She turns to me. "If that gap stays open and the boundaries fall, it will release a potentially infinite amount of evil into the world. If this monster escapes, people will *die*. It's our responsibility to stop it!"

"Which is why we want to close the gap," Theo says quietly.

"That does not absolve us of the responsibility."

"Absolve *us*?" My anger boils over, and I'm standing before I even intended to move, nerves snapping under my skin. "You're not taking on any risk—you just keep pushing it on to us! If you're so concerned, *you* become the Witch!"

The tips of Louisa's hair start to curl. "I can't. I don't have the strength needed to fulfil the role. But we need a Witch to defend our borders. Not only will nothing be able to get out, but were anything evil to seek you out, you'd be able to fight it. Becoming the Witch would give you that power!"

"I don't *want* that power!"

"It's your duty to keep this town safe," she says firmly, and then her voice drops. "You'd have greater control of your magic."

I know exactly what magic she's talking about, but I didn't expect her to use it against me. The breath leaves me in a rush. I should have known she wouldn't let this go. Everything always comes back to this; it always has. Whatever threat she imagines is coming, whatever she thinks we have to be safe from—she'll never let it rest until one of us finally does what she wants, whether we like it or not.

My fingernails gouge into my palms, rage turning my vision red, and then—

"Cass?"

Will touches my hand. His expression is worried, his tone placating. Almost apologetic.

Something turns cold in my gut.

"What's the downside of this?" he asks. "It *does* seem like the best option."

Will has always been on my side. Until now. When he doesn't know what he's talking about, what he's saying I should do.

Maybe it's the feeling of betrayal. Or my exhaustion. But the thin rein I have on my temper snaps.

I wheel on him. "Do you know what it means to become the Witch?" I demand. "Not *a* witch, but the Witch of Fallow Creek?"

Will pulls his hand back. "I—"

"You die," I snarl. "You *die*, alright?"

The room goes very quiet.

Everything has a price. I've known it since I realised bewitching butterflies made me dizzy, since that day in the woods when Will choked to death in my arms.

I've known it since the day six years ago, when Louisa sat us down around the kitchen table and explained what was required to become the Witch, and how one day, one of us would be expected to perform the rite. Since she explained how my mother had failed, dying alone on the floor of a forest, her blood soaking into the leaves. Since my older sister left our house forever, raging about the deception, about how we'd been born and raised to die, because our lives had never been ours.

"To become the Witch, you have to die," I repeat. "You go into the woods. You find the clearing. Then you take a really sharp knife, and you stab yourself in the heart. Or you can slit your own throat, I suppose, I doubt it matters. You just have to die."

Louisa has gone pale. "Cass, don't—"

I ignore her. "If you're *really* lucky, and your blood is magical enough to get you through the rite, then you come back as the Witch. You have all the power you could ever want, and you're responsible for every single supernatural thing in Fallow Creek. And you can say goodbye to any dreams you might have had, because once you're the Witch, you're trapped in this stupid little town forever, because you never get to leave! And I mean *forever,* because *the Witch is immortal.* They don't die until someone murders them to take their place. But if you're *not* strong enough, and you don't become the Witch, you don't have to worry about any of that, because you get to die alone in the fucking woods!"

The words taste like blood in my mouth, but at long last I've said it. It's all out in the open, the things I've thought for years and have never been able to say. I've spent so many nights imagining myself dying in those woods, wondering if I'd bleed out in the same spot my mother did. So many nights imagining myself as the Witch, bound to this town by the same power I'm supposed to want, an outcast forever, watching everyone age and die around me.

Most nights, I can't decide which fate would be worse.

Will looks like he's been struck, staring at me with wide, shocked eyes. I'm too furious to stop, so instead I turn, jabbing a finger at Louisa.

"And you raised us, *knowing* what you're trying to force us into! You know we could die! Our mother did! You think you're not strong enough—there's no guarantee any of us will be any stronger! All of us could die attempting that rite, but I guess it's still better to make us do it, to make this *our* fault, than to do it yourself!"

My voice has risen to a shriek, and once I'm finished the silence is startling. Louisa looks down, saying nothing. Pen picks at the sleeve of her pyjamas, and Theo's eyes have dropped to his knees, his shoulders hunched. I'm too afraid to look at Will. Or maybe I'm too angry.

I stand there, chest heaving, and feel utterly alone.

There's a small sound as Merich shifts, sitting forward in his chair. "Perhaps it is a necessary role," he says carefully, "but not one anyone should rush into. If you want to try something else first, then that's what we'll do."

At the same time, he touches my wrist. I start, and then his hand slips into mine. My palm aches with how forcefully I've driven my nails into my skin, but his fingers are gentle, easing my fist open.

I glance at him, feeling strangely ashamed. His expression is deliberately empty, but his eyes are soft. Understanding.

My rage dims.

"You know more about this than us." The words are a rasp, like I've screamed myself raw. "If we close it—the gate, the gap—will we be safe?"

He gives my hand a squeeze before releasing me. The absence of his touch feels like a loss. "Evil things will always be drawn here. The power in this house, in this town, is a beacon to them. But if the gap is closed, then yes. The trouble should stop."

I nod. "Then we try to close the gap."

"And if we can't?" asks Pen.

"If we can't..."

The woods. The clearing. The knife.

"I think we can." Theo's voice is soft, and he doesn't look up as he speaks. "I worked it out with Mosi last night. We—well, *he*—thinks it should be possible to close it using wards, and a lot of magic. But it's only a theory."

"Everything is a theory until you see if it works," Merich says.

Pen sighs. "I don't suppose we can throw some dynamite in there and solve the problem that way."

I start to roll my eyes, then pause, looking at Merich.

"Can't say I've tried it," he says drily.

"Anyway," I say, contemplating hurling a stick of dynamite through the gate, "the gap isn't getting closed until the kids are out."

"How are we going to do that?" Will asks. He doesn't meet my eyes.

"Throw them a rope," suggests Pen.

"No." I swallow. I knew it would come to this, but that doesn't make it any easier to face it, or to say the words. "I'm going to go in there and get them."

For a moment nobody speaks.

Then everyone reacts at once.

"Hell no," says Will.

"Absolutely not!" Louisa croaks.

"There must be easier ways to kill yourself," Pen adds, but she's gone white.

Merich gets to his feet. "It would be suicide," he says, his eyes burning black. "You'd be entering an environment that isn't designed for beings from our world."

"You said yourself it could be a middle ground," I remind him. "If Max is alive in there, people must be able to survive."

"That was only a theory!"

"Everything is a theory until you see if it works," I reply. He glares at me. "Besides, I'm not planning to build a house and live in there. I'm going in, finding those kids, and I'm getting out. Then we're sealing the gap for good."

"And if you die?" Louisa's face is so still it could be carved from marble, her lips pressed into a thin line. "Have you thought about that?"

I lift my chin. "Then you seal the gap with me inside."

Pen makes a strangled sound.

Theo sighs, dragging a hand through his hair. He suddenly looks very tired. "This is a stupid idea, but it's the only one we've got." His eyes cut to me. "I should go in. I'm older than you."

"You are," I agree. "But I'm the one who can blow up monsters. If I go in, I might die. If you go in, you'll *definitely* die."

"Then I'll go with you, at least. Not into the gap. I'll wait outside."

I frown. "Why? Wouldn't you rather wait here?"

"Merich says those creatures are drawn to us," he says quietly. "And the Hounds are still around."

There's an odd swooping sensation in my belly as I realise what he means. "Oh."

"It *is* possible that when you enter the gap, any entities in the area will be drawn to the disturbance," Merich says. "They may come running."

Theo gives me a half-hearted smile. "Maybe if I'm there, I can stop them from cutting off your exit."

I stare at him, struggling to find a response. If he comes with me, he could save my life. He could also be killed.

"It's a good idea," Merich says calmly. "I'll go with him."

Relief floods Theo's face, but before I can start to feel better, Pen sits up. "I'll come too!"

"No, you won't," says Louisa.

Pen bristles. "I *want* to go."

"I know." Some of Louisa's composure has returned; she won't look at me, but the high points of colour in her cheeks have faded, and her hair has stopped moving by itself. "But there's a good chance everyone involved in this is going to die horribly. When you're older you can decide if you want to follow in their footsteps, but for now I'm in charge, and I say no."

Pen looks furious, switching her focus to me. "I can come, can't I? You could use more help!"

I consider letting her come with me, just to see what happens, but I'm reasonably sure it would annihilate whatever relationship Louisa and I have left. Also, we *could* very well die horribly, and I'd rather it didn't happen to Pen.

"Sorry," I tell her. "Someone needs to stay here."

She slumps, scowling. "I never get to do anything."

"I could die," I point out.

"Oh, whatever."

"I'm coming too."

I turn. Will rises from his spot on the couch, his face set and still. He meets my eyes, and the challenge in them is clear.

I hesitate. "Will—"

"*Don't.*"

"Will." I extend my hand. "Please."

He doesn't take my hand, but he follows me out of the room, into the dim hallway. The window at the far end hasn't been covered, and autumn leaves are drifting through the empty panes, coming to rest on the floor.

I stop beside it, in the hazy yellow light. Will is ready for me, stepping in close. "You can't possibly expect me to go away and let you walk to your possible death like it's nothing," he hisses.

"There's nothing you can do," I say.

"Yes, I know!" He takes a deep breath, looking away. There's something close to devastation in his expression, and my heart clenches. "Why didn't you tell me? Why didn't you ever say anything?"

Will has known for a while that there's a difference between being *a* witch and being *the* Witch. I've known since childhood, so of course I told him—I never thought it was a secret. But then I learned the price, and suddenly it wasn't something I could share with him. How do you tell someone you're slated to die? He's always viewed it as some kind of promotion.

I'd say that illusion has been thoroughly shattered.

"What would you have done?" I ask him. "What would it have changed?"

He says nothing, glaring at the wall. I can't remember him ever looking so angry.

I wrap my arms around myself, trying to remember how to breathe. "There's nothing you can do if you come with me," I say. "There's probably nothing Merich or Theo can do, either."

"They can do more than I can." His jaw works. "I could bring a gun. Anyone tried shooting one of those Hounds?"

"Not to my knowledge. What do you plan on doing if it doesn't work?"

Dying, I think.

Maybe Will thinks it too, because he finally looks back at me, his eyes full of hurt. “You want me to abandon you,” he whispers. “To pretend this isn’t happening. And I’m supposed to be okay with it?”

“You’re not abandoning me.” I huff out a rough breath. “How am I supposed to do this if I’m worrying about you? You’re supposed to get married next month. What do you think Stephanie will do if you get killed by monsters? What do you think *I’ll* do?”

“What do you think I’ll do if you don’t come out of those woods?” he asks softly.

I have no response.

We stand in silence for a moment, unable to look at each other. I can’t relent now. Not after I’ve spent so long trying to protect him. And yet each second I say nothing, it feels as if a chasm is opening between us.

An idea occurs to me. “You want to help?” I ask. “Join the search party.”

He frowns.

“You know the area the gap is in,” I continue. “You could steer people away from it. What happens if they stumble across us while we’re using magic? Or if they run into the Hounds?”

Will winces. “They might run into them anyway.”

“If we’re using magic, it seems more likely they’d be drawn to us,” I say. “Everyone else should be safe. Well, safe enough.”

Will is quiet for so long I wonder if he’s going to leave without saying a word. “Do you still have that walkie-talkie?” he asks suddenly. “From when we were kids?”

I blink. When we were young, he had the idea to buy walkie-talkies so we could whisper to each other at night, long after we were supposed to be in bed. It was a lifeline out of this house—a way to talk to someone who wasn't buried in a book or accidentally setting things on fire with magic. But once Will's family moved, he was out of range, and my walkie-talkie was put away in a box and never touched again. I haven't thought of it in years. "Somewhere. Why?"

"Change the batteries in it and take it into the woods. I'll take mine. Then I can know roughly where you are, and I can try to lead the search party away."

"That's brilliant. If you can hear me…"

"We're too close to you." He nods.

His anger is gone, but there's still tension in the air. I can't remember the last time I fought with Will. He's the one I've always gone to when I fought with someone else. This awkwardness is unfamiliar, and it leaves me unsteady, like I'm standing on thin ice with no idea where to put my feet.

"You could meet me here," I say tentatively. "When I get back."

"If," he says. "If you get back."

In the main room I can hear Pen complaining about how she never gets to be involved in anything. There's a conspicuous silence from the others, as if they're trying very hard to pretend they aren't there.

"I'd better go," Will says. "Catch up with the search party."

My heart sinks. "Yeah. Alright."

He begins to walk away, and I let him go, the horrible feeling in my stomach growing. Then he stops. Shakes slightly.

He turns back, and I'm stepping into him before he's even stopped moving, his arms closing around me.

"I'm sorry," I say. "I'm sorry I didn't tell you. I didn't know how."

"It's alright," he whispers. "I know I'm not—I can't help you. I just wish you could trust me more."

Then he releases me, walking out the door without looking back. I stand alone in the gloom, watching him leave, and can't help feeling as though I've lost something.

16

I PREPARE TO ENTER THE ABYSS ON A BEAUTIFUL AUTUMN morning.

Bees hum through the lavender in the backyard, their fat little bodies hovering over pieces of broken glass. A clamouring chorus of birdsong carries out of the woods, and the trees stretch into the distance under a perfectly blue sky, their leaves a sea of emerald and orange.

The walkie-talkie is clipped to my waistband. I take comfort in the weight of the scratched purple plastic. With Will gone, I can't tell if it works, even with the new batteries. If all goes well I won't hear from him at all, but it still feels like I'm carrying a lifeline.

While Pen glares down at us from her bedroom window, Louisa stands on the back porch to see us off. She's silent and pale, watching as I attempt to tie my shoe.

"I don't know how long we will be." My fingers fumble with my shoelace, and I curse, starting over. "We don't know how time works inside the gap."

Down by the garden gate, Theo and Merich watch the treeline. Will has already sent word that he's with the search party. All the wheels are in motion; I can't stop this now. And every minute we delay is a minute another child could vanish.

Maybe it's the mounting sense of urgency making my fingers tremble, but right now I just look like an idiot who can't tie a knot.

"Hopefully we'll be back by tonight," I babble. "But if we're not—"

Louisa sinks into a crouch, batting my hand aside, and I fall silent, watching as she ties my laces into a perfect little bow.

"You don't have to do this," she says softly.

"What?"

She looks up at me, her expression strained. Golden hair falls loose around her face, brushing the collar of her white lace shirt. There are faint bruises on her skin, and a shiny new scar through her eyebrow. In the dazzling morning light, she looks like a battered angel. "You don't *have* to go through the gap. It can simply be closed, Cass."

I stare at her. "You want me to leave the small defenceless children to die?"

"I don't *want* you to, no." She sighs. "It's not a choice anyone should have to make. But when you agreed to help, you never agreed to this. Nobody expects this of you. They could just… stay lost."

I've always known Louisa wanted to stay out of the spotlight. If people want the help of a witch, they come to her. Otherwise she stays out of the way, and she makes us do the same. She's so desperate to keep us safe that she'd rather we never did anything at all, unless we want to risk death during the rite. That alone is acceptable, as if whatever she's afraid of is worth the risk, worth the potential loss.

And she *is* afraid of something. That's one thing I'm sure of, after the last few days. Something scares her so badly that she values the protection of a Witch above all things.

But to suggest sealing the gap with those kids inside…

I love Louisa. But right now, I can't help but feel like I don't know her.

"If one of us were missing, would you have done it to get us back?" I ask quietly.

Louisa's eyes shutter, and she pulls her hands away.

Once I'd have felt guilty for asking such a question. Now all I want is answers.

"What happened?" I ask. "What happened to make you live like this? You're so afraid for our safety that you made us *outcasts*. Why do you want a Witch so badly? What are you afraid of?"

Louisa gives me a long, long look. I almost think she's going to answer.

Instead she says, "I hope you know what you're doing."

And that's all.

I step back from the porch, my throat tight. Upstairs Pen pokes her tongue out, and Louisa watches me, her face blank once more.

I turn away, following Theo and Merich out of the garden and into the woods.

By day there's nothing foreboding about the trees. Merich's presence is reassuring, the sword at his hip even more so, but I still feel jittery as we leave the sun behind. The light within the woods falls dappled and green, and the shadows are deep.

I could be walking to my death. I might never come this way again, never *go home* again. I fight the desire to look back, desperately wishing I had Will's voice in my ear to distract me.

Even so, when Merich speaks I jump with fright.

"Your aunt." The words come slowly, as if he's waiting for me to stop him. "Is it always… like that? With her?"

I should have known he'd be listening, especially with what he witnessed inside the house. My cheeks burn at the memory of my outburst, and I glance ahead to where Theo is tromping through the undergrowth. He's never happy when there's conflict in the house, so he definitely can't be happy about what happened earlier.

"You know how it is," I say lamely. "Family and stuff."

"No." Merich's voice is perfectly even, his eyes flooded back to black, making him impossible to read. With Will gone, he's dropped all pretence of looking human. "I don't have any family. I don't know what it's like."

"Oh. I'm sorry for your loss."

He snorts. "They're not dead. Well, I assume they're not. They're probably around somewhere. But things are different for immortals. We live so long, move around so much—relationships are difficult. We don't usually have families."

"Oh." I blink, then squint at him. "How old are you?"

His mouth twitches. "Older than you."

"Right."

What's the harm in telling him the truth? He saved my life last night and watched me totally lose my temper this morning. There's nothing like a near-death experience to give you a feeling of closeness. And I could *actually* be dead in an hour, so why does it matter?

"It's been like that since I was a teenager." I speak softly, so Theo doesn't hear. "We don't get along."

"Why not?"

I sigh. "There are four of us. Helen is the oldest. She was perfect—perfect grades, perfect behaviour. She and Louisa always got along, until she learned what it took to become the Witch. She didn't like being lied to, so they haven't talked since she left. Theo's never done anything wrong, so Louisa loves him. And Pen..." I shrug. "Pen's the youngest. So they're the closest."

"And you?"

"Things used to be fine. But after Will..." I swallow. For a moment I'm eleven, lost in the woods and covered in blood, and Louisa is running toward us, her face whiter than snow. "I don't think she knew what to do with me. With the power I have. And as I got older, I tried making plans to get out of Fallow Creek. School, travel, whatever. Maybe she assumed I'd get us all into trouble." Though I *am* about to walk through a gate to another world, so maybe she had a point. "Maybe she just doesn't like me much," I finish.

It's plausible. I'm hard to like. I wonder what will happen if I don't come back. Maybe she'll be upset.

Maybe she'll be relieved.

"Are all witches so wary of unfamiliar magic?" Merich asks. He sounds puzzled, and when I glance over I see his nose is scrunched. It's oddly charming.

"Yes. You probably wouldn't understand since your magic doesn't have a price. But if you know every spell should come with a cost, and someone performs magic that shouldn't be possible, you start wondering how they're paying for their power."

"So the power that comes with being the Witch..."

My chest tightens. "You pay for it with your life."

He doesn't respond, his head tilted as he considers it. In the dappled light his hair is as dark as fresh soil, his eyes as black as beetle carapaces. "You don't get to leave the territory?"

I shake my head. "Once you're the Witch, you're more powerful. But you draw your power *from* the territory. I could leave, technically. But..."

"But?"

I shrug, keeping my gaze down. "Magic corrupts. If I left, all that power would eat away at me until there was nothing left. You said magic attracts monsters; it creates them, too. If you try to take the power of the Witch without protecting the place where the power came from, without following the rules..."

It's all too easy to imagine. That power turning inward, devouring someone whole, until they're only a husk. Or worse, turning them into something savage and hungry. Something not even recognisable as human.

"And your aunt? She said she couldn't do it."

I pull a face. "Louisa always says she's not suitable for the rite. Not strong enough." I slap aside a reaching branch, the sting against my palm making me wince. "But I remember her doing powerful magic. I think she stopped after my mother died, but I *remember.* So I think she just doesn't want to do it."

"Maybe that's fair," Merich muses. "If she'd failed the rite, what would have happened to you? Your siblings?"

"It's fair," I agree bitterly. "But it's hypocritical. She could have tried it, once we were old enough to take care of ourselves. We haven't had a Witch in ages, and the world hasn't ended. She could have waited, then done it herself, and she didn't. Why do *I* need to give up my life because she thinks I need to take responsibility for everyone else?"

"Aren't you already taking responsibility?"

And I suppose I am. Like Louisa said, nobody is expecting this of me. Nobody told me to walk into another world. I just think someone should.

"There's a difference between *wanting* to do something," I say, "and having no choice."

For a moment I worry he's going to keep pressing, but he simply makes a thoughtful sound, continuing to walk alongside me. We've travelled far during the conversation, the woods growing darker, deeper. My heart races, my eyes searching for black shapes among the trees.

"You knew," I say finally. "Didn't you?"

Merich looks down at me. "You'll have to be more specific."

"You knew I could kill the Hound."

He slows, and I match his pace, watching him.

"That," I continue, "or you took an *enormous* risk by shoving me in front of a monster last night." When his face doesn't change, I sigh. "Come on. I'm spilling my darkest secrets. It's your turn. Cough up."

Last week I could never have imagined speaking to one of the Fae at all. Now I'm pestering one as I walk to my probable death.

Merich scoffs. "You think *that's* dark? Other than raising the dead, you're practically dull." He pauses. "You're not wrong, though. When you weren't brutally killed the first time the Hounds showed up, I assumed you had something up your sleeve, but I had suspicions before then."

"How? You've only known me a few days."

He's quiet, stepping delicately through a tangle of thorns. "I'm a Warden of the Woods. I hunt monsters."

"This had *better* not be you calling me a monster," I say flatly.

He laughs, a small, rasping huff, and my stomach lurches. "Hardly. Magic has a very faint sound. Humans can't hear it. Few of the Fae can, but it's a necessary part of my skill set to know any creature of magic, be it monster or witch or one of the Fae, makes a sound. Like a faint vibration."

"So we're like dog whistles."

"Closer to a hum. Like an electrical current. Monsters make a very deep sound—ugly, really. It makes them easy to hunt. Your average human makes no more sound than a brick wall. But most human magic-users make the same sound, like you're all on the same frequency."

I nearly trip over a rotting log, torn between watching my feet and watching his face. "And me?"

He looks at me. "You make a different sound. Very close to the others, but at a slightly different pitch. I noticed it when I first met you. It's… stronger."

I don't respond. I don't know what to do with this revelation.

"So yes," he says. "I suspected you could kill the Hound. If I'd been wrong, of course, we'd have both died horribly."

"The type of magic I can do," I say slowly. "Nobody taught me how to do it. And Louisa said my father could do strange magic too. Do you think it's hereditary? That he might have been a witch, or something else?" With my eyes fixed on the undergrowth, I can voice the fear gnawing at me. "What if he wasn't human? How would I know?"

I'm so caught up in my thoughts I don't notice him moving, not until he brings us to a halt and his fingers gently close around my chin, tilting my face up.

Every intelligent thought exits my head, and I forget to breathe as Merich examines me. "You look human enough to me," he murmurs.

"Would you be able to tell if I wasn't?" I croak.

We're close enough to kiss. It would barely take an effort.

The ghost of a smile crosses his lips, and I tear my gaze up. A narrow beam of sunlight falls across his face, setting pinpricks of gold glittering in his eyes.

"Not necessarily." He releases my chin, fingers skimming my skin as he withdraws, and the world moves again. "I don't know what kind of magic you're using. You're not one of the Fae, and if you were a Halfling, I'd be able to tell. Therefore it stands to reason you're human. Maybe just… odd."

"Odd," I echo, pretending my heart isn't pounding.

He shrugs. "I know someone who could taste your blood and give you a clearer answer. They'd then also be able to ask any favour of you they like, which is unlikely to go well for you."

The moment dies, and I pull back, catching sight of Theo waiting impatiently ahead. "Noted."

After that we're quiet for a long while, picking our way through the woods. The walkie-talkie taps against my hip, comfortingly silent. Nothing happens. Nobody speaks, as if words will cause the stillness and growing quiet to break.

Then it starts.

An ink-dark tree appears ahead, the branches sagging, splitting down their centres like overripe fruit. Sap weeps from the cracks like black ichor, and fallen leaves turn to sludge around the crumbling roots, forming a thick, poisonous coating on the earth.

Merich looks around, his eyes glinting. Any softness I might have imagined in his face is gone—now his expression is intent, watchful, his sword a shimmer of light in his hand. Theo sticks close to my side as we weave through more decaying trees, their trunks cratered to reveal ashy wood.

The canopy above us is silent. The rustle of leaves is the only sound.

I don't falter. I know where I'm going this time, as though the scrying spell has burned the route into my head. I move through thickets of barren vines as if I'm following a magical line once more, like the phantom footsteps of a missing child are leading the way.

I step gingerly down a rocky slope. At the bottom is a dead bird.

It rests on its back, small head covered in blood, but its chest is open to reveal a tiny cluster of bones. The flesh around them is stained black.

As I step over it, its wings give a tiny, desperate flutter.

Theo sucks in a breath, and I squeeze my eyes shut.

It only gets worse as we carry on. There are whole flocks of birds, fallen in groups among the roots of infected trees, lying in the mud. There are rabbits too, standing motionless, watching us go through dead eyes. Once Theo's fingers close around my arm, and I follow his gaze to see a deer. The flesh on its flanks sloughs away, exposing red-slicked bones. Its antlers crumble like wood burned to ash, and its eyes are black and dead and leaking blood.

I lead us on. Theo takes quick, nervous strides, surveying the trees as though he's waiting for something to sneak up on us. Merich stays beside me, as calm as if this carnage is an everyday event, and whenever I glance at him he smiles, small and tight, like he's trying to reassure me.

Then, finally, the woods fall away.

The silence is all-encompassing, the clearing a dark cathedral of decaying trees and crumbling branches, the gate standing like an altar in their midst. The black iron gleams dully, the curlicues like coiled snakes. Black sap crawls down the tree trunks. Even the earth itself has turned dark, as though the life is being leeched out of it.

And around the edge of the clearing, like a thicket of blood and bones, is a ring of dead animals.

Truly dead, this time. As if that undead suffering we saw on our way here was only a prelude to this, everything slowly travelling to this space, only to perish the instant they arrive. I see feathers and fur, hooves and paws, and bones, and bones, and bones.

"Oh, *fuck this*," hisses Theo.

I take a deep breath, the taste of rot and iron lingering on my tongue. "This is from the gate?"

"From the presence of whatever is inside." Merich's voice is even, but very low. He keeps his sword in his hand. "It's contaminating the world in this area. You can't feel it?"

I focus, but I feel only a deep dread I suspect is my own. "No."

His mouth presses thin. "The leech is seeking something to fuel it. It's tainting the earth, the trees, the…" He trails off, waving a hand toward the ring of ruin. "It's sucking the life out of everything it can reach, to gain the strength to emerge. The stronger it grows, the further it can reach."

I remember what he said about parasites and plagues. Is this what he meant? A wave of contagion, poisoning all it touches?

"The kids," Theo rasps. "Are they…"

"Humans are different. More life to them. Thoughts, willpower, imagination." Merich grimaces. "I can't say what state they'll be in, but I imagine whatever stole them would have taken care to lure them in unharmed."

The thought is chilling. I picture Hannah and Max, lured here deaf and blind to the dying woods around them, drawn closer by whatever lovely vision led them through the trees. What are they facing inside the gap? It can't be better than this.

I gnaw my lip, wondering when my mouth got so dry. "Why can you feel it, but I can't?"

Merich's expression is as dark as I've ever seen it. "The Fae are more open to magic. Humans feel other things. Fear. Paranoia. Dread."

It makes me feel a bit better to know this fear isn't my own, but not much. "So you can feel what's really there?"

He nods. "There's something in there. And it wants to get out."

"Cool," Theo says lamely. "That's not at all terrifying."

My skin ripples with cold, and I can't tell if the turmoil in my stomach is from terror or the desire to be sick. *Hannah. Six. Max. Seven.*

The gate awaits.

I take a deep breath. "Okay. Let's get this over with."

Theo shudders, stepping over the carcasses and into the circle of death. "This… border. It obviously means something that they all died *here*."

Merich moves slowly after him. "This may be where the power is the most concentrated. So these animals can survive if they're further away, but once they reach this area, the leech drains them dry."

"Like they're in the centre of the web." Theo looks around. "If we start warding outside this ring, then move inward, it should trap the magic inside. Then we can push it back into the gap and seal it."

So easy. So complicated. "Did your friend say that would work?" I ask.

Theo's eyes lower. "It was the best we could come up with."

My stomach clenches. Wards are such a normal, everyday kind of magic. Using them to seal some kind of horrific otherworldly entity away feels like trying to stop a tsunami with a single flimsy wall. "Will it be enough?"

"Do you have a better plan?"

I don't.

I follow them into the clearing, approaching the iron gate. Even in daylight it seems shadowed, somehow undeniably *evil.*

"Here." I pluck the walkie-talkie off my belt, passing it to Theo. "Will is with the search party. If he gets within range of you, tell him to take them in another direction. If anyone sees this, we'll all be burned for witchcraft."

He doesn't laugh, his eyes creased with worry. "Are you sure about this?"

"No."

"That's reassuring." Theo pauses. "Cass, if you don't come back..."

I don't let myself think about the words before I say them. "Seal the gate."

He doesn't respond, staring at me. Can he seal the gap with me inside? I try to put myself in his shoes, to reverse our positions, but my brain shies away from the idea. Would I be able to seal the gap if he were in my place, knowing I'd be dooming him to die?

"I'll come back," I tell him. We both pretend my voice isn't uneven, that fear isn't choking me. "I promise."

"You'd better," he says. "If you don't, I'm going to have to become the Witch."

That hadn't occurred to me. If I don't come back, or if sealing the gap doesn't work, someone will have to risk the rite. It will most likely be Theo. He'll do it so Pen doesn't have to. And if it works, he'll end up bound to this tiny town, forever viewed as a sinner and an outcast.

He probably considers it an even worse fate than I do.

"It won't come to that," I tell him. "It won't."

He says nothing, nodding. He doesn't move toward me or offer me a hug. Physical affection isn't a big thing in our family. Maybe it's like he said, and we don't know how to have normal relationships. Most of my hugs come from Will, who is usually as affectionate as your average Labrador. But he's not here.

I could still use a hug, though.

I turn away, facing the gate. No amount of delaying will make this easier, or less terrifying. "Okay," I say. "I'm going."

A hand closes around my arm.

"Don't do this," says Merich.

I stare at him. "The whole point of coming here was to do this!"

"I know." He swallows, his fingers tightening around my elbow. "But… Cassandra, the Fae have too many stories about the abominations that live alongside our world. Things of unimaginable evil, intent on devouring everything living. I'm only *theorising* there's something beyond that gate. You could step through it and be annihilated from existence. You might not be able to get back. And even if you can, those monsters, the ones that aren't quite real in this world? They will *all* be real through there."

A cold feeling pools in my chest. "I can't just leave them. Max is alive in there."

Merich holds my gaze. "Or something that sounds like him."

My throat closes.

"Don't do this," he says softly. "Some paths aren't meant to be walked."

I consider giving in. Turning away and sealing the gap, walking back through the ring of the dead and going home. I can sleep in my own bed knowing the woods are safe, and nothing like this can ever happen again.

Knowing I abandoned two children to die.

"I have to," I whisper.

I wonder if I imagine the regret that flashes across his face. Merich's eyes close, and he sighs. "Then try to come back." He releases me and opens his jacket, reaching inside. "Here."

He presses a knife into my hand. The blade is formed from silver-blue steel, the hilt from something like white stone. It's impossibly light, and it fits in my palm like it was made to be there.

"This is a knife," I say weakly. Theo cranes to see over my shoulder.

"I assumed you didn't already have one," Merich replies. "Everyone should have a knife."

"It's like your sword."

"I know. It was made by the Fae, and it's great for killing things. There's a good chance you'll need it."

My gut twists, and terror crashes through me. "What good is a knife going to be?" I demand shrilly, pointing at the gate. "If the monsters don't have actual bodies—"

"There are no physical forms on the other side of the veil," Theo interjects. "We're working on the assumption you're not actually going through the veil, remember? It's a middle ground."

"What if we're wrong?"

"Well, you won't need the knife," says Merich.

I glare at him, and his expression softens.

"If it's a middle ground, physical forms must exist. Otherwise Max wouldn't be alive. That means the monsters may have physical bodies too. And in there, they bleed."

I let out a shaking breath. Theo watches me, a worried crease to his forehead. If I stay any longer someone will ask me if I want to turn back, and I don't know if I have the strength to say no.

I close my hand around the knife. "Get ready to close the gap," I say, hoping my voice sounds steadier than I feel. "I'll be back soon."

And as they watch I turn away, push the iron gate open, and step through.

17

FOR A WHILE WHEN I WAS IN SCHOOL, I WAS ON THE swim team.

It was one of the few extra-curriculars Louisa approved of. I think she liked how it kept me out of trouble. It's easy to feel normal when you're part of a team. When you're all wearing caps and swimsuits, there's little to differentiate one person from another, and there was a certain peace in performing laps, one after another, where you only had to think about your breath and the water.

My favourite part was the diving: the surge of sound and descent into silence. The stillness beneath the surface.

This is a lot like diving, but instead of the bottom of the pool, I find another world.

For a few seconds after I step through the gate, I can't breathe. The air—and there *is* air, so that's a bonus—is thick and stagnant, like the air inside a coffin after days in the dirt. The fact I'm choking means I haven't been annihilated from existence, but it doesn't stop me from panicking.

Merich's knife brings me back to my senses. The stone hilt is cold in my palm, and it seems to be growing colder still. The chill of it is something to focus on as I suck in one breath, then another, and as the initial terror fades, I take in where I've ended up.

It's the woods.

The shock startles me, a final wheeze escaping my throat. It's the woods, but… not *quite.* It's the woods as if they were created by someone who had only ever seen a forest through a filthy window. There are trees, but they're enormously tall and perfectly black, like silhouettes. Featureless leaves hang motionless at the end of branches that twist like forks of lightning, all of them utterly motionless against a sky—

I stare at the sky. It flickers like static.

"Well," I mumble. "I don't like *that.*"

I tear my eyes away before fear can overwhelm me, quickly turning around. Theo and Merich are gone. The gate stands behind me, identical to how it appeared on the other side of the gap.

My breathing seems harsh. Too loud. Then I realise there's no other noise. No birds, no wind. Nothing but a terrible silence, as though I'm the only thing in the world.

Okay. So, I'm alive. This is already going better than I expected, which isn't saying much, but it could definitely be worse.

I clutch Merich's knife to my chest, taking a tentative step forward. My foot comes down on soil littered with grey leaves, but they make no sound, no crunch or rustle. They may as well be printed on the earth for all the presence they have. Almost as if they're—

Fake.

It's all fake. This place could just as easily be a blank space, a dark hole for the leech lurking here. It can't really *care* how the trees look, and once it lures its prey through the gate, it probably doesn't care what they think. There's no reason for this level of effort.

Unless it's trying to acclimatise. To prepare itself to exit the gap.

I shiver. The sooner I find Max and Hannah, the better, but I can't go around blindly shouting for them. The longer I can stay unnoticed, the higher my chance of getting back to this gate alive, and screaming my head off in a place full of monsters seems like a bad way to achieve that.

Then I frown.

The gate is still here. So why didn't any of the children attempt to go back?

I look at it suspiciously. Maybe they couldn't get back through it. The thought sends a brief bolt of panic through me, but I can't even test the theory—if I go back now, I'll never bring myself to set foot here again. But the children were lured here in a trance. Maybe once they entered this strange world, they simply kept walking wherever the leech wanted them to go. Maybe once they woke up, they couldn't find the gate again. Maybe it *moves*.

What if the gate vanishes the second I leave this clearing? A moving gate makes sense: if a monster is luring children here, it wouldn't want them to find the way out. But if the gate disappears, I won't be able to find the way out either. I need to make sure I don't end up stranded.

Don't use any magic. They notice that.

Merich's warning sends a chill down my spine. Does it apply here? I know there are monsters about, but is a single spell more or less likely to be noticed now? Is the threat of being noticed worse than the threat of never finding my way home?

Biting my lip, I stretch my mind toward the gate, searching for a link. An anchor-point leaps into my head: the iron. Strong, immovable. It might be a doorway between worlds, but the gate is real enough. Something to tie myself to.

I knot my thumbs together and tug.

The spell strikes me like a blow, sending me reeling. The location of the gate is locked in my head, bound to me like an anchor, but the magic ripples through me in waves. The effect of the spell is stronger than any I've ever experienced. Summoning it into existence was easy.

But if this whole place is made of magic, why wouldn't it be?

I take an experimental step away from the gate, and there's a tug in my chest. I grimace. Pain, then. It's not an uncommon price for magic: every step I take will hurt, but as long as I keep the spell running, I'll be able to find the gate again, even if it moves.

I tighten my grip on Merich's knife, taking a deep breath. *In there, they bleed.*

Then I walk away from the gate.

My footsteps are silent. My heartbeat thunders in my ears, made louder by the lack of all other sound. It's an unnatural quiet, like the start of a horror movie right before the scary stuff starts happening. Sticks should be snapping as I move through these woods, leaves whispering as I pass beneath motionless boughs. But the trees are as lifeless as cardboard cut-outs, and nothing moves. There's only this silence, this terrible stillness, that—

That breathing.

Breathing. Deep and laboured, like it's coming from a wounded animal.

I whirl, looking around, and see nothing but grey haze and black trees. There are no footsteps. There's no way to tell where the sound is coming from, but it's close, and the knife in my hand suddenly seems very lacking.

A guttural moan travels through the woods.

Terror burns in my veins, and I lunge for the nearest tree. It's surrounded by a mass of roots, protruding from the ground like huge dead limbs, and I throw myself among them, burrowing into the dirt. I force myself to huddle down, holding still as the breathing gets louder.

Closer.

The air changes, turning thick with a stench like bog water and rotting flesh. I gag, burying my nose and mouth in my sleeve.

On the other side of the tree, something groans.

My chest aches with the urge to scream, but I force myself to remain silent as the creature releases a few deep, slow breaths. Finally it moves past, pausing up ahead.

And because I'm terrified and stupid, I crane my neck and peer over the roots.

The creature is a stag, eleven feet tall and furred in black. Its antlers are enormous and branching, but they're not the antlers of a normal stag. Instead of smooth, elegant lines, these are jagged and thin, like razors jutting from the creature's skull. Its eyes are empty holes, and blood streams from its lowing mouth in rivulets, pooling black and fetid on the forest floor.

Its ribs are exposed, revealing a tangle of flesh and organs. I see throbbing intestines. A pulsing heart.

A mass of circulating, half-devoured corpses.

Rabbits. Birds. Mice. They roll and revolve, over and over, a slick red mess.

Among them is a flash of blue. A glint of metal, bright and brassy.

A dog collar.

The stag moans, sloping away into the trees. I cower among the roots until it's gone, and then I turn over and vomit.

Those devoured animals were from *my* world. Which means that thing, that un-stag, was in *my* woods.

Some creatures can pass through the veil more easily than others. *Little monsters,* Merich called them. But if that was *little,* and the leech stealing children is even worse…

A whimper slides between my teeth. I bite it back.

Max. Hannah. Emma. Morgan. Jacob.

I repeat their names in my head until I slide back to sanity. Five little kids, lost in a nightmare. The sooner I find them, the sooner we can go home.

I drag myself off the ground, taking comfort in the pain linking me to the gate, and continue into the woods.

•••

It's not the bodies that bother him.

Theo has seen dead things before. Roadkill. Dead birds. During hunting season it's common to see people emerging from the woods, the elegant forms of dead deer sloped over their shoulders.

It's not as if he *enjoys* being surrounded by a ring of carcasses, of course. But it's the stillness making him nervous. It's unnatural, even for death. There are no flies. There's no stench. Only a mass of silent corpses.

He keeps his eyes down, methodically carving wards into the earth. For now they're simply shapes, blank and useless, but when Cass comes back they'll pour magic into every symbol at once. A giant surge of power—it should be enough to seal the gap.

If Cass comes back.

He glances up. Merich stands in the centre of the clearing, arms crossed over his chest. His eyes, black from rim to rim, never leave the gate. Theo's just glad he doesn't have to look at it. If he had to watch it, waiting for something to emerge, he'd probably snap.

Eyes down. He traces ward after ward, gradually circling the gate. When he decided to devote the time to learning wards—and there are a lot of them, so it was more akin to learning hieroglyphics than anything else—he never expected to use them for this. There's more than a few he doesn't understand, only using them because they're carefully drawn out on scraps of paper, sent to him through midnight messages. Meaningless shapes, designed to close a gap in the world.

He hopes.

God, he hopes.

"Something is coming."

He blinks. Merich has turned away from the gate, but there's a tension to his shoulders that makes Theo think all of his attention is on that silent space.

"What?"

"*Something*," Merich says tightly, "is *coming*."

Dread crawls up Theo's spine, like the slide of cold fingers. "How do you know?"

"I can feel them." At some point Merich has drawn his sword again, and it glints in his hand, as sharp and bright as a slice of moonlight. "They don't belong here."

"Hounds?"

"Maybe," Merich replies, in a tone suggesting any alternative will likely be worse.

Theo looks around the clearing, his heart sinking. The wards spread across the space, like a web of earthbound constellations, but he's nowhere near finished. They can't seal the gap. And Cass isn't back yet.

There's not enough time. The Hounds are coming, and there's nothing they can do.

"We can't fight them," he whispers. "We're screwed."

"They're on their way," Merich says calmly. "If we close the gap they'll either die or be dragged inside."

"We *can't* close the gap! Cass is still in there!"

"So we need to hold them off until she's back."

Theo gapes at him. "We have no idea how long that will take."

"It will take as long as she needs."

Merich seems unconcerned. Unflappable. Or maybe he's been driven to insanity by the confidence that comes with having a stupid fancy sword. "So we die," Theo says weakly.

"No."

Merich's response doesn't invite further discussion, but there is no time for it anyway.

Theo knows they've arrived before he sees them. There's a shiver through the undergrowth. A crawling across his skin. A silence, like the world is holding its breath.

He sees the arm first. Long fingers, curling around the trunk of a tree. The bark beneath the black touch withers and sloughs away, turning to something like soot.

"Merich," Theo rasps.

"I see it."

The first of the Hounds emerges from the woods.

It slinks forward like a cat, moving with disjointed, humanoid limbs. Sometimes it walks on four feet, then rises to lurch through the trees on two. Regardless of how it moves, it stalks steadily toward them.

It has no face. None his mind remembers, anyway. But if he concentrates, he can see empty white eyes.

The Hound is followed by another.

Then a third.

And a fourth.

Theo's breath catches. "*Merich.*"

"I know."

The Hounds begin to circle them, and Theo spins, trying to keep all of the beasts in view. At least one is always behind him, and he backs toward the gate, heart thundering.

"If you know a way to hold them off that doesn't involve us getting *eviscerated,*" he hisses, "now would be the time!"

Merich doesn't reply. Instead he faces the woods, lifting his palms skyward.

The earth shudders. Bones snap, rotting wood splintering as the air suddenly grows solid, darkening like glass stained by smoke. As the darkness spreads it becomes a wall, moving to circle the clearing, and the light grows dim as it rises. When it closes the two of them are left standing in a dome of magic, the surface glistening like an oil spill.

Merich's eyes open, gold flashing across the black, and when he speaks his voice rings with power.

"Let them come."

•••

I don't know how long I walk for. The sky doesn't change, and there's no sun to judge the time by. I still feel the tug of pain anchoring me to the gate, so I suppose the gap still exists. I can't have been here long enough for Merich and Theo to give up, sealing me inside.

Yet I feel as if I've been on my feet for days. The air is heavy in my lungs, and a cold white mist wreaths the trees, turning everything soft and blurred. My hands and knees are filthy from the number of times I've thrown myself to the ground to hide from more creatures. Each time I do so it takes more effort to get up.

Something stalks through the woods in the distance, booming roars announcing its presence. Whenever I hear it I go in the opposite direction, but I can't keep walking forever.

Finally I sigh, leaning against a tree. There's no way to know how big this place is. Merich once called it a *pocket space*, but who knows what that means? It could go on for miles, and there's no sign of Max or Hannah.

They could be dead already.

No. I roll my neck, taking a deep breath. They're not dead. I refuse to accept that, not after I've come this far.

My foot slips in something wet, and I look down.

Lines of black sludge cross the ground beneath my feet.

That's new. Certainly a change in the scenery. The lines stand out like veins in the earth, shining slightly, as if they're wet. I can't bring myself to touch them, but they're the realest thing here.

They lead further into the woods, where the trees seem to be thinning.

I push myself upright, quickening my pace. More black veins slide between the trees, obvious now I'm looking for them. Some of them link up, melting into slick black threads. I move faster, almost at a run, until the trees fall away.

The earth ahead slopes downward, becoming a dark, shining crust, almost volcanic in appearance. The veins weave across it, creeping down the surface.

They vanish into a hole.

I pause at the edge of the woods. The sloping ground leads to a cave, resting at the bottom of a pit like the opening of a throat. The entrance is certainly big enough for a child to get through, but there's nothing visible within.

It looks like a den.

Nope. I mouth it to myself. Using words here feels wrong, like screaming into the silence of a tomb, but I feel the need to voice how adamantly I don't want to go near that hole. Every nerve in my body is telling me to get very far away from here, preferably at a very high speed.

Then I squint. Something rests near the opening of the cave. Something purple.

With pink laces.

I close my eyes, mouthing a soundless chorus of profanity. Off in the woods, something roars.

I start toward the hole.

Nothing moves as I approach, and I crouch at the entrance, peering in. The opening is big enough for me to get through, but inside there's a drop, leading into a tunnel.

A burrow, my mind whispers. I tell it to shut up.

I should be able to stand once I'm inside. The only thing worse than going in there would be having to crawl around, but there's another problem.

The tunnel quickly disappears into darkness.

Creating light is easy enough, but I've already used one spell here, and I can't let go of my link to the gate. If I use more magic, I'm at risk of being noticed. The alternative is wandering around blind in a monster's den.

I look down at the shoe. It's so small.

"Jesus Christ," I mutter, flinching at the sound of my own voice, and I lower myself into the tunnel.

The tunnel floor is soft, a puff of ash rising as my feet hit the ground. I reach for the wall to steady myself and the surface is damp and tacky.

Black streaks weave across the floor, leading deeper into the tunnel.

I think of the rot Hannah left in her wake through the woods, the disease seeping into the trees. Is this where it comes from?

Well, I think grimly. *I'm about to find out.*

I flick my thumb across my fingers, my peripheral vision vanishing as light blooms in my palm. The magic linking me to the gate trembles as I split my attention between the two spells, and panic lances through me. Without light, I'm blind. Without the link to the gate, I'm lost. How long can I keep up two spells?

Don't think about it. I swallow hard, moving deeper into the tunnel.

The walls are formed from dark earth, covered in a thin sheen of… something. The tunnel twists and bends, the air cold and reeking, and the deeper I go the colder it gets. Each time I turn a corner I scratch a mark into the wall with Merich's knife, hoping I'll be able to spot them on the way back.

The light flickers.

I pause, frowning at my hand. The light shouldn't flicker. It comes from *me*. It's my magic. It shouldn't flicker unless I want it to flicker, or unless—

The air is *so* cold. Draining, almost.

Whatever creature lurks in that space, it's only there while it gathers the strength to push through the door. To exit the gap.

Humans are different. More life to them.

A wave of fear sweeps through me, and this time I can't shrug it off. My thoughts leap to the ring of dead animals surrounding the gate.

This is what happened to them. They got too close to the leech, and it drained them dry. The longer I walk, the more tired I become, and now it's weakening my magic. Maybe the only reason I'm still alive is because the leech doesn't know I'm here.

But it finds children more appealing than animals. And if humans give it more sustenance, what kind of power could the leech gain from me? Enough to reach even further into my world? Enough to exit the gap altogether?

If simply being here is enough to drain my power, what damage could the leech itself do?

I stare at the light, waiting for it to flicker again. Hoping against hope that it won't.

Somewhere ahead, there's a sob.

My head snaps up.

It's a small sound. It falls strangely in this empty place, landing without an echo. It's quiet. But close.

Max.

I edge forward, my palm extended to light the way, clutching the knife in my other hand. Merich's words about something impersonating Max ring in my ears, and I bare my teeth, forcing myself to continue on.

Another sob. A sniffle.

A corner looms ahead. Whatever is waiting, it's around the bend.

My fingers shake on the hilt of the knife, and I take a deep breath.

Then I plunge around the corner.

The light spills onto a small, round face, surrounded by a tangle of dirty blonde hair. The girl squints, peering up at me with perfectly green eyes, the colour of light through leaves.

She's barefoot.

The shock of it freezes me in place. I said I'd find her. I *tried* to find her.

I never thought I actually would.

"Hannah," I croak.

She blinks at me, wiping her nose with the back of her hand. "What?"

I hardly hear her. I'm too busy staring at the second, smaller girl Hannah has her arm around. She has a halo of curly black hair, and the biggest brown eyes I've ever seen.

I know her face. It's been burned into my memory from the leaflets shoved through the mailbox and the posters plastered on every flat surface around town. From the photo at the tiny shrine at the start of the trail where she disappeared, while on a picnic with her family.

Emma Carfax. Aged four. Five now, I guess. It was her birthday three days after she vanished.

"Oh my God," I whisper.

"Who are you?" Hannah asks. Her arm tightens around Emma. The younger girl says nothing, watching me silently.

I pull myself together. "I'm Cassandra. I'm—I'm here to rescue you."

Neither of them respond. The light in my hand flickers. "Hannah, is there anyone else here?" I ask. "Have you seen any other kids? A boy named Max?"

Her lips press together, but her eyes dart to the left, to another corner. I follow her gaze, then move in that direction.

There's a gasp, and something scrambles away from the light. "*Go away*! *Leave me alone*!"

My heart hammers. "Max?"

There's a long silence.

"Who are you?"

I take a deep breath, my knees trembling. "I'm Cass. Max, is that you?"

There's movement in the shadows, and then a small group of figures press forward, huddling against each other. I see tiny flashes of rainbow lights, and the suspicious scowl of a dark-skinned boy. *Morgan.* And there, behind him, so covered in leaves and filth it's hard to make out his face. Jacob, the first to vanish.

And at the front, the boy I recognise from photographs in a sterile house. His green jacket is zipped up to his throat.

Max.

They're all here. They're all *alive*. They barely look as if they've been gone a day, let alone weeks, but they all look pale. Drained.

Less.

"I know your voice," Max says slowly. He has his sister's startlingly blue eyes, ghost-grey in the light. "I heard you calling me."

A lump forms in my throat. "Yes. I was looking for you."

"She's one of *them*," Morgan hisses. "It's a trick."

"No," I whisper. "I'm not a trick. I'm here to take you home."

"You can't." The voice comes from behind me, and I glance back to see that Hannah and Emma have followed me around the corner. Hannah looks at me, her face expressionless. "We can't get back."

I feel for the tug in my chest. "I know how to get back."

"How?"

The question comes from one of the boys. I can't tell which. Max has crept to the edge of the light, but the others hang back, their faces shadowed. They look fierce and half feral, and desperately afraid.

What is this experience going to do to them?

"I can do magic," I say. "I have a spell that shows me how to get home."

They're quiet as they take this in. Nobody accuses me of lying; I suppose carrying around a ball of light is proof in itself, and they *are* standing in a tunnel in another world.

"You can find it?" Hannah asks. "The gate?"

I nod. "How did you get here, anyway? What did you see?"

"I heard it." Max stares at the light in my hand like he's staring at the sun, his cheeks ashen. "I heard it calling me. It looked like... someone. I don't remember who. But then I couldn't stop walking, and once I got here, I didn't hear it anymore. And I couldn't get home."

"I don't remember what I saw," says Hannah. "I just remember here, now."

Ice seeps through my veins. "It doesn't matter," I say. "I'm here, and I know the way out. I can get you home."

"I don't remember home," Morgan murmurs.

"We can't get out." One of the boys at the back says it, his voice hollow. "It won't let us."

My stomach plummets to my feet. "It?"

Max looks at me. "The monster," he whispers.

In the depths of the den, something lets out a long, howling scream.

18

THE DARKNESS SHIVERS.

My skin erupts into goosebumps, the light in my hand wavering, but I hardly notice. The sound is everything. To call it a *scream* is to call the approach of a tsunami a rumble; it ignores the terror and the fury, the roar of power behind the thing making the sound. This is the noise the universe might make if someone pierced a hole in it. This is the sound of emptiness. The sound of hunger. The sound of something that shouldn't exist.

Max's face goes white, and Hannah cowers against the tunnel wall, bent double with fear. Emma whimpers.

"It's coming," a boy whispers. "It knows you're here."

The tug in my chest is frantic now, the gate calling me back. "I don't care if it knows," I say. The words sound brave. I wonder if the kids can hear the lie in them. "We're leaving, and no monster is going to stop us."

The children stare at me, their faces cast in black and white. I can't tell if they're in awe of my bravado or if they think I'm insane. I'd like to believe it's the former.

But none of them move.

I resist the urge to scream. Every moment wasted is a moment the leech is getting closer, but I can't drag five children who don't want to run. And with what they said before...

I just remember here, now.

Maybe they think following me can only lead to a worse fate.

I tuck Merich's knife into my waistband, then reach my hand toward Hannah. She looks at me warily, and I force myself to speak calmly.

"Your mother misses you," I say.

She blinks.

And then her face crumples, all her bravery crashing down with four little words, and she puts her hand in mine.

Thank God. "Let's go home," I say brightly, turning back the way I came. I wait for a moment as frantic whispers and scuffles erupt behind me, but I don't panic. If I have one of them, I have all of them. Nobody is going to want to be left behind, even if there's only a small chance I'll lead them home.

Plus, I'm the one carrying the light. And I can't imagine how it must feel to be down here in the dark.

I'm so busy enjoying my victory, I barely hear Hannah hiss, "Do you want it to get hungry again?"

Nerves flutter in my belly. What does the leech do when it's hungry? Nothing good comes to mind, so I clear my throat, hearing silence fall behind me. "We're going to run now," I say. "We're going to be very quiet and sneaky, and you're going to stay close to me. And we're going to get out before it finds us. Okay?"

I risk a glance down. Hannah watches me doubtfully. She doesn't seem reassured.

To be fair, I don't feel very reassured either.

"Okay," I whisper, mostly to myself. Then I start running.

But running with small children is infinitely more difficult than running by myself. I have to go slowly, taking their shorter legs into account, and now that they're committed to moving keeping them together is harder than herding cats. The boys push to the front, but Emma is small, sniffling as she follows along in our wake. Hannah refuses to let go of my hand, which wouldn't be a problem if she weren't so heavy. She drags at my arm like an anchor, as though she barely has the energy to run.

A second scream echoes through the tunnel. This one sounds angrier. As if the leech has realised something is missing.

My pulse spikes. "We're going to go a little bit faster now," I whisper.

"I'm *tired*," Hannah whimpers.

"I know." I keep my eyes on the walls, searching each corner for the marks I made earlier. "Keep going."

"If it touches you, it makes you sleepy." This murmur is Emma's, her hand clutching at my jeans. I find her staring fearfully up at me, tears staining her face. "It makes it hard to breathe."

For the first time I notice the hollows in her cheeks, the darkness beneath Hannah's eyes. *I just remember here, now*.

The leech sucks the life out of the trees, draining it from small creatures that venture into its invisible web. But Merich said humans were different: they had willpower, imagination. If the leech is gathering strength by siphoning it out of children, what exactly is it taking from them? Their blood? Their thoughts? Their life?

Somewhere behind us there's an echoing shriek, followed by a thick *crack*, like the slap of wet meat against cement. The sound makes me flinch, but Emma bursts into tears, and one of the boys looks back at us, his eyes as black as stones in his white face.

"It's looking for us," Hannah croaks.

"Probably," I say tightly. I glimpse a flash of light ahead, like a slit in the dark. "There. Go. *Go*."

They take off. Even Emma finds a renewed speed, hurrying after the bigger children. Their breaths rasp like a harsh wind, echoing through the tunnel, but even over that I can hear a growing hiss.

It's coming.

The entrance to the den appears before us, and I let the light in my hand die as the flickering sky illuminates the tunnel. It's no wonder the kids couldn't escape—the cave mouth is too high for any of them to reach alone. As soon as they were lured inside the cave, they would have been trapped like fish in a barrel.

I glance back into the dark. The low hiss continues, my skin crawling at the sound, but nothing is visible.

Yet.

"Okay," I say, keeping my voice low. "I'll boost you up so you can get out, and then you'll wait for me up there. Once I'm out, we'll all go home."

The grey light falls over their frightened faces, giving their skin a strange, dead pallor. I quickly look away, and as my mind screams at me to run I force myself to one knee, linking my hands before nodding at Max.

"You go first."

He doesn't protest, setting his foot in my hands and gripping my shoulder. As soon as he's secure I boost him up, and he catches the lip of the hole, scrambling to safety. Even before he's pulled himself to his feet I'm kneeling again, gesturing for another child to come forward. "Quickly. Come on, quick!"

The hiss is getting louder. It's a dragging sound, like flesh sliding across dirt.

Another child. Another. *One, two, three*. My shoulders ache, and the link to the gate pounds in my chest as I shove the kids out of the tunnel and into the false daylight. *One. Two. Th—*

The leech rounds the corner.

The first I see of it are two long, white arms, curling around the wall as it drags itself forward. The air turns cold, and as the world slows, the arms are followed by a body.

It would resemble a human torso, if the torso were conjured from nightmares. Its ribs are as stark as the bones of a shipwreck, its shoulders as twisted as a body at the bottom of a cliff. Two more sets of arms bloom from its sides like tentacles, overlong and over-jointed, bending to unnatural angles.

Below the torso the leech is a mass of rent flesh. I see shadows and bones. Wet, flapping meat. A bridal train of half-formed shapes, slithering along in its wake.

I tear my eyes away from the grotesquery, fighting a retch, and look into its face.

My scream catches in my throat.

It's human. And not. A malformed skull presses tight against its skin, two round white eyes bulging from their sockets like those of a fish. It has two ragged slits for a nose, and its flesh is slimy and pale, pitted with holes and sores.

The leech's mouth hangs slack and open, the parody of a grin splitting its face from ear to ear.

It's trying to look human. It's gathering its strength, building itself a body, trying to form itself into something that might pass in the outside world.

The sight of it scares me senseless.

I take a step back, and my heel strikes the wall. To get out of the tunnel, I'm going to have to turn my back on the leech.

There's no sound from above me. The air is heavy with the silence of children, too frightened to breathe.

The leech stares in my direction, cocking its head. Maybe the creature is blind. Those eyes don't look as though they can see. Its fingers drum against the tunnel wall in a slow, deliberate beat, but it doesn't move. As if it's listening.

I smother my breathing, carefully sliding my hand up the wall. All I have to do is stay quiet, get out, and run like hell.

I reach for the edge of the hole.

A low whispering fills the tunnel.

I go still. The noise is distant, but familiar—enticingly so, like a song I had almost forgotten. At one point I swear I can hear a laugh, brief and barking, and I feel a strange pang of sadness.

One of my feet slides forward, and I claw my fingers into the wall, anchoring myself. The desire to walk deeper into the tunnel is strong. I want to hear that laugh again, to find the source of the sound—

The lure.

I snap back to my senses.

This is the lure. It begs to be followed, but when I clear my head there's no real sound there. No laughter, no voice. Just a soft susurrus, coming from…

The leech doesn't look like a monster anymore. Its shape shifts, as if hidden in shadow. White eyes could be blue, or black. That hideous body suddenly seems human, familiar. Comforting. I see arms spread wide, like an embrace I'd want to step inside, a softness that could be hair, black or blonde or bronze. The two shapes overlap each other, creating a tangled form, one that hurts to watch and calls me forward all at once.

I close my eyes, taking a deep breath. I am stronger than a lure. I am stronger than a monster.

And I refuse to let this thing loose in my world.

My eyes open.

And with a scream of rage, the leech lunges.

The illusion shatters, leaving only a mass of flesh surging toward me. I leap aside, hurling a hasty fireball, and the leech recoils with a shriek as flames sear its face. I grit my teeth and throw another fireball, driving it back.

Magic comes easily here. Anchors leap out at me, stunning in their clarity, but my attacks have little impact. As quickly as it retreated the leech is scuttling forward once more, moving like an enormous centipede.

I edge away from the cave mouth, my heart slamming in my throat. If I can force the leech further down the tunnel, maybe I can buy some time to get out of here. I push a wall of air at it, hoping to send it tumbling, but the monster doesn't react.

Fire, then. I summon more flames into my hand, and the leech lets out a piercing scream.

I stagger, gasping. The sound lances into my head like a spear of pain, my vision blurring as my eyes water. My hip hits the wall, my ears ringing—

There's a flash of white to my left.

The leech swipes at my chest, its fingers glinting as if riddled with blades. I twist away and the blow carves a gouge into the wall, the earth parting like butter. I flinch back as chunks of dirt sting my cheeks.

The leech strikes me in the head, and the world spins.

My forehead cracks off the ground before I even know I've fallen, the ash on the floor choking me as I gasp for breath. I smell blood, feel the heat of it trickling down my face, but when I try to get to my feet my limbs refuse to respond. I hear my own strangled wheezing as I stretch my fingers across the floor, searching for something solid.

There's movement at the edge of my vision.

And the leech creeps into view.

Its overlong limbs splay out like the petals of a hideous flower, hanging limp and fleshy. It clicks slightly as it walks, its innumerable joints popping and revolving, and as my sight steadies it stops, hovering over me.

I lay frozen, too terrified to breathe. Pain echoes through my skull, but my attention is fixed on those round white eyes, as blank and shiny as pearls.

I can only watch as the leech reaches one hand toward my face, its fingers like sharpened bone. It moves slowly. Ponderously. One gleaming point descends toward my eye, and I can't even find the air to scream.

Then it slips down, and the leech touches my throat.

Ice floods my veins, freezing my heart, and my muscles lock. My hands claw, my heels digging at the ashy soil, but the movements are mindless reflexes. I have nothing to fight with. My chest seizes as the leech surveys me, a spider contemplating the fly trapped in its web, and I am totally, utterly helpless.

Its slack mouth widens, and the leech begins to drain me.

No. My protest is a croak, a faint huff of air. My fingers are too stiff to move, and the ringing in my head erases all thought of magic. The world narrows until all I can feel is the leech's pointed finger as it traces up my throat, finding the spot below my jaw where my pulse races under my skin.

My sight darkens.

Do something. Do anything. I search for a spell, but my mind slips away from the task, my thoughts muddling. My eyes slide closed.

My lungs turn solid, and my next breath doesn't come.

I'm going to die. Fear pierces through my daze, sharp as a razor. *I'm going to die here—*

The finger touches my cheek, and my fear evaporates as warmth creeps through me, my body relaxing into the dirt.

Images flash through my mind. The gate. I remember the creak of iron, a girl with green eyes. I hear a child crying softly.

I came to get them out—

The thought vanishes. Pain reverberates through my chest, as urgent as a warning light, and fingers claw greedily at my temples, my skin parting under their touch. More memories flit through my head: Pen, sticking her tongue out. Will's crooked smile, Theo watching grimly as I entered the gate. Merich's eyes, obsidian flecked with gold.

There.

Gone.

Those are mine. I feel a dim spark of anger and throw my mind around it, clinging to the emotion. *Mine.*

The leech is stealing my memories. Sucking them away along with my energy, dragging them out of my head. The sound of my breathing reaches me through the fog, tiny and quick. My eyelids are so heavy they feel weighted with stones.

Mine.

I force my eyes open.

The leech looks different. More solid. Its torso is *expanding*; before it ended just below the ribs, but now I see the start of a stomach, moving as it feeds. Its fingers are wet with my blood, streaks of scarlet smeared around its gaping mouth.

It's taking me to make itself. So it can create a body, a *real* body, and leave the gap to feed on others. If it takes enough, maybe it can make itself look like me.

That spark of anger grows, taking root in my chest. It doesn't get to steal me, and it doesn't get to eat my memories. I *refuse* to die like this.

But magic is beyond my reach, my mind too shaken to search for an anchor-point. Even if I could find a spell, the leech is right on top of me. There's no room to fight it; anything I try will undoubtedly hurt me too.

My body shudders, a pitiful whimper escaping me. The imagined warmth is gone, and cold clamps around my bones. The spell linking me to the gate tugs weakly, barely holding on, and in my panic my fingers spasm, clawing across the ground.

They brush something solid.

In there, they bleed.

I seize Merich's knife and slash upward.

The leech squeals. Something wet and reeking splashes my face, and bladed fingers tear across my scalp, leaving lines of fire in their wake. White limbs flail in the air over my head, and though my sight is blurred I see limp flesh, flapping loose across the monster's ribs.

Good. And not enough.

I grit my teeth, readying myself. Normal magic is out of my reach. But I'm not totally normal.

I open my mind and find the anchor right above me, hanging over my head like a dark star. Then I curl my frozen fingers and seize it.

The leech screeches, grasping at my throat. My stomach heaves at the touch, and I hurl my remaining energy into the spell. I force all my power out, away from me, and *push*.

The ash on the floor explodes into a storm of grey, and the leech is thrown backward, crashing into the opposite wall before collapsing in a squealing heap. I drag myself to my knees, sucking in stale air, and claw my way up the dirt wall until I'm standing.

The leech writhes, trapped on its back like a beetle, but its limbs are twisting, dislocating as the monster tries to right itself. I bare my teeth, then clench my fist and wrench.

One groping white hand snaps, bones splintering. The leech wails, the sound warbling like a siren howl, but it doesn't stop. As one hand breaks, another grasps at the wall, seeking purchase.

And from that horrific mockery of a torso, something presses against the underside of the skin, swelling as it pushes outward.

The start of another arm.

Fear drives me into action. If the leech can regenerate, maybe it's impossible to kill. If it can't die, it'll just keep coming after us, and I'm not confident I can outrun it.

Before it can right itself I stagger over to the cave mouth, digging my toe into the wall and hauling myself up. Small hands snatch at my sleeves, dragging me into the open air. Grey light stings my eyes, already blurred and streaming, and bolts of pain shoot through my skull. When I press my hand to my forehead it comes away stained with blood, both red and black.

"It's getting up!" a shrill voice says.

I peer down into the cave. The leech is bending in on itself like a centipede, the awful mass that forms its lower half thrashing as it attempts to right itself. The monster meets my gaze and shrieks.

I grimace. "No, it's not."

I push past the pounding in my head, ignoring the ache in my bones. As the leech slithers forward I reach for every anchor I feel in the dirt, every atom of bizarre magic thrumming in the air around me. This time it doesn't feel strange, or unfamiliar. It feels like mine.

I seize the earth, and I force it down.

With a deafening roar, the tunnel collapses. The leech screeches as the ground folds inward, and then it vanishes, crushed under a hail of falling earth. The cave mouth disintegrates as howls erupt among the trees, and I shepherd the children backward, waiting for a grasping hand to claw free of the ruin.

But the dirt settles.

And nothing moves.

Several seconds pass. "You killed it," Morgan whispers.

"Looks like it," I croak.

Yet a deep unease settles over me. I might be horrendously dazed, but something seems… wrong.

Merich said this could be a pocket space, a lair created between our world and another.

What happens when the beast that made the lair dies?

I glance up. The smeared grey sky flickers.

And I find myself praying the leech isn't dead.

A hand clutches mine. Hannah looks up at me, her eyes full of fear. "What do we do?"

I take a deep breath, my chest aching, and listen. For a terrifying moment I think it's gone, the spell falling away during the fight, but then there's a tug, like a hook in my heart.

I sigh with relief. "Right. Okay. Now you're all going to stay very close to me, and we're going to run. Alright?"

None of them object. Their faces blur and spin before my eyes, and I swallow hard.

"Alright," I repeat. "Let's go."

And as a bestial wail rises in the woods, we run.

Emma flags first. She's the smallest, her legs the shortest. The first time she trips over a root Max tugs her to her feet. The second time I pick her up, letting her hang off my back in the world's worst piggyback ride.

I don't have to slow myself down this time. I'm already limping, my run closer to a stagger than a sprint, and each footfall sends spikes of pain through my bones. I try to keep track of the children, but they move with wild panic, their heads weaving back and forth until it seems as though they're multiplying. The sight is nauseating.

Finally I pause, leaning against a tree for support as I gasp for breath. As I look down, fighting the urge to vomit, I see torn earth around the roots.

Here. This is where I hid from the stag.

"We're almost there," I say. *Thank God.* I straighten, adjusting Emma's death-grip on my neck.

There's a rumble in the distance.

I freeze. The children flinch, looking around as if they expect something to come charging through the trees, but my eyes are drawn upward.

The sound came from further away. Like thunder on the horizon. Like a great, deep shift.

Like the tether holding this little world in place just snapped.

"Let's go," I bark.

The kids need no encouragement. They hurry off, peering over their shoulders to make sure I'm following, and with a final glance at the sky I run after them. My legs tremble, my muscles on the brink of failing, but I force myself on.

We've barely been going for two minutes when the ground jolts, bucking as if in the throes of an earthquake, and I trip, trying not to panic as a small chorus of screams rises around me.

Then—

"Look!"

We stagger out of the trees, and in the middle of a clearing, iron black and gleaming, stands the gate.

I lower Emma to her feet, trying not to drop her in my exhaustion. "This is it."

I expect them to fight over who gets to go through first, but none of them move. I watch blearily as they look at it, then at me, terror on their faces.

"What if it doesn't work?" Hannah asks shrilly.

"What if it goes somewhere else?" asks Jacob.

"It—" Pain crushes my skull, and I rest my hands on my knees. Black spots dance in my vision. "It won't."

"But what if it *does?*"

If it does, then we're probably dead. If it does, all of this was for nothing.

"If it does," I say, the words thick on my tongue, "I'll be with you."

Before any of them can reply, there's a deep and terrible *crack.*

My stomach sinks. Once more, I look to the horizon.

But it's not a horizon anymore. What was once a vast expanse of empty skies and black trees is now rapidly closing in. The grey sky is darkening, like burning paper curling in at the corners, and there's a distant roaring, growing closer by the second.

The noise is vast. It's the heaving, colossal approach of an avalanche. The high, desperate shriek of animals in a forest fire. The world-ending scream of a mother in a morgue.

My mouth goes dry. "Go. *Go.*"

I shove Hannah toward the gate, not daring to breathe.

If this doesn't work, we're all going to die.

With a final look back she steps through the iron gate—

And disappears.

I want to weep with relief. "Go!"

Emma is next, running after Hannah. Then Max, his eyes wide with fear.

The horizon races closer. Half the woods have been devoured by the grey.

The next child goes through. Then the next. Then the next.

And when there's no more, when there's just me and that second heartbeat pounding behind my ribs, I turn away from the dying sky.

The end of the world roars up behind me, and I step through the gate.

19

MY KNEES STRIKE DIRT, AND I BREATHE IN AIR THAT tastes like blood.

"Oh my God, Cass—"

A body collides with mine, a pair of arms crushing me, and I whimper as Theo's shoulder thumps against the side of my head. "Sorry," he says, then squeezes me so tightly it hurts.

I don't mind.

"Told you I'd come back," I mumble, clinging to his arm. I take in the woods surrounding us through bleary eyes. The trees are all comforting shades of green, even if they do look hazed in darkness. The blurriness only adds to my nausea.

Theo laughs, the sound uneven, and tugs me to my feet. "I'm glad you were right."

"Do this *later*," Merich's voice snarls. "We need to finish this."

I drag my head up, and I'm so startled I almost forget my exhaustion. Merich stands in the middle of the clearing, his hands raised as if he's holding up the world. The muscles in his arms strain against his skin, and enclosing the clearing is a sphere of shadow, as if smoke has taken on a solid form.

Dark shapes prowl past on the other side of the screen.

I tighten my grip on Theo's arm. "What the hell are those?"

"Hounds," he says grimly.

"And what's Merich doing?"

"Magic." He lowers his voice. "It looks cooler when the Fae do it."

I peer through the gloom inside the sphere, finding Max, then Emma, then Hannah. They stand in a little huddle, their faces melting together, but I assume they're all present. "Ah," I say. "That's… good."

Ignoring the small collection of children watching him like he's God or the Devil or both, Merich shoots us a furious glare over his shoulder. "This isn't as easy as it looks," he snaps. "Get your shit together and *seal the gap*."

Theo looks appalled. "There are *kids* here."

"That's nice! They'll all be dead in a minute if you don't get on with it!"

Theo blinks, flustered, and pulls away from me. "Oh. Right. Cass, here. I've drawn these."

He gestures, and I examine the ground. A web of carefully drawn wards covers the entire clearing, spreading out around us like the spokes of a wheel. Each careful line of symbols leads to the gate, and though they flutter and move as my sight wavers, I get the idea.

"Wards of sealing," I rasp, closing my eyes. It makes sense; it's how you'd make sure a door stayed shut against intruders. Though this seems like a much bigger intruder than we're used to.

"But they're magnified," Theo says. "And there—wards of deterrence, silence, strength. And some others. All leading inward."

It takes me a moment to put the pieces together. "You're going to block the gap."

Theo nods. "The gap does two things: it pours out evil, and it sucks in life. Any life, any *power*. Once we start putting magic into these wards, the gap is going to try to absorb their power. The wards should overwhelm it, pushing all the evil inward. It will block the leech from getting out."

I remember that mockery of a world, crumbling as I fled through the gate. "The leech is dead."

He brightens. "Good! Then this will be easier." His finger traces a line of symbols. "The wards are designed to race toward the gap from all sides. If we can shove enough magic at it, coming from every angle at once, it won't be able to handle the strain."

It takes me less time to figure this out. "It won't be able to absorb all the magic at once."

"It should essentially turn itself inside out." Theo looks extremely satisfied with himself. "We won't have to worry about any other monsters escaping, because the gap should just vanish."

"*Should?*"

"Well, I don't know for certain!" The confidence on his face flickers, and he suddenly appears almost desperate. "I've never closed an opening to another world before, Cass! We're only guessing this will work!"

"It *has* to work," I croak. "The pocket space inside the gap is *gone.* Whatever is on the other side of the veil is right through that gate!"

Merich looks back at us, his expression sharpening in a way that tells me he's heard everything. "Then this needs to be done now. If there's no middle ground, then that gap is a big flashing beacon to every monster in the vicinity. The longer it stays open, the more things will be drawn to it. To *us*."

My heart stutters. More things like the leech? Like the terrible, flesh-eating stag?

Theo nods, striding across the clearing. "Alright." He puts his shoulders back, and by the time he turns around any sign of worry has vanished from his face. It's as though he never doubted himself at all. "Merich, on my mark, drop the barrier."

"Oh, sure," Merich snaps. "I love a good massacre."

"There won't be a massacre."

"The Hounds will come straight for you."

"That's the plan." Theo looks at me. "Cass, you're going to need to throw all your magic into those wards. The Hounds will be caught up in the surge. If we put enough power into this, they should be sucked straight into the gap."

That little *should* again. But what other choice do we have?

I nod, ignoring my thumping headache, and brace my feet. Wards spiral out around me like I'm standing atop a labyrinth, and the sight of them sets my vision spinning. I am definitely injured, certainly in need of healing, but there's no time for it now.

"Cassandra?"

Shit. I'd already forgotten about the kids, standing there watching our every move. Perfect prey for a Hound. "Get down," I call. "Get down and stay together. *Do not move*. Do you understand?"

There's no reply, only shuffling and fearful whispers. Hopefully they've listened to me; I don't have time to corral children. The world is smeared and blurring, and I'm already sweating from effort. Frankly I'm just hoping we can pull this off before I pass out.

There's a sharp word from Merich. A faint shimmer is appearing around the gate, a pale, indescribable colour that hurts to look at, and as a shiver of fear runs through me I reach for my magic. It hums against the underside of my skin, building without an outlet, and I keep my eyes down, waiting for Theo's call.

It doesn't come. I sway, my teeth bared. "Theo?"

"Here."

I look up.

Theo stands with one hand raised, pointing skyward like a prophet or a rock-star. The air burns white around him, crackling in a halo around his head, turning the usual grey-blue of his eyes electric. His hair curls at the tips, his shirt billowing in unnaturally slow waves.

He looks, I realise, *like a Witch.*

The power builds beneath my skin until I feel breathless with it, and Theo meets my gaze. "Ready?"

I nod.

"*Now*."

Merich drops his hands, and the dark barrier falls away. Bounding black shapes leap out of the woods, and behind me I hear a chorus of small, panicked screams—

I press my palms to the earth and force my magic down.

The wards burst to life, flaring a searing white as they erupt around my feet. As the magic races outward more symbols wake, each one initiating the next in the sequence until the clearing glows, as though bathed in midsummer sunlight. Power hums in the air, tainting everything with the scent of lightning and steel, but even as the light blinds me I can see the beauty in the web Theo has created, the cleverness in the trap.

My magic meets his.

And the clearing explodes.

Wind rushes past with a muffled *boom*, and the breath tears out of my lungs. The thrum of power is replaced by the roar of the void, laced with a piercing, otherworldly shriek. My knees hit the dirt, my ears ringing, and the world drags at me with the force of water flooding a submarine, until I'm sure I'll drown in the flow.

I feel a faint, indescribable *turning*. The sensation of something reverting.

Gasping, I slit my eyes open. Black shapes move in the brilliance, their howls lost in the storm of sound. I watch as they're slowly dragged into the centre of the clearing, where the light is almost too bright to look at, and the shrieking grows, and grows—

And stops.

My hair falls limp around my face, and I take a deep, desperate breath. The light fades.

The clearing is empty. The ring of ruined carcasses now circles a glade filled with shining silver wards.

The Hounds are gone.

Relief turns my muscles liquid, and I sink to the ground, curling into myself. My forehead grinds into the dirt. I revel in the silence. The stillness. The smell of blood is thick in my nose, and my fingers are grey with the ash of another world.

It's done. It's done. It's done.

I hear a metallic rattle.

Theo moans.

And though it feels impossibly heavy, I drag my head up.

The gate is still there, and it's vibrating. It shakes in its stall, the hinges shuddering as if the entire thing is about to come apart.

This isn't the stillness of a closed gate. Of a sealed gap.

"It didn't work." Merich moves into view, his face hard as he surveys the gate. "It's not sealed."

"Well, that's it then." Theo throws up his hands, sweat beading his forehead. He sits with his legs splayed, his chest heaving. I wonder if he feels like I do. hollow between his ribs, the effort of all that magic leaving him drained. "We're totally fucked."

I close my eyes, sighing. I'm so tired it might actually be a relief to be devoured by monsters. At least I won't be in this much pain anymore, or not for long, anyway. And sure, this will look really bad when the townspeople eventually find this clearing, but I'll be dead, so it won't be my problem.

"Not totally." Merich's voice reaches me even through my exhaustion. "You didn't fail. The Hounds were forced back through; you drove the darkness back into the gap. The only thing remaining is to seal it."

"What do you think we were trying to do?" Theo snarls. "We *can't* close the gap."

Merich simply looks at him. "You don't have a choice."

Despair hits me like a punch, and a tiny sound escapes me. Nobody else can do this, but I don't want to do this anymore. I have nothing left to give. I can't seal a gap. I don't even think I can *stand.* I want to burrow into the dirt and disappear and never think about this again. I want to crawl into bed and pretend this has been one long nightmare.

A hand touches my back, and I blearily look up.

Merich is crouched beside me, the gold in his eyes as bright as a thousand tiny suns. His expression is soft. "One last thing, Cassandra," he murmurs. "One last thing, and then this is all over."

Somewhere nearby, a child is crying. *One last thing.*

I can't do this.

But I refuse to do nothing.

I hold my breath, pushing myself to my knees. Merich's hand on my shoulder is the only thing keeping me steady, and I try not to lean into him as I turn to Theo. "We have to do it," I rasp.

"But it didn't *work*!" He yanks at his hair, his eyes wild. "We can't do this! The price for using wards is energy, and the two of us weren't strong enough to do this the first time! You're half dead! We can't do this with just two of us, and there's no time to go looking for help!"

I glance at the gate. The shudders are becoming more violent, the rattle of iron intensifying.

"What about with three of us?"

Theo frowns at Merich. "You?"

Merich nods.

I think about the wall of shadow he held up earlier, like a screen of dark glass. It was beautiful, like no magic I've ever seen. "Would that work?" I ask.

"I don't know." Theo's brow furrows as he thinks. "We'd have to try the wards again, force even more power into them. And I don't know if the Fae can even use our wards."

"I can't use them," Merich says. "They mean absolutely nothing to me. But I don't have to use them. You just need to throw your power at the gap, and that's something I can do too. I can push my magic inward, like you can, but with more force. If we do it at the same time…"

"It might overload the gap."

Merich nods, his voice growing urgent as the gate jerks. "Your wards—the sealing, the deterrence—I can amplify them. With the gap gone, we can make this place a dead zone. Nothing magical will ever be able to appear here again; not from this side, and not from the other."

Hannah lets out a shriek, and I flinch as the gate shakes, the hinges screaming. Emma starts to cry.

"Wards fade eventually," I blurt out. "We can't keep this spell running forever."

"I can if my power is involved," says Merich. "I can keep every ward in this clearing active for as long as I live, if need be."

"How long do you live?"

A wry twist appears at the corner of his mouth. "As long as I damn well want."

A high whine pierces my skull, and a sickly burning smell permeates the air. "We don't have a choice," says Theo. "We have to do it. *Now*."

With that he throws himself back into the spell, the wards brightening around him. Merich presses his hands to the ground, his jaw set, and as my vision swims I summon the scraps of my magic, tying them to the wards in my half of the clearing.

They flare white—

And flicker out.

No.

"Cass!" roars Theo.

I gasp, searching myself for any hint of magic. I look for an anchor-point, *any* anchor-point.

I find nothing. Nothing happens. No power bursts forth from my hands. I am completely drained.

The clearing brightens, wards stretching out around Theo, but the gate remains a skeletal black silhouette. I squint at it, my heart in my throat.

And I see it swing open.

There's movement in the gap.

"*Cass*!" begs Theo.

I can't bring myself to look at him. This is it. We're going to die.

"Cassandra."

The voice comes from my right. I glance over and find Merich. His fingers are buried in the dirt, but his eyes are locked on me.

"Cassandra," he repeats. I hear him through the roaring and the rattling, as clear as if he were speaking into my ear. "You have power. *Use it*."

I stare at him, and something steels inside me. This is my job. I started this.

Now I'll finish it.

I take a deep breath, and instead of grasping for magic that won't come, I reach for the strange power lurking at my fingertips. It spills forth eagerly, flooding my veins, and once it boils beneath my skin, waiting for the right moment, I hurl it into the earth.

The wards erupt with light.

But instead of the blinding white they were before, these are molten silver, like the flash of sunlight off a mirror. They radiate power, and as my bones tremble, my body threatening to come apart with the strain, I send all of that power toward the gate and that gap in the universe.

It collides with something dark and seething, a faceless presence.

Something is trying to push through.

I hiss through my teeth. *These are my woods. This is my world.*

The gate shudders, cracks forming in the iron bars. It inches closed as the wards swarm around it.

Shadowy fingers reach out through the gap.

A snarl tears out of me. *These are* my *woods, and you do not belong here.*

The fingers claw at the dirt—

And I scream, forcing out every last atom of rage and magic. The world turns white. Leaves rip free of their branches as the wind shrieks, the ground trembling, bones pushing loose from the bodies surrounding us—

An iron latch closes with a soft, metallic *click.*

The light dies. The wind falls.

The woods go quiet, and I look up.

The ground is glowing: the wards have turned a solid silver, like hardened mercury, steaming slightly as they dim.

And the gate is closed.

Theo lets out an uneven cry, burying his face in his hands. Merich springs to his feet and strides through the smoke, then lashes out with a kick, his boot meeting iron.

The gate collapses, crumbling to black rust.

The children stare, stunned into silence, and I close my eyes.

The air is cool and crisp, ripe with the smell of rot and autumn, and slowly, as if just remembering how, birds begin to sing.

•••

From there, things get hazy.

We start back through the woods, moving past dead grey trees, great grooves carved into their trunks. But there's no sign of any blackness, no unnatural, weeping sap. No should-be-dead animals watch us as we go. Instead their corpses lay silent and still, relaxing into the decaying leaves, resting at last.

Before long the clearing is lost behind us. Nobody will ever find that ring of bodies, or those frozen wards. As long as the spell is in place, anybody drawing near will suddenly decide to head in another direction. Wards of deterrence work better on people than monsters. The bones will be swallowed by the earth, and the iron rust will disappear.

The gap is closed. It will stay closed.

Theo takes the lead as we walk. I'm glad—I can barely manage to stagger along at the back of the pack, the thunder of a false world echoing in my skull. As my adrenaline fades pain spreads through my body in vicious tendrils, and the wounds across my throat and face ache, my skin tacky with blood.

Every so often a small hand takes mine, as if seeking reassurance, or offering it. I don't look down to see which child it is. Doing so makes me feel dangerously close to passing out. In fact, I'm not even sure how I'm still walking.

My foot catches a root, and a wave of dizziness runs through me as I stumble. My vision darkens, and I catch a glimpse of blank white eyes, slashing fingers, a slack mouth open in a scream—

My breath hitches, and a hand closes around my elbow.

"Cassandra." Merich's face appears before me. "Can you hear me?"

His eyes are as black as a moonless night. I remember the feeling of his shoulder under my cheek, his skin lit by flames as my bedroom burned.

Some of my fear eases. I still have my memories. They weren't stolen by those pale, grasping fingers. "I hear you," I whisper.

I straighten, trying to steady myself, and Merich tuts. He pulls my arm across his shoulders, slipping his own around my waist, and I sag gratefully against him.

"You must be so sick of me by now," I say thickly.

I hear him laugh, catching a flash of bronze as the sunlight catches his hair. "Never."

He smells like green plants and summer. I rest my head against his shoulder, and his arm tightens around my waist.

"Almost home," he murmurs. "Almost home."

The rest of the journey passes in brief peeks through my eyelids. I see Theo, carrying the little form of Emma. The multi-coloured drift of falling leaves. Jacob staring as cracks of blue sky appear through the canopy, gaping as if he's never seen them before. Max's feet dragging, his head drooping with weariness. Hannah watching me over her shoulder, her eyes worried and green.

There's a faint electronic crackle. And someone speaks.

"*—anyone there?*"

A voice—Theo's—replies, and I try to look up. The world rocks and I gasp, reaching for something to stop me from falling. My fingers catch on soft fabric, and I realise I'm grasping at Merich's shirt.

I don't have the energy to be embarrassed. "Sorry."

"Don't worry about it," he says. "I have you."

The light grows, searing my eyes. The birdsong reaches a crescendo. Static buzzes and a walkie-talkie crackles, burbling.

"*Cass?*"

The voice is very distant, but I hear faint footfalls as Theo runs back toward us. "Shit, they're coming. Merich—"

The arm around me retracts, the warmth of Merich's body disappearing, and his murmured words are lost in the confusion. I open my eyes, but he's already gone. A small, cold hand slips into mine, and a child speaks, high and terrified, and then—

"*Cass?*"

"Oh my God—"

"Hannah? *Hannah?*"

"*Daddy?*"

And then the woods are full of screaming and shrieking and a flurry of colour and movement. I hear Theo shouting, and the hand in mine vanishes as someone bursts into hysterical tears. Children run in every direction, vanishing into the swarm of dumbstruck people.

I see Hannah's blonde hair, barely visible over her father's shoulder. Fleur Elbridge stands motionless, sobbing as Max sprints toward his family. A woman falls to her knees, wrapping Morgan in her arms, and a black-eyed boy stands in the middle of it all, watching.

A figure pushes through the chaos. His hair is a dusty brown, his eyes so very blue. My vision fades as he shoves toward me, and his voice cracks with relief as he says, "Cass."

"Will," I breathe.

Then I collapse into his arms as the search party swallows us.

20

IT'S THE TWELFTH DAY OF OCTOBER.

It's a golden dusk, the sky a haze of deep oranges and reds, the trees standing below like shadowy sentinels. Bees hum as they weave through the garden, drifting through fragrant lavender and rosemary. Beyond the white picket fence winter is creeping in, but here it is always slightly warmer than it should be.

I'm not complaining.

It's the twelfth day of October, and there are no missing children in the woods.

I sit on the porch steps, my cup of coffee growing cold beside me as I watch the sun sink. Inside Pen and Theo are bickering in the kitchen, and the faint smell of burning is seeping through the screen door. Then there's a crash and a burst of laughter, Pen letting out an indignant screech.

I smile to myself.

After a moment the door squeaks, then gently closes. When I glance back Louisa is hovering behind me, one hand on the doorknob.

"I come in peace," she says timidly. "I thought you looked a bit lonely."

There's a clear question in the words, and she doesn't step toward me, as if waiting for a rejection. My stomach twists with nerves, but I nod.

In the two days since I emerged from the woods, our reputation in Fallow Creek has hit unprecedented heights. People routinely drop off cooked meals, and our freezer is full to capacity. We have so many baked goods we will never conceivably be able to eat them all, though Pen is making a valiant effort. Each day a strange new assortment of pretty rocks, fresh eggs and home-grown vegetables is respectfully left on the doorstep, as if nobody is quite sure what witches might want.

The story goes like this: Theo and I found the missing children in some kidnapper's den, the villain fleeing when he realised he'd been discovered. It was easier to explain my head injury as the result of a blow from behind rather than an attack from an otherworldly monster, after all. It helps that the children are vague on the exact details of their disappearance. They all agree on being held somewhere, and Max and Hannah have both said a figure lured them into the woods. I was sure the story would collapse under questioning, but everyone seems to believe it.

Maybe the kids truly don't remember, or maybe they just aren't talking. Either way, the adults involved have put the rest of the details together in a shape they can make sense of. *Isn't it lucky Cassandra wasn't killed,* they whisper. *Isn't it remarkable how she led all those children to safety after regaining consciousness? Such a shame the kidnapper got away, but they'll get him eventually. They always do.*

The parents of the children have come by in sets, expressing their gratitude in floods of tears. Hannah's parents were first, but afterward I started hiding whenever there was a knock at the door. I've never had anyone be so genuinely happy to see me before. It's disconcerting.

Louisa has been the one fielding the calls and greeting the visitors, but despite everything, she and I have been circling each other, unsure how to act. She and Pen were delighted to see us return alive, of course, but the past few days hang between us like an ugly spectre. Neither of us can forget my outburst, or the things I said.

Neither of us can forget how she never denied any of the accusations I threw at her.

But she's been respectful. Kind. And because I don't know what else to do, I'm respectful and kind back.

She hasn't actively tried to talk to me, though.

She takes a seat on the step above mine, delicately tucking her skirt around her legs. I don't say anything, watching the colour bloom across the sky.

"You did very well, you know," she says finally.

It's a good start. I wait for the *but.*

"I know I'm hard on you," she continues. I keep my eyes on the clouds, unwilling to move in case she stops speaking. This feels like a speech she's been thinking about, and I'm both interested and afraid to know what she'll say. "I know I don't give you enough credit, or as much attention as the others. It must seem unfair. But… Pen is Pen. She needs more help. And I don't have to worry about Theo—"

"Because Theo doesn't do anything wrong." I pluck at a strand of rosemary, irritation stabbing at me like a splinter. "I know."

"No," says Louisa. "Because his talents lie in safer directions. I don't have to worry about him getting hurt."

My annoyance fades, and I risk looking up at her. The low light turns her eyes a strange lilac colour, and she rests her chin in her hand, watching me thoughtfully.

"You're more powerful than both of them," she murmurs. The words have the air of a confession. "I always suspected it, even before the day you brought Will back to life. You were born for magic. You were doing it before you could walk. I knew your mother and I remember your father, and sometimes I think you might have the best of both of them, that you drew from their power and became something better. But when you're more powerful, there are so many more ways that power can backfire on you."

I stare at her. This is only the second time Louisa has mentioned my father, and I can count the number of times we've discussed my mother on both hands. But she's saying I'm like them. She thinks I'm *powerful.*

"You said my father could do strange magic too," I say. My voice comes out weak and uneven, and I clear my throat. "Was he a witch? Did I get this power from him?"

Louisa shakes her head. "He couldn't use magic, and magic couldn't touch him. Maybe that's what your mother found interesting about him. He was an oddity. He saw things other people didn't. Monsters. Secrets. Sometimes futures, I think." Her expression darkens, her gaze growing distant. "Your mother always kept him separate from me. She was always secretive. She never kept her men around long, never told me anything about them. She moved through them so fast it was as if she was searching for something, and never finding it."

I swallow. "But… was he human?"

"Of course."

Human. I'm human.

"I thought you didn't like me because of my magic," I say quietly. The admission is cradled by the faint rustle of leaves, the soft squeaks of the early crickets in the bushes. I flex my hands, looking at my ragged fingernails. "I thought you believed there was something wrong with me."

"Didn't like you?" Louisa's hand finds my shoulder, squeezing. "Cassandra, I *love* you. You thought I didn't?"

I shrug, feeling about five years old.

Louisa sighs. "I love you," she says again. "I've always loved you. So much I worry about you constantly. I'm sorry if you ever thought I didn't. You have a power I don't understand, and… it scares me." Her eyes crease. "Like calls to like, and there are creatures out there that will be drawn to power like yours. Creatures you don't want to meet."

A cold feeling settles over me, sinking into my skin. "Is that why you want one of us to become the Witch?" I ask. "Those creatures?"

Louisa looks at me, and for a moment she seems far older than her years. Her expression turns strangely sad. "I want you to be protected," she murmurs. "That's all."

I have no response.

Together we sit in silence, listening to the wind. The woods sway and whisper, dark in the twilight.

Louisa's fingers brush my cheek. "You would be a good Witch," she says softly. "If you decided it was what you wanted to do. It's possible your power would help you."

No anger rises in my chest. "We don't need a Witch," I point out. "Look at what we did without one."

"You did beautifully," she agrees. "But if you ever wanted to take on the role… I think you'd do well at it."

I grimace, and she laughs a little. The sunset turns her hair to molten gold, and then she tilts her head, smiling.

"You have a visitor."

I look around. Merich is standing at the fence, watching us.

"Oh." This is awkward. "Do you want me to tell him to leave?"

She snorts. "I don't see much point in that now."

With a wave of her hand, the garden gate swings open.

As I blink Louisa pushes to her feet, brushing imaginary dust off her skirt. "I do love you, you know," she says simply.

A lump forms in my throat. "I love you too."

She smiles once more, then heads inside, closing the door behind her.

Merich walks carefully across the garden, his eyebrows raised. "I must admit," he says, his voice clear in the evening stillness, "I half expect to be struck by lightning."

I grapple for control of my emotions. "You seem to have been given permission to enter."

"It's an honour, I'm sure." He halts at the edge of the porch, resting one boot on the bottommost stair. His eyes appear human today, but they're still blacker than black, the dying sunset lending them a red shine. "You look considerably better than when I last saw you."

My cheeks heat, my fingers drifting to my temple. Louisa healed my head injury, and the aches and pains are fading after several days of bedrest. The real challenge came from the gouges the leech scratched into my face with its sharp fingers: some faint lines mark my jaw, but others were far deeper, scattered around my temples and on my scalp. Those took more effort to heal, and they left white scars which may never fully fade.

I try to pretend Merich's scrutiny doesn't bother me, but those scars are all I can think about. "I *had* just fought a monster," I point out.

"You had."

"And killed it," I add. "Which *you* thought I couldn't do."

"You did," he agrees. "And have you actually recovered?"

"Yes." I narrow my eyes. "You seem surprised."

"I expected you to die, in fairness," he says plainly. "You stepped into a space between worlds. For all I knew, if you did manage to return, you could have come out totally insane, or with your skin inside-out. Or bleeding from your eyeballs. You might have spontaneously combusted."

"Charming. Do you often spend time thinking up terrible things that could happen to me?"

"I had plenty of time to do so while I waited for you to come out of the gate. I alternated between worry and boredom."

I grin at him. "You worried about me?"

Merich gives me a disdainful look. "Well, I'm regretting it *now*."

I'm not sure I totally believe him. He's probably teasing me. Even so, I decide not to tell him how it took a day for the ringing in my ears to subside. Or how my nightmares are vivid and terrifying, and that I wake up screaming into my pillow, feeling the touch of sharp fingers at my throat.

"Well, here I am," I tell him. "Not dead."

"Not dead," Merich echoes. "And apparently in one piece."

This feels more believable. The faint mockery in his voice seems to come far more easily than the startling admissions of worry. "Sorry to disappoint you."

"Not at all." His mouth quirks. "I find I rather like you that way."

I wait for him to laugh, to shoot me his knifelike grin. All he does is smile slightly, watching me.

There's a wild, terrifying flutter in my stomach, and I swallow. "What about you?" I ask quickly. "You disappeared the other day."

In fact, even though he vanished moments before the search party found us, I haven't seen Merich since. I don't know what I expected; the job is done. We sealed the gap, I found Hannah, Merich protected the woods. We both got what we wanted. He wasn't hanging around for fun, and I'd be fooling myself if I expected this strange partnership to last any longer. There was no reason for him to stop by afterward.

Still, I can't pretend I'm not disappointed.

"I thought it might be concerning if a bunch of missing children ran out of the woods with an immortal being in tow. That sort of thing tends to upset people." He thinks about it, then smirks. "I also seem to recall you had concerns about being burned for witchcraft, and I can't imagine my presence would have helped."

I don't remember our exit from the woods—I passed out as Will found us, and he had to carry me home, barely conscious. But I expect Merich's appearance would not have gone down well among the frantic townspeople. "You're probably right," I admit.

"I usually am. I did keep an eye out, however. Today was the first time I saw you outside."

"You were watching my house?"

He looks at me like I'm an idiot. "You *had* just fought a monster," he says, echoing my earlier words. "I was hoping for a sign you weren't dead."

So he didn't disappear. He was waiting. Like he actually cared. "Oh," I say softly.

"Yes." He rolls his eyes. "*Oh*."

And then there's nothing left to say.

I try to ignore the uneven thumping of my heart, dragging a smile onto my face. "Well, thank you for your help, Merich. You had no obligation to give it, but I'm glad you did."

He lifts a brow. "Because you'd have all died without me?"

"Yes. Because we'd have all died without you."

He rocks back on his heels. "I can't say I enjoyed it. It was infinitely more interesting than what I normally get up to, but there was far more suicidal bravery than I'm comfortable with. Even so, you're welcome."

As I thought—it's not as if he's hanging around for fun. "I'll make sure not to call you next time something weird is going on," I assure him.

He pauses, cocking his head. "On the contrary. I'd be disappointed if I were never to hear from you again. I'm immortal.

Things get boring after a while. It's not often I get to spend my time in such an interesting way, let alone in such appealing company."

Heat blooms across my chest, the blood rushing to my face. "I'm sure I remember you calling me abrasive and unpleasant."

Merich smiles. This is no teasing smile. This is a curling, dangerous grin, and my heart stops beating in response. "I've re-evaluated my opinion."

I search for a reply and find nothing, too flustered to think. His eyes remain fixed on mine, yet the moment doesn't feel awkward.

Instead, it feels far more intense than it should.

The back door bangs open, and we both jump. "Merich!" Theo brings a whiff of burning food with him as he flings himself down onto the step beside me, lounging across the stairs with the boneless fluidity of a cat. "You're inside the fence."

All trace of intensity is gone from Merich's face. He's now as cool and polite and distant as always. I almost wonder if I imagined it. "I appear to have been given special privileges."

"I'd say you earned them." Theo leans back on his elbows, yawning. "Something we can help you with?"

"No. I'm just checking in. It's been a difficult week."

"That it has," Theo agrees. "Thanks for all the help, by the way."

"Don't worry about it. I'll simply call in the favour one day. Expect it to be a big one." Merich looks at me. "I'll leave you to your evening."

"Thank you," I say. "Take care, Merich. Don't be a stranger."

"I know where to come if I find any evil lurking." The corner of his mouth curls, and then he bows as he did when we first met, low and mocking. "Until next time, witchling."

Then he turns, strolling across the backyard and melting into the shadows, disappearing so quickly it's like he was never there at all.

Theo frowns after him, a crease of worry between his eyebrows. "He was kidding about the favour, right?"

I'm still wondering what might have happened if he hadn't burst through the back door. "I don't know. Probably."

He huffs, but doesn't say anything else. For a while we simply enjoy the silence as the colour in the sky deepens, darkening to a livid violet at the edges.

"You know," Theo says finally, "I'm proud of you."

I snort. "Very funny."

"I'm serious!" His voice softens, a faint flush entering his cheeks. "You did a really good thing, even though everyone else thought it was a bad idea. *I* thought it was a bad idea. But you did it anyway, without any guarantee it would work out. I think that makes you a better person than the rest of us."

I squint into the woods, hoping the sunset hides my embarrassment. "Oh. Well, uh. Thanks."

"You did a good thing, and I'm proud of you."

"You're sounding distinctly *brotherly*, Theo."

"Shut up."

I bump my shoulder against his. "Thank you for doing the good thing with me, though."

He sighs. "You're my sister. It's my job to deal with your dumb shit."

The first stars are appearing, the last of the day's warmth leaving the air. A chill arrives on the wind, stoking the aches in my bones.

Theo hums to himself. "Five kids are going to sleep in their own beds tonight because of us," he says.

"Six," I say.

"What?"

"There were six kids." I close my eyes, wincing as the stair digs into my back. "People think you're a hero, at least get the details right."

There's a pause before he replies. "No. There were *five*."

His voice is so serious that I open my eyes, finding him watching me warily.

An uneasy feeling comes over me. I think back to our journey out of the woods, the pounding of my head turning it into a blur of people and sound. But there were six kids. I remember them. There was Hannah, small and blonde, and Max, the last to go missing. Emma, who wailed as her mother hugged her, and Jacob, so covered in leaves he looked as if he belonged in the woods. Morgan, his shoes lighting up in a different colour with each step he took, and—

And the sixth.

The one with eyes so black they seemed to swallow the world. The one whose face fades in my memory as I try to recall it, his features sliding away. The one who held my hand, his skin icy, only to vanish when Merich came near, as if to avoid his notice.

The one who looked on as the search party arrived, no parents racing toward him. Like nobody saw him at all.

He was there in the woods.

Beyond the gap.

In the cave.

"Cass?"

"Theo," I breathe. A cold feeling crawls through my chest, like a creature made of fear is making a home inside my ribs. "*Six* kids came out of the gate."

The blood drains from his face. "Only five went missing."

"I know."

"Then..."

We stare at each other. Theo's throat moves as he swallows, all trace of peace gone from his features.

"The gap is closed," he says.

I nod.

The gap is closed.

But something got out.

Inside the house I hear Pen and Louisa laughing, but my eyes are drawn to the woods. The last of the light is finally fading from the sky, and the shadows of the trees fall long and dark, stretching toward us across the whispering grasses. It's a lovely evening, and night is falling under the boughs, forming a deep, impenetrable gloom.

That darkness could hide anything.

Anything could be watching.

Return to Fallow Creek in

2022

ABOUT THE AUTHOR

Claudia Cain was born in the North Island of New Zealand and continues to live there, sharing a home with an assortment of animals and an excessive amount of books. When she isn't writing, she's probably reading.

www.instagram.com/cainbooks
claudiacain.com

Printed in Great Britain
by Amazon